"Emma," Derri~~ck~~ ... hard. **"We could complicate things."**

"I know," she whispered. She couldn't seem to stop her wayward hands as they slid up his hard torso to wrap around his neck. Derrick's arms went around her waist. He closed his eyes, dragging her against him.

Emma gasped and he groaned softly, deep in his throat. Then his mouth was finally, blessedly on hers again. And there was nothing tentative about his kiss, regardless of his doubts. He tenderly drew his fingers along the side of her neck, moving his mouth to the delicate line of her jaw, then following the trail of his fingers.

Instinctively she eased away from Derrick, pushed on his shoulders. It wasn't a shove, she wasn't strong enough for that, still wanting—craving—what he was giving her, but knowing she didn't have the control needed to protect herself.

"Maybe, you're right," Emma breathed, willing her head to stop spinning, her legs to stop trembling and her heart to stop pounding. "But if I don't have you, all of you, I might just lose my mind..."

* * *

Be sure to check out the other books in this exciting series: **To Protect and Serve**—
A team of navy military operatives and civilians are called to investigate...

THE AGENT'S COVERT AFFAIR

BY
KAREN ANDERS

First Published in Great Britain 2017
By Mills & Boon, an imprint of HarperCollins*Publishers*
1 London Bridge Street, London, SE1 9GF

© 2017 Karen Alarie

ISBN: 978-0-263-93049-8

18-1017

Karen Anders writes a suspenseful and sexy mix of navy and civilians investigating murder, espionage and crime across a global landscape. Under the pen name Zoe Dawson, she's currently writing romantic comedy, new-adult contemporary romance, urban fantasy, syfy and erotic romance. When she's not busy writing, she's painting or killing virtual mmorpg monsters. She lives in North Carolina with her two daughters and one small furry gray cat.

To the men and women in the shadows.
You're the only ones who know who you are.

Chapter 1

Navy Housing Complex
La Mesa, California

The baby-faced teen who walked across the lawn, his sights set on Lily St. John's door, didn't look like an assassin.

Until someone looked into his eyes.

He bypassed the front and stole around to the back. A dog barked and he hesitated, then realized it was coming from next door. Not that he couldn't handle a dog.

His orders were clear and concise.

The dark green landscaper's shirt was a tad too small. The material stretched taut across his back, roping his biceps just above the distinctive tattoo, the blood staining the back collar barely noticeable. That old man had put up quite a fight, but in the end, the teen knew how to kill too fast and efficiently. He needed the uniform so these suburban housewives wouldn't get too nervous.

He popped the door with ease, pulling the knife at his waist free of the sheath and removing his shoes. The blade glinted in the light from the window behind him as he crept to the bottom of the stairs. A muffled female voice crooned softly as he started up, his steps light.

If she was unlucky, like the old landscaper dude, and saw him coming, that would be too bad for her.

He'd be the last thing she ever saw.

NCIS Headquarters
Camp Pendleton, California

Special Agent Derrick Gunn shut down his computer, the workday at NCIS coming to a close.

"Personally, I think it's the Lakers. They had Kobe," Special Agent Amber Michaels said, her honey-blond hair in a ponytail as she walked into the office with Special Agent Austin Beck.

He shook his head. "You're crazy, girl," he said, looking over at Derrick. "Tell her, Derrick." Today Austin's shaggy, two-toned brown and blond hair was tamed, almost.

"The Bulls," Derrick said, shrugging into his suit coat. Even after three years at NCIS, it was still jarring to Derrick that he was part of a team. His time as a CIA operative in a war zone was one of secrecy, lying to just about everyone he knew and screwing over people. That was what Derrick did for a living. Coming from no one with no family, he'd found it easy to hide what he did. Keeping things casual with women was a fact of life. Even now he found it difficult not to keep to himself. Even with the cases he'd worked on with both Austin and Amber, covering their backs and working together, Derrick still felt detached. It was his mind-set. It was what he had used to survive in a hostile environment for most of his life.

"That's what I'm talking about," Austin said, reaching his desk and shutting down his computer. He grabbed his hoodie.

Stopping in front of Austin, Derrick fist-bumped him, and both of them turned to find…empty space. Amber was gone and their boss, Supervisory Agent Kai Talbot, a dark-haired woman in her midthirties, with a quick stride and a tough-as-nails disposition, was fast approaching with the look on her face that spelled…overtime.

"We've got an injured petty officer in La Mesa Park. At a glance, it looks like she fell down the stairs, but take a closer look and make sure that's all that happened. She's at the base hospital. Check it out. Here's her address."

Derrick took the slip of paper Kai offered and turned to look at Austin. "Oh, Amber's good."

Austin sighed. "She's smarter than the two of us put together."

"Get us talking about basketball, then she hightails it out of here." Derrick couldn't help a small smile. Amber was motivated after her marriage to Tristan Michaels; she wanted to be with him as much as possible. Derrick swallowed, suddenly thinking about his past with the opposite sex. Most of the beautiful faces were a blur, except for Afsana, and everything about his love for her had been a disaster. She was an asset and she should have remained that way, but the intensity of the situation, the danger and the work he did, changed their dynamic. For the first time in his life, he'd connected with someone, and he knew it was a doomed relationship from the get-go. The only redeeming quality was that he didn't have to lie about who he was.

They headed for the elevator. "Well, to be fair, neither of us has someone waiting for us at home. She has good motivation." Austin pushed the button and the door slid open.

Too true. Derrick had no one waiting for him, but he'd been on his own for so long, first as a kid; then living with the man who had adopted him had been almost like living alone. Jerome Thornton III had groomed Derrick to take over his vast fortune. But with no loyalty to the cruel, heartless and exacting miser, the minute the old bastard kicked the bucket, Derrick liquidated everything, giving half to charity and depositing the rest into a bank account. The only thing he'd kept was an island, which suited him fine. It was as isolated as he was. Then he'd joined the CIA. There was something compelling about becoming a spook, a shadow, moving around the globe incognito, that completely appealed to him. He had the skill set from fending for himself in that money-grubber's house. Hiding from him had become a sick cat-and-mouse game.

Arriving at the hospital, they went up to the ICU floor and stopped at the desk. Flashing his badge, Derrick said, "We're here about a petty officer—" he looked down at his phone "—St. John."

The nurse at the desk said, "Yes, she was admitted about thirty minutes ago."

"What can you tell us about her condition?" Austin said.

"She's in a coma. She's critical—cuts, bruises, broken ribs, broken arm and leg."

"If her condition changes, could you let us know? We'd like to ask her some questions," Derrick said. Both Derrick and Austin handed her their cards.

They backed away from the desk and Austin asked, "Think she fell or was she pushed?"

"It's possible, but I'm not taking anything at face value until we thoroughly investigate."

"Agreed." They turned toward the elevator. "How about I drop you at her town house, and I'll go and talk to the military police who found her?"

"That's a plan," Derrick said. Fifteen minutes later, Austin drove away and Derrick walked the perimeter of the town house, but found nothing suspicious. Lily St. John had the end unit of a row of Spanish-inspired homes, pink stucco, painted tile, curves and arches with black ornamental ironwork and terra-cotta roofs. He knocked on the neighbor's door adjacent to hers, but no one answered. A woman in a white top and jeans came out of the house a door over. "Oh, she's not home. She's one of them military lawyers—JAG. Works late."

Derrick walked off the porch of the neighbor's town house and approached the woman. He flashed his badge. "Her name?"

She studied the badge and said absently, "Lieutenant Gail Baker." Then she looked at him. "NCIS?"

"Naval Criminal Investigative Service, ma'am. We're federal agents," he said, jotting down the neighbor's name.

"Criminal? Oh, I saw the ambulance a bit ago. Is Lily all right?" Her face was pinched in the fading light from the setting sun.

"You know her?"

"Just to say hi. She is so sweet and her little boy, Matthew, is a doll."

Derrick stiffened. "Her little boy?"

"Yes, he's just a baby—um, nine months, I think. Is he all right, too?"

"What is your name?"

"Samantha Robbins."

"Did you see anything suspicious this morning?"

"Oh, heavens no. I sleep in, as I have a late shift at my bartending job. But my husband, Sergeant Rod Robbins, is up at the crack of dawn and so is Gail."

He handed her a card. "Have him call me when he gets home. Thank you for your time." Derrick reached for his phone and dialed Austin's number as he headed for Lily St. John's town house. Once inside, he climbed the stairs two at a time and stopped dead when he hit the first room on the left.

A nursery.

He took in the crib, the changing table, the baby blue walls and the whimsical animals painted on them. Pain sliced at him but he dismissed it. This wasn't about him and the child he'd lost. This was about Lily's little boy. He called Austin.

"She has a baby," Derrick said, his gut in knots. "Nine months old."

"Where the hell is the kid?"

"That's a damn good question. I'm searching for her phone. Check to see if it was with her personal effects. We need to find out if she's got relatives, a babysitter or day care." He headed for the door. Going to the master bedroom, he noted how the house was very neat and tidy, the bed made. He found the charger on her nightstand, but no phone.

Urgency burning in him, he rushed downstairs into the living room. A female voice ordered, "Hold it right there."

"I would suggest you stand very still and keep your hands where I can see them," Emma St. John said, pointing her 9mm directly at the powerful back of the man standing in her sister's living room. "Slowly turn around and don't make any sudden moves. I'd really hate to end the day with killing someone. It was going so well. Besides, blood is really hard to get out of the carpet."

The man did as he was instructed.

Whoa.

Emma straightened, her stomach giving a funny little lurch when she saw him. It took all her professional private investigator willpower not to react to the man's gorgeous features. He certainly didn't dress like a thief, but Emma never took any unnecessary chances. That suit was expensive; the tie, too. He looked a bit tired—his eyes gave that away—but other than that, nothing. She absorbed the details she could, her observation skills her biggest asset. But she was frustrated when this man didn't reveal much.

She didn't know what she'd been expecting, but this man wasn't it. Big and wide-shouldered, he stood framed in the light from the lamp in the living room. His fingers were long and well shaped, and there was something almost deceptively casual about his stance, about the way his hands weren't quite relaxed. Something lethal and a little too careless, as though he had small regard for danger.

Experiencing a strange flutter at the unexpected thought, Emma clenched her palm around the grip of the gun. She was looking for her sister, and she had a gut feeling that something was terribly wrong.

Lily had to work late tonight and Emma had agreed to pick up Matty from day care and watch him until Lily finished her shift. Except, when she'd gone to the base, they'd told her Matty hadn't been dropped off today, nor had Lily called in to let them know he wouldn't be there.

"Who are you?" she demanded, her fear for Lily over-riding anything else.

"Drop the weapon and kick it over here," a male voice said from behind her. "I also would prefer not to kill anyone today."

She complied, the voice of the man who had the drop on her firm and commanding. Feeling as if her heart was going to come right through her chest, she watched the guy in front of her approach, her heartbeat stopping completely when he reached into his suit coat. He was stern and unsmiling as he met her gaze with an unreadable expression, his chiseled features neutral.

A warrior. That was what he was.

A cop, she thought a moment before he pulled out the NCIS badge and showed it to her. Navy cops. What were they doing here? "Oh, God. What happened to Lily?" she said, dropping her hands and taking a step toward him, her voice compressed.

"Who are you?"

"I'm Emma St. John, Lily's sister."

The man who had been holding the gun on her came around to face her, and he was very different. Much more casually dressed in chocolate pants, a baby blue Polo and deck shoes, his hair a mixture of blond and brown— very California beach boy. He flashed his badge. "I'm

Special Agent Austin Beck, and this is Special Agent Derrick Gunn."

She took another step as the men exchanged glances and her stomach plummeted. "Why are you here? What happened to my sister?"

"She was found at the bottom of the stairs hours ago. She's at the base hospital. It appears she fell."

"I've got to go."

A strong hand gripped her wrist, and something wrenched loose when she met Agent Gunn's flat, unreadable gaze. Grasping her shoulder, he drew her over to the sofa and guided her down to the cushions, his tone firm when he said, "I know this is terrible news and you want to be with your sister, but we need to ask you some questions. Where is your nephew?"

Cold to the bone and scared to death, she sank into the sofa, the solid pressure of his hand on her shoulder strangely reinforcing. She stared at him, her heart hammering in her throat; then she drew a deep, stabilizing breath. "Oh, man, that's why I'm here," she said, brushing at her hair. She was trying to recover, to catch her balance. She clasped her hands between her thighs, aware of the panic rising and trying to remain calm. Getting hysterical wasn't going to help the matter. She needed to think like a PI, not a panicked family member. "I—" She paused and took another deep, shaky breath, then said, her voice still unsteady, "I was supposed to pick Matty... Matthew, up from day care."

"Do you normally pick up your nephew?" Austin asked.

"No, Lily had to work late today, and I was going to watch him." Fear twisted up her stomach. "I knew something was wrong," she said as her voice dropped into a distressed murmur. Agent Beck turned away and pulled out his cell. After dialing, he started to talk. He was speaking to someone about notifying NCMEC. Emma didn't know what NCMEC stood for, but before she could say anything, Agent Beck stopped talking and asked for a description of Matthew.

"What is this for?" she asked.

"National Center for Missing and Exploited Children," he replied.

Emma pulled up her phone and navigated to a recent picture of him, sending it to his phone when he requested it. Then he was focusing again on his conversation.

"Ms. St. John—"

"Emma is fine," she said, absently caught up once again in her shock. This couldn't be happening. She was supposed to watch out for her baby sister. But they'd had an argument and Lily was being stubborn. She was still absorbing this information. Matty gone? Lily hurt. "How bad is she?" Their argument had been intense, but Emma was always there for Lily and she knew that. Their conversation had been strained, but for the sake of Lily's job and Matty's care, they had both agreed they would talk again with more level heads. Work things out.

"Critical. She's in a coma. I'm sorry that you have to go through all of this, but we're here to help." Concern showed in his unique deep blue eyes. "Where is the boy's day care?"

"On base—Naval Amphibious Base Coronado, NAB." She took a fortifying breath. "They told me Lily hadn't dropped him off. At first I thought maybe Lily or Matty was sick, and she forgot to call me. She can be flighty, but she's been so responsible since she joined the navy and had Matty—much more responsible."

"I need you to confirm his age for me," Austin said as he stopped talking into the cell, waiting for Emma's response.

"Nine months," she said, her voice catching. "I tried to call Lily several times, but there was no answer, so I came over to make sure everything was all right. What is going on? What happened to my sister? Where is Matty?"

She knew the sound of her shell-shocked tone was edged with anger. She wanted answers. Had to have answers. Lily was the only person she had left from their family. Their grandmother didn't count.

"I understand the need for answers, and I understand your anger even if I don't completely know what you're going through," he said, his voice now warm and soothing. "We don't know at this point, but we're going to do everything in our power to find who did this and find out what happened to your sister."

"The phone dump is in progress. The boss wants an update as soon as we have one."

Derrick nodded. "Canvass the neighborhood. I'm taking Ms. St. John back to the office for more in-depth questions."

Agent Beck nodded. "See you back at Pendleton."

Derrick nodded and escorted Emma out the front door and to his car.

She moved as if in slow motion, as if her limbs had been frozen and were now just thawing. Once inside the car, she looked over at him, their eyes clashing in the silence; his heart skipped a hard beat. Her face was stiff and only her mouth quivered, her eyes moist, devastation there in the striking blue depths. She stared at him as if her whole world had just crashed and burned. Derrick stared back at her, his expression neutral. He was trying to remain professional. Remain detached, and for the first time since Afsana, he was struggling.

She broke eye contact and faced forward, her head bent as she just stared down; a curtain of shoulder-length copper hair fell on either side of her oval face, her forehead fringed with thick bangs. Something about her moved him, stirring sympathy and deep interest.

He felt as if someone had just dropped a load of bricks on his head.

The woman was beautiful, the kind that stopped a man's heart. But her beauty wasn't what affected him; it was those eyes, thickly lashed and straightforward, filled with the kind of courage he'd seen on the battlefield. This woman was a fighter through and through.

She looked like trouble wrapped up in a redheaded package.

With everything that had been stirred up during the mission with Dexter Kaczewski and coming face-to-face with his tumultuous past in Afghanistan, then that harrowing jungle adventure with Kaczewski's brother Rock, Derrick had needed more recovery time than he'd gotten. It was all messing with his head.

It had been easy to handle his emotions when he didn't have to see the boy or interact with Afsana. His colossal mistake had jeopardized his mission and her life. He regretted his lapse in judgment, compromising himself and the safety of the troops in the area. But he'd fallen in love for the first time in his life and hadn't known how to deal with it. He'd made a mess of it by getting her pregnant.

Derrick's guilt, even after eight years, was still fresh, his remorse even more of a bitter pill. He had a son and he could never see him or be a father to him like he wanted. His only consolation was that Afsana had married a good man.

When he walked into the office, he ushered Emma to the conference room. Pouring her a cup of coffee, he watched her out of the corner of his eye. Damn, she was striking. *And off-limits*, he reminded himself. He wasn't about to muck up an investigation by thinking inappropriate thoughts about the victim's sister. This was at the very least a suspicious incident, and at the maximum, a child abduction with Lily's attempted murder. His gut said kidnapping. He fully expected someone had thrown a five-four, one-hundred-ten-pound woman down the stairs and abducted a nine-month-old infant. The child was the key if they could figure out why someone would want to snatch him.

Reaching out, he clasped the woman's arm, but she shrugged off his touch and stepped back. "Have a seat. I need to ask you more questions," he said, keeping his voice calm and soothing, yet urgency churned in his gut.

For a moment she stared at him, the color gone from her face; then she closed her eyes and drew a deep breath, as if it hurt her to do so. She folded her arms around herself. Turning, she sat down wearily at the table and cupped her hands around the mug. Still, he couldn't help but look. She was beautiful, really beautiful.

He settled into the chair diagonally from her and said, "Tell me about your sister. There's a clue in there somewhere that will give us information that may point to who took your nephew and what happened to Lily."

She looked away and there was resistance written all over her face as if their past was something that was painful and guarded. And again, he couldn't seem to help his response. He knew exactly what that was like.

He tempered his reply as best he could, but this copper-haired woman got to him, even with his formidable skills in deflecting complex human emotion.

"We lost our parents in a car crash when Lily was six and I was eight," she said, her voice also filled with dissent. "We were raised by our…grandmother." There was a discordant undertone to her words now. "She wasn't exactly sympathetic or tolerant of two little orphaned girls." She didn't waver, her gaze steady and strong on his. "My sister was pure, trusting and kind. She always got herself into situations she needed help getting out of and I was there for her, until we grew up and went our separate ways. Lily was always looking for love. She wanted it desperately enough that she rushed into relationships, hoping and praying it would work out. She ended up going from inappropriate boyfriends to abusive boyfriends to indifferent boyfriends."

Emma sipped her coffee, then said, "She acted on impulse and danced to music no one else could hear and there was no holding back with her."

It surprised him that Emma's sister was a sailor. The navy was all about conformity and rules. Where did the child at heart fit in? "It makes me wonder how she ended up in the navy."

Emma sighed and shook her head. "She met a sailor and, on a whim, joined the navy, but she landed on her feet and seemed to love it. Maybe it gave her structure."

"What is this sailor's name?"

"Petty Officer William Samuels. I don't believe they are together anymore."

"Was she married?"

"No, she was secretive about the men in her life lately.

I think she was seeing someone, but she wouldn't tell me who. I suspect she thought I wouldn't approve."

"And the father of her son?"

"I don't know. She wouldn't say. Maybe he's married? Maybe someone she works with."

"An officer?"

Emma shrugged. "I wish I could be more help there."

Derrick reached for one of his cards and slid it across the table toward her. "If you think of anything else, Emma, please call me."

She rose at the same time he did. He was far, far from the touchy-feely sort. That was why he often worked with Austin or Amber. They were the ones who got all sympathetic and supportive. It wasn't that he didn't have compassion, it was that he chose to channel everything he had into a case. It worked the best for him, but this woman always seemed to be shifting the firm ground beneath his feet into sand.

For a moment they stood there while this "thing" passed between them. Finally, she reached into her purse and pulled out a card. She handed it to him. "Call me when you find out any information. I want to know everything, no matter how small."

He nodded, not trusting his voice.

Then she slipped past him and the door closed behind her. He felt instant relief that she was gone. Not since Afsana had he had such an instant connection, an interest that he couldn't shake. But it went deeper than his feelings for the woman he'd lost. There was the case to consider and her vulnerability. No matter how much she tried to hide it, he'd seen it. He was damn good at seeing beyond barriers.

Except now he knew that she was attracted to him, too. She was fighting it just as hard and that suited him fine.

He looked down at the card, then swore softly under his breath. She was a private investigator. It didn't require a stretch of the imagination to think that Emma would want to be involved in locating her nephew and finding out the mystery of her sister's attack. The reason the boy was abducted had to be directly tied to the mother. Investigating Lily St. John was where they would start, but it sure wouldn't be where it ended.

He knew Emma's type and she was definitely the sort from the top of her copper head down to her feet. He had to wonder if she had either military training or she'd been a cop. Something he was going to find out right now.

There was no time to screw around. They had a missing child kidnapped by unknown persons. That had to take top priority.

God help Emma if she got in his way.

Chapter 2

Gathering his composure and pissed that he had to actually pull himself together, Derrick turned and left the conference room.

He went right to Austin's desk and said, "What have you got so far?"

Austin looked up and his eyes narrowed. "Why are you cheesed?" In the past he'd been able to hide his emotions, but now Austin and Amber were tuned in to him. Something he was still getting used to.

"I'm not," Derrick ground out. Amber looked up from her desk with a dubious expression on her face.

"Oh, sweetheart, yes, you are." She smiled at him and his heart softened. She got up and walked over to his desk and Austin rose, too. Derrick settled behind it, turning the card over and over in his hand. He knew it was stupid, but it felt warm to the touch, as if Emma's heat was trapped in the paper.

"You can talk to us," Amber said, her tone muted. She glanced at Austin, who grinned and opened his mouth. She nudged him. "Stop teasing him."

Austin's grin disappeared and he cleared his throat. "At the risk of sounding touchy-feely, we always have your back. You should know that by now."

Derrick was well aware. They had proved it so many times, Austin just this evening when Emma had had the drop on him. He huffed a hard breath and said, "I know that. Still not easy for me."

"After this we need to get drunk and you can spill all your secrets, and if a certain agency that shall remain unnamed should come up, we'd be sworn to the utmost confidentiality."

"I never said I was with the CIA." He didn't know where it came from, but there was a pressure in him to tell them, get the aching pain out, but his oath to the company and his lone-wolf need to be separate from the pack interfered.

At the looks on their faces, Derrick, for the first time ever, felt their disappointment keenly. How could he ever be part of a team when he didn't trust its members completely? Except trust was hard-won with his background, his childhood had been anything but idyllic and years of keeping everything to himself made him bottled up tight inside.

He snapped the card right side up. "She's a PI."

Both of them groaned. "Ah, all of us know she's going to be a pain. PIs always want in on the action, especially when it's something as personal as this. My heart goes out to her, but getting involved in a family member's kidnapping is a bad idea," Amber said.

Austin nodded. "Yeah, I got the sense she's a ball-buster and won't easily accept no for an answer."

These were Derrick's exact thoughts. They were all completely on the same page.

"Far be it for me to break up this little tea party, but can we get on with it?" Kai said as she entered. "We've got a major dirtbag to find," she ground out, her mood mirroring Derrick's.

Derrick clenched his jaw. Someone had injured a mother—a petite, sweet, unassuming woman. It was time to run him to ground.

Austin threw her a glance and nodded. He walked over and picked up the remote. Clicking once, Lily St. John's navy profile photo popped up on the plasma.

Amber sat on the edge of his desk and gave her attention to the screen. "Lily Leigh St. John, raised by her grandmother, Elizabeth Grayson St. John, Esquire," she said as Austin passed her the remote.

"The Ice Queen lawyer?" Derrick said. Bess was a no-holds-barred District Attorney who practically ran the justice system in DC about ten years ago. She had a reputation of taking on the worst cases and winning them, made a name for herself. It was telling that he'd never heard she had a family or that she had raised her grandchildren. In Bess's case, he was sure children were to be seen but not heard.

"Yes. She's retired now. She had a son, Matthew, who graduated from Harvard and was being groomed for the DA's position, and a daughter-in-law, Laura. They were killed in a car accident when the girls were eight and six. Lily's only sibling was Emma Jean St. John, former LAPD detective and now a private investigator with three offices in California."

Austin groaned and Amber made a face.

"Yeah," Derrick said. "She gave me her card," he said to Kai. He studied Lily's photo, and his gut clenched for Emma. He immediately switched his thoughts to keep his mind off Lily's attractive sister. The focus needed to be Lily and her son. "Lily wouldn't tell Emma who the father of her child was. She was tight-lipped and secretive."

"Hmm. Usually means the man isn't free," Amber said.

"He sure isn't," Austin said, settling behind his desk. "While you were questioning Emma, I was looking into her phone. The hospital found it in her personal belongings and sent it over."

"You have something to share?" Kai said with an arched brow.

"I found what is described as a 'semi-anonymous chat app' on Lily's phone. They are supposed to be anonymous, but aren't. Far from it. It took me all of ten minutes to find out who she was chatting with."

"Who?" Kai said.

"Her CO, Commander John Ward. Married."

Kai did a *tsk-tsking* noise and before she could say anything, Derrick growled, "I'm taking him. Here or at the office?"

"Here," Kai said. "And since you didn't ask, you have lead on this. Your interrogation skills are top-notch. So step all over his toes and then some."

"Yes, ma'am," Derrick said with relish. This is where his interrogation experience with the CIA would come in handy and wouldn't tweak his conscience one bit.

An hour later Derrick entered the interrogation room.

"It's about damn time! What is this about? I was dragged out of my home and in here like some common criminal!"

"Commander Ward. I just discovered that you were brought to the wrong place," Derrick said, his voice conciliatory as he entered the eight-by-ten room with blank gray walls, one table and three chairs. It was designed to maximize a suspect's discomfort and sense of powerlessness. It was imperative in this particular case because Commander Ward was used to being in charge. Kai, Amber and Austin were all in the observation room watching through the two-way mirror. He pulled out the chair and sat down. "We apologize for the mix-up, but since we're already here, we might as well discuss Petty Officer Lily St. John. Would that be all right with you?" Derrick smiled. "Can I get you something to drink?"

"Water," he said, partially mollified, but still wary, especially after Lily's name was mentioned. He didn't seem to notice how Derrick had glossed over his acquiescence in staying in the interrogation room. Either he was playing it cool or he was trying to play Derrick.

"What does this have to do with Petty Officer St. John?"

"What were her duties?" This question was key. The first rule of interrogation was to create a baseline, forcing the suspect to access different parts of his brain. Asking nonthreatening questions that required access to memory or the other part of the brain required for thinking broadcasted nonverbal clues to Derrick. Ward's eyes went to the right, a cue that he was remembering, accessing the part of the brain used for memory.

"She's an E4, Petty Officer Third Class, a mass communication specialist. She performs graphic design in support of the public affairs mission, designing and managing official websites and performing high-speed, high-volume graphic reproduction."

There was a knock on the door. Derrick rose and accepted the bottle of water from Amber's hands. Ward's gaze darted to the two-way mirror. Yeah, this guy had something to hide. Interrogation was all about human nature. Set the subject at ease and get them to talk about things that were true. Then delve a little deeper and drop the big bomb. It made it more difficult to lie effectively. A nervous suspect got nervous for a reason. Derrick had enough experience with simple and complex interrogations. Some were sanctioned and others were dark-ops related. He didn't judge himself. His judgment was all about justice, and it was his bottom line.

"How would you rate her as an employee and sailor?" Warmth flooded Ward's eyes as they moved to the left, indicating that Ward was thinking and activating his cognitive center.

He smiled and said, "She's exemplary at both. Punctual, always willing to go the extra mile. She has a sweet disposition. Her output is top-notch and she's a hard worker."

"What is she currently working on. Anything sensitive?"

For a moment Ward stared at Derrick, his eyes sharpening as if Derrick was accusing Lily of something criminal. The disbelief on his face was added to Derrick's mental database. Then he looked right, a sure sign that he was accessing his memory banks.

"She's working on the navy's Birthday Bash website. We're gearing up to sell tickets and plan the event. All the employees in public affairs handle sensitive matters, but if you're insinuating that Lily…Petty Officer St. John… is in any way acting against her country, you must be mistaken," he said, disgust evident in his voice and face.

"When was the last time you talked to her?"

"Yesterday. I didn't see her today. I was busy and in meetings." Ward looked to the left instead of right, indicating to Derrick that he was lying. He had had contact with Lily the day she went down those stairs.

"Were you in a meeting at six this morning?"

His eyes shuttered and his lips pinched, Ward shook his head. "No. I was home getting dressed to go on base. Why do you want to know where I was at six a.m.? Is Lily in some kind of trouble?" He was telling the truth.

It was time to confront this suspect, to get a confession out of him and hopefully the possibility of getting a lead on Lily's son. "She's in a coma. She was tossed down the stairs, Commander. She was found this afternoon." Derrick opened his folder and spread out the photos on the table.

The blood drained from the commander's face as his shocked and suddenly moist eyes stared at Derrick. "No," he whispered, swallowing hard. "That can't be. No wonder she didn't answer me," he added desolately.

"Answer you?"

He cleared his throat, blinking rapidly. "How did this happen?"

"You have special ops training, correct?"

Ward stiffened, broadcasting loud and clear he knew exactly why Derrick was asking him. "I washed out of the SEALs, but that's no disgrace."

"You'd have the strength to toss her down the stairs."

Ward's face contorted in anger and anguish, then with a small, explosive move, he pushed the photos toward Derrick. "I didn't hurt Lily! I wouldn't do that... I love her." His voice fierce, he leaned back and his eyes moistened again.

Leaning forward, Derrick pushed the photos back; it was time to discover why Ward had committed the crime. It was all about setting up a confession. Derrick leaned in again, dropping his voice to one of understanding. "I get it. You're a married man. Maybe she was getting sick of waiting around for you. Maybe she was pushing the issue, threatening to tell your wife."

"No, that's not—"

"Not to mention the charges you would be brought up on if the brass discovered that you're fraternizing with an enlisted sailor under your authority." This time Derrick pulled out a photo of Matthew and set it down. "One you got pregnant. Where is your son, Commander?"

"I didn't do this!" he said vehemently. Then his face softened as he looked down at the baby's picture. He picked it up. "I have two sons of my own." He raised his eyes and said, his voice subdued and filled with concern, "Matthew's missing? Who would do this to her?"

"I know this must be hard, considering your career, your livelihood, the scandal, but this is a baby boy who has an aunt and a great-grandmother who want him back. Tell us where he is, Commander. It'll go better for you."

"I don't know. I didn't take him. I'm getting divorced. I've already filed the papers, and I'm retiring from the navy effective a month from now. They've hired me on to work with the office in a civil capacity. We would have been able to be together. I was going to marry her. Matthew isn't my son, but I intended to adopt him." His voice caught, then broke. "I know cheating isn't admirable, but it just happened. My wife and I have been unhappy for a long time. She and I made this decision together and it's completely amicable. You can talk to her if you like. I've already come clean about Lily. She knows."

Derrick wasn't getting any kind of lying vibe from him. "How can you be sure Matthew isn't yours?"

"Because she was pregnant before we started having

an affair. She came to me, panicked and scared. I gave her a shoulder to cry on and we got closer and closer. After she had Matty, we got physical, but it was only about eight weeks ago. I'd already filed the papers." He swallowed hard and his eyes narrowed. "Why don't you ask her sister about Lily's 'accident'? They had a terrible fight about her taking that assignment in Okinawa, Japan. We were going together, and Emma didn't want her to move so far away. It was a sweet deal of a job for Lily, would help her get promoted. Lily was determined to go against Emma's wishes. Maybe they fought over Matty and it got heated. Maybe it was Emma who pushed her down the stairs by accident. She's the sweetest, kindest person I've ever known… Damn, where is she?" He covered his face and sat back, his shoulders shaking.

The man was genuinely upset and that meant Derrick had come to another dead end. William Samuels was an explosive ordinance disposal tech on the EOD Mobile Unit that had been at sea during three months of Lily's possible pregnancy and was currently still on sea duty. After contacting the captain of the *U.S.S. Pioneer*, it was established that Petty Officer Samuels wasn't recently in San Diego as he was out to sea. He couldn't have pushed Lily down the stairs and abducted her son.

Hours later, after poring over all of Lily's personal information and looking through everything on her phone, including pictures she'd taken on a cruise where she looked tanned, fit and happy, Derrick left the quiet, darkened office. Emma's shocked and devastated eyes haunted him through all his waking hours as something undefined stirred in his gut—nothing sexual, more elusive than that. A kind of soul-deep restlessness. What would calm it? Finding out who had done this to Emma's sister, giving her the closure she needed. He wanted to find the infant and return him to his family. His insides scored with memory, he clamped down on his pain.

He'd been adopted after spending many years in the foster care system. Derrick had been…troubled, with no memory of his biological family. No one even remembered where he came from and it left him feeling detached, lost. When Jerome Thornton had found him and adopted him, Derrick thought he might have found the family he craved. But Thornton was a cold, calculating man. He'd wanted a kid with street smarts, wanted to groom him into Thornton's likeness, make him into someone just as ruthless.

Thornton was a corporate raider, gleefully planned hostile takeovers to sell companies for profit, no matter who it hurt.

Derrick had lived in luxury, had had everything he could have ever wanted, except what he always craved—family, connection, a sense of place and self.

He didn't want to delve too deep as to why. He didn't need to know why; he just needed it. He also didn't want to analyze his deep-seated belief that Emma couldn't have hurt her sister like Ward had suggested. He shifted to ease the flip-flopping sensation in his chest.

The sun would be rising by the time he got back to La Mesa. He stopped at a coffee shop on his way out of Pendleton for an infusion of caffeine, his mind wandering back to Emma St. John.

His cell rang and he answered. "You're heading back to La Mesa, aren't you?"

Kai Talbot was one perceptive woman, and it was

unnerving how she read him. "Why aren't you sleeping, boss lady?"

"There's a missing kid—that always puts me on edge."

He didn't know her story and, still unused to sharing anything even with his team members, he remained closed-lipped about his. He knew what it was like to be abandoned and lost as a child; he knew what it was like to lose a son. He wasn't going to stop until he found this kid.

"We've had a call from the complex reporting one of their landscapers is missing. Check it out when you get there and keep me posted. But, Derrick, don't burn out. Get some rest."

"I'll talk to you soon."

He pulled up to Lily's house, dislodged the crime scene tape and went inside. Donning gloves, he looked around. Sometimes sifting through a crime scene gave him clues to follow. He went to the back door. This was where the possible intruder had gained entrance.

It wasn't clear whether Lily had let him in or he'd walked inside; the normal floor scuff marks could mask a break-in. If the intruder had gotten inside by forcing the door, that wasn't evident. There had been debris that suggested the kidnapper had removed his footwear. Frustrated, Derrick went back to the front door. Through the window, he saw a car pull up into the parking space next door. Looked like Lily's next-door neighbor, Gail Baker, was burning the midnight oil. She wearily rubbed the back of her neck, her uniform rumpled and wrinkled. She walked up the path and disappeared from his view.

He left Lily's house and knocked on Lieutenant Baker's door. Moments later the pretty, middle-aged woman answered. Derrick flashed his badge and introduced himself and his purpose. She was dismayed at the news of Lily's condition. Her face went sad and white.

"Please come in," she said, ushering him into the living room. "I was just getting ready to go to bed."

"Your neighbor said you were a lawyer. JAG, right?"

She nodded. "I've been working on a big case. Just got in." She folded her arms across her chest. "It's terrible that someone hurt Lily? Why?"

"We're still working that out."

"And Matty is missing? That is so disturbing." She shook her head. "Can I get you some coffee? I have one of those nifty personal brewers. It would only take a minute."

He nodded and while he sat down at the counter, she pressed buttons and handed him a cup. "I'm heartbroken about Lily. She's a beautiful person. So sweet. Do you know where she's been hospitalized?"

"NAB, but she's in a coma, so it might only be family members allowed to visit at this point. She's also under guard, just in case." He sipped at the hot brew. "Did you know her well?"

"Yes and no. We talked a bit. She loves that boy, but was in quite a turmoil when she first got pregnant. She wouldn't tell me who the father was, if you're looking for that information."

"I was. Did you notice anything suspicious or out of the ordinary yesterday?"

"As a matter of fact, I did. There was a teen here who I didn't recognize. He was probably about sixteen or so. Black hair, hard-looking eyes. I'm very observant. Comes with being a lawyer." She shrugged. "Anyway, he had on this landscaper's shirt, a dark green color. The same shirt our landscaper wears, too. An older man, Kevin. He's a sweetheart."

"What was out of the ordinary about the guy wearing a dark green landscaper's shirt?"

"It was too small, ill-fitting. He also had this disturbing tattoo. It was on his upper arm, and it was of this woman, but creepy, as if a skeleton's mask had been placed over her face. There were these curlicue designs on her forehead and chin, stitching across her lips. Both eyes were blackened with studs around them, but the left eye had this red X with blood dripping down."

"Would you be willing to sit with an artist?"

"Yes. I can do that. I was supposed to be back after sleep and a change of clothes. Let me call the office." She picked up her cell. "There's one other thing that I wanted to mention. When I took out the trash, I noticed an unfamiliar car out back, a black sedan. It was a rental."

"How do you know that?"

"It had shiny new plates, unadorned by dealer badges, and had a bar code sticker in the back window. The rental agency uses a bar code to scan the car when it goes in and out of the lot, in order to keep track of it."

"Did you happen to get the plate number?"

"I did." She wrote it down and handed him the paper. "Lily's sister was here this morning. You just missed her. She's a PI and I told her everything I told you. I'm surprised she didn't get in touch with you."

Derrick clenched his jaw and thanked Gail. He left her town house and scanned the neighborhood. His eyes stopped roving when he spied a dark green pickup truck with a metal trailer on the back, carrying a mower, several tools—rake, clippers, blower and an edger, along with an orange and white cooler. He headed toward it and, as he got closer, he spied the name on the side. The Green Thumb. That explained the dark green color of the truck and the shirts.

Derrick approached the flatbed of the pickup and when he glanced inside, there was a tarp that looked like it was used to cover the equipment on the trailer. His gut clenched when he spied a distinct bundle underneath it.

Reaching into the vehicle, he flipped the tarp away.

The dead face and open eyes of an older man looked sightlessly up at him, his chest bare.

An hour later, after he'd gotten Gail Baker to confirm that the dead man was Kevin, and NCIS forensic medical examiner, Ray Sotheby, had found a puncture wound at the back of the dead landscaper's head, Derrick decided that tracking down Emma St. John for her safety and to keep her from doing something foolish was a good plan of action. He wouldn't admit to himself that he was only concerned about her as a course of his duty. There was nothing personal about it.

He tried calling Emma, but there was no answer. He accessed DMV and found her home address and drove over there, but when he knocked at the beautiful stone and clapboard house, there was no answer. After peering in the garage, he discovered that her car was gone. He got back in his car and drove over to her office.

St. John Investigations was located in downtown San Diego in a stone building. Walking inside, he went to the receptionist. "I'm looking for Emma St. John."

"I'm sorry, sir, you just missed her." It was clear the woman was well versed on not giving a thing away.

"Did she say where she was going?" Derrick pulled

out his badge and flashed it. "This is important and involves a federal investigation."

Her lips thinned and she said, "I'm not exactly sure." But it was clear to Derrick that she knew exactly where Emma had gone, but was given strict instructions not to say. "I don't believe she'll be long. She has an appointment in the next thirty minutes. If you'd like to take a seat—"

"No. I'm not waiting. But never mind. I think I know." There was only one thing on Emma's mind right now, and that was finding her nephew and discovering what had happened to her sister. Derrick smiled slightly and turned away.

Chapter 3

Emma stood resolute, her eyes gritty, her body weary, but her determination to find out who took Matty and hurt her sister burning hot. She'd already snagged a blue smock from Crown Car Rental Agency and was behind the counter. The trick to getting information as a PI was looking the part she was playing. She accessed the computer and typed in the license plate that Gail Baker had given her and when it popped up on the screen, she scanned the data.

George Douglas. That was the name of the man who had rented the black sedan that had been parked behind Lily's house.

"Excuse me," said a male voice, nicking the edge of her focus. She was already memorizing the information. Some compelling force made her look up. Her gaze collided with that NCIS agent. The one who looked like a rough and tumble James Bond was staring at her across the counter.

She would recognize him anywhere, the angles of his face so achingly perfect, the straight, beautiful nose, a firm, sensual mouth accentuated by the beard stubble darkening his jaw—and those eyes, cobalt blue under dark lashes, undeniably intense, unconditionally unwavering... unequivocally locked on to hers. She had to work to not get distracted by those piercing blue eyes. Mr. Gorgeous wasn't happy, but that was too damn bad. She didn't answer to him or to anyone. It was clear the navy cops had their own club and giving a victim's family member any information or allow them to participate in the investigation was as likely as an elephant flying. She was going to change their minds. She was tailor-made to help with this investigation.

"May I have a word with you?" he said coolly.

She lifted her chin, having talked, fought, or blustered her way out of almost anything. But this guy. Wow. He was looking at her long and hard, his eyes dark, intense and filled with enough raw power to make a shiver go down her spine.

Emma came around the counter and walked outside with distracting Agent Derrick. No way in hell did she want to even feel the least bit attracted. Men like him were closed-mouthed and unemotional. They were also usually married to their jobs. She got along with just about everyone; it was imperative in her business to be people savvy. But with Special Agent Gunn, she found herself getting all distracted and confrontational with him. A little hot and bothered was on that list, too. Okay, so maybe it was a lot hot and bothered. One look at him and it was easy to see herself kissing those lips, getting close to him and getting an even better whiff of that cologne he was wearing, something like him, spicy and clean.

It was very disconcerting for a woman who found

herself in her early thirties and completely devoid of any type of romantic relationship. Not that Derrick was a good candidate. He just reminded her that in all her travels, she'd never been this interested, turned on or this tempted in her life. But it was completely out of the question and impossible. Special Agent Derrick Gunn was one of the investigators on her sister's and nephew's cases. She couldn't jeopardize it with any kind of personal relationship with him.

She was picky and to allow someone in her personal space, he had to be special. So she had encounters instead of relationships. That suited her and her physical needs just fine. Not that she was looking for a husband or even a boyfriend, for that matter. That was Lily's hope—to have a family. Emma wasn't sure she could open up her heart wide enough for that. Her grandmother hadn't nurtured them in the least and Emma had learned to be just as tough. Vulnerability equated to weakness in Bess's book. With Lily's injuries she was beside herself with worry, determined to make a difference here. It had been them against the world for so long.

"What the hell do you think you're doing?" Those piercing blue eyes bored into hers. He was scruffier than when she'd first met him at Lily's. His medium length hair was tousled from either his fingers or what looked like a sleepless night.

That struck her. She'd been a dedicated cop when she'd been on the force, had spent many nights working to break a case, but Agent Gunn had been not only dedicated enough to get either very little sleep or no sleep at all, but also to take the time to track her down. He was concerned about her. He might not act it, but she was sure he had the information about the license plate. It was why he was here. He'd spoken to Gail and she'd told him what she had seen. Why did he care about a PI sticking her nose into the investigation, family member or not?

"Getting the information I need to go after my sister's intruder and my nephew."

"Looks like you're impeding a federal investigation to me," he said, his voice deep, smooth and compelling.

"I was going to give you the information after I found out who rented that car and if it had anything to do with my sister."

"Does it?"

"You tell me. I'm sure you already have the information."

He made a soft laughing noise that had nothing to do with humor. "You're absolutely right. We have the information and we're going to follow up on it."

"Fine. Then why are you wasting your time tracking me down and busting my chops?"

He set his hands on his hips. "These are dangerous people, Emma. We found the complex's landscaper murdered for his shirt."

"I was a cop for ten years, and have been a PI for three years. I deal with extremely dangerous criminals every day. That's not going to scare me off. I have every right to hunt for my nephew and nothing you say will stop me. So either arrest me for *impeding* your investigation or get out of my way." Oh, shoot. This man brought out the worst in her.

She was just about to apologize when he said, "Your gun?"

"What?" she bit out. He held out his hand. "I have a permit."

"I'm sure you do." He did a "gimme" gesture with

his fingers. She pulled the gun she carried in a holster at her lower back and set it in his palm. He checked the safety and pocketed the weapon. "Turn around," he said through gritted teeth.

She huffed and did as he asked. When she felt the cold steel against her wrists, and his hot skin against hers, she swore under her breath. "There's no need for this. I'm just trying to help." She gritted her teeth against the re-action her body experienced when he touched her. His wide chest and broad shoulders, all that muscled power beneath his expensive suit…

He was close behind her and when he leaned in to speak into her ear, his warm breath made her shiver. She tried to chalk that up to reaction, but she knew she was lying to herself. "Civilians helping is something NCIS frowns on, Ms. St. John. It could muck up the evidence." He marched her to his car and opened the back door.

Emma sighed, ducking her head to get inside. She couldn't let her emotions get to her. "Exactly. I could work with you."

At his dubious look, she swallowed hard. How could she convince him? "Don't cut me out. I can help you." The need churned in her gut and wouldn't go away, no matter what she did, from this moment to the day she stopped drawing breath. If she didn't see this through, it would haunt her every waking hour.

She'd taken care of Lily since they'd been kids, pro-tected her against their indifferent and mean-spirited grandmother, who resented them for messing up her per-fect life and interfering with her work. It had been them together against the world and she couldn't just let NCIS take over and handle the investigation. She couldn't.

Derrick turned around and stared at her; she bit back

the tears. This was too important. She had to act professional. Not like a grieving sister and panicked aunt. Getting her nephew back and making the person who hurt her sister pay would be the only outcomes she could handle.

He sighed. "We don't make a habit of arresting grieving sisters, Ms. St. John. I resent you for making me do it."

He turned back around and put the car in gear. "Well, then, we're even, Agent Gunn," she said softly to his suddenly stiff shoulders. "Are you going to tell me if you found this George Douglas or not?" she asked when the pressure to know got too much.

"My pal at NCIS is looking for that car right now and tracking down the guy who rented it. With traffic cams all over this city, the AMBER Alert active, we'll spot it and that will give us some clue where he might have gone." He pulled onto the highway and said, "I did interrogate Lily's CO. They were having an affair."

"What?" If Lily had kept this from her, what else had she kept secret? Had she been too afraid of Emma's interference? Had Emma driven her sister to keep these secrets?

"He seems like a decent guy. They were planning to get married and he was offered a position in Okinawa. They were going overseas together."

Trying to ease the sudden knot in her throat, she tightened her bound hands into fists, the hard wad of tension in her belly intensifying. Experiencing a flurry of emotions—pain, guilt, anger and hurt—Emma had thought she and Lily had an unshakable bond. But when Lily had shocked the hell out of Emma with the news that she was taking an overseas assignment in Japan, Emma had voiced her disapproval. The fact that her sister would be too far away for Emma to keep an eye on her fueled the worry that had made Emma's words harsh. And, to Emma's incredulous surprise, Lily had pushed back, hard. She'd told Emma to mind her own business for once and stop crapping all over her rainbows, dampening her happiness and pointing out problems. Lily had stormed out and she hadn't heard from her in days. But they'd reconciled somewhat when Lily had asked Emma to watch Matty. Now she was in a coma and might never wake up, all that promise gone. Had she been too heavy-handed in Lily's life? Was that because her own had been so empty?

"So maybe you didn't like that idea and you two fought."

Emma stiffened and glared at his back. "What are you saying? I pushed Lily down the stairs because I couldn't let her go to Japan? I hired some thug to abduct my nephew, and I have him stashed away to keep him safe?"

"Did you? Do you have him?"

She leaned forward and said, her tone glacial, "No. I would never hurt my sister. Never deprive my nephew of his mother, no matter how much I disagreed with her."

"I have to ask these questions," he said, meeting her gaze briefly in the rearview. "It's nothing personal. Just the fact that well-meaning family members can get carried away."

"I didn't," she said as his eyes flicked away. "We fought. Sisters fight, but we would have worked it out."

He pulled up to the Pendleton office and got out of the car. Helping her out, he kept his hand on her arm. She wanted to shrug him off, but she didn't want it to matter, so she endured his touch.

Once they emerged from the elevator and entered the

bullpen, his teammates all stared at him. One woman looked nonplussed and rubbed at her forehead. "What's going on?"

"I arrested her."

"Derrick," a tall woman with honey-blond hair said, clearly appalled at his treatment of her.

"Take her to the conference room and remove the cuffs," the first woman instructed.

"Yes, ma'am," he said and escorted her into the conference room. He unlocked the cuffs and slipped them back into the pouch under his suit coat.

She rubbed her wrists. His eyes went there and he looked away, another little frisson of heat sizzling through her. Damn that reaction.

"You're pretty self-assured about everything you do, aren't you?" Okay, so maybe she was picking a fight. That helped to neutralize this…thing between them.

He didn't answer and she sighed. Did she peg him or what?

Emma hadn't had time to research the tattoo Gail had mentioned, but the sound of it gave her an idea of what it was. To get her mind off the vibes she was getting from Derrick, and give him some information that might be helpful, she said, "That tattoo is *Santa Muerte*, Saint Death. It's usually depicted by a woman with designs on her face and stitched lips, chalky white skin. Many Mexicans revere her as a popular icon. You can ask her for love, money or wealth, but it's also insanely popular with drug dealers or criminals and acts as protection. Connecting with death hopefully will protect them."

"You're pretty knowledgeable about Mexican culture."

"I've cleared several cases in Mexico. I saw firsthand

the tattoos and the worship of her. I speak fluent Spanish. I could be an asset."

"You think someone is going to ransom your nephew?"

"No, I don't think he will be ransomed. I think he was taken for a reason and my sister stood in the way, but I have no idea for what purpose."

He pulled out his cell and gave the person on the other end the information about the tat.

His boss entered the room and she came forward. "Supervisory Special Agent Kai Talbot. Have a seat, Ms. St. John."

Emma sat, keeping her eyes on this woman. She was formidable in a nonthreatening way and Emma liked her. It was inordinately easier to deal with her than to have to interact with that gorgeous, pushy alpha male.

Even with her attention on Kai, she was aware of him looming in the background, his presence palatable, distracting her all over again.

Emma leaned forward and said, "Does he have to be here?"

Kai smiled and nodded. "He's one of the best." She sat forward and said, "I have more information." Emma steeled herself to hear about what had happened to her sister. "She has defensive wounds. She fought hard before she was thrown down the stairs. It's the doctor's assessment that she didn't break her fall—a human reflex. She would have had to been unconscious when she tumbled."

"My little sister fought. I'm so proud of her."

"This all likely happened very early yesterday morning. He's had all this time to take your nephew anywhere. But we have a Be On the Lookout—BOLO—alert in progress."

Derrick was watching her, and for one single moment

she wondered how it would feel to have his arms around her, comforting her just like his body language and his eyes broadcasted he wanted to as she allowed herself to look over at him. Her eyes filled up with tears as she tried to swallow. Derrick inhaled sharply and started toward her, almost as if he didn't remember Kai was even in the room.

Her heart jumped into overdrive, pounding so hard it felt as if it would come through her ribs. She shifted her eyes to Kai, feeling her face drained of blood, but Kai's expression and eyes softened, too. Emma looked down, trying to keep her composure, her pulse laboring, her breath jammed up in her chest, fighting her anger and anguish, all mixed up into a surging desire to maim someone.

Compelled, she looked back at Derrick. Holding his gaze, she stared at him this time with the pain and desolation she couldn't hide bare, tears spilling over.

Dragging in a ragged breath, he swore viciously and quietly to himself. Snatching up a box of tissues on the table, he walked over and offered her one. It was clear to her he considered it a paltry offering, but she pulled one out of the box and sat there as the tears rolled off her jaw.

They gave her a few moments of silence to absorb the information and handle her grief.

"Emma, Derrick arrested you for a reason. We can't have civilians—"

"I wouldn't say I was a civilian."

"We have a murder now included in this investigation."

"A murder? Who?"

"The landscaper, Kevin Sherman. He was a grandfather and husband, had two grown daughters. Found him in the back of his pickup truck."

Her heart went out to the family, but she'd already been involved in solving more grisly murders. "I used to be an LAPD detective, and I worked homicide. Now I'm a private investigator and successful enough to have offices in San Francisco, LA and here in San Diego. I want the people who took my nephew and hurt my sister."

"So do we."

"Not as much as I do," she said fervently, meeting Kai's eyes straight on, blotting her eyes with the tissue, showing her need to actively participate and see this through. Emma's meaning struck home as Kai acknowledged her right to be involved. "He's my family. I want in on this."

"We don't think that's a good idea for you to be personally involved," Derrick growled, pushing through his already disheveled hair and yanking on his already displaced tie. The smooth skin of his chest peeked out from between the open collar of his dress shirt.

Why did she have to have this reaction to him? How was it that he projected so much from those hard, flinty eyes without really saying anything and she had to resist the urge to shiver? Deep down he cared, and his sense of justice was evident in the cadence of his voice. But Emma had just lost the stable world she'd constructed for herself, Lily and Matty. She was broken and hurting, feeling horribly guilty, and she didn't know any other way to handle this. She might have been struggling, but she wasn't defeated. "I'd be an asset. As I said, I speak fluent Spanish and I've been to Mexico many times. I have even negotiated for a kidnapped businessman and worked with the FBI. I'm fully qualified with a handgun. I can do things federal agents can't because I have fewer restrictions on the letter of the law. I can help in this investigation." She pulled an envelope out of her purse. "Here is my résumé."

Derrick strode over and turned her chair. "You're too close to this."

She stood and faced off against him, her temper tripping, the grief igniting her deep-seated need to protect her sister and the agonizing realization that she'd failed so utterly. She had to do this. Be involved. There was no other way and she'd die trying because she had to. It was the only way she could live with herself.

"You can't stop me from investigating if I choose to. I don't care if I lose my license or you throw me in jail. I'll get bail and then I'll do what is necessary to find out who did this. You can either allow me to work with you or I'll do it on my own."

He took a step closer and she tensed, not because he was threatening her. She didn't need this distraction. It would be so much easier to deal with Kai alone. This man already had a way of seeing past her defenses, to some other place she was unaccustomed to people reaching. It was like he knew what it was like to have to keep every shred of vulnerability under wraps. Like he understood. She rejected that. It wasn't possible to understand what she'd gone through, what Lily had to endure at the hands of their grandmother.

He stood his ground, kept his gaze steady on hers. She had to grudgingly admit that this man wasn't intimidated by her like so many were. "Let us handle this. We'll keep you fully informed—"

Both their cells rang and they answered in unison.

Then looked at each other, their gazes triumphant. Disconnecting the call, Kai said, "We found the vehicle."

They both headed for the door and Emma was determined she wasn't going to be left here to ponder ineffectually while the "professionals" conducted the investigation.

"No," Derrick said, holding up his hand.

She went around him, and he grabbed her arm.

"Let her go, Derrick."

He threw a surprised and questioning look toward Kai.

"Maybe she'll spot something we miss."

Shaking off his hand, she followed them out to the bull pen, to the big plasma screen where they were already running footage of the black Crown sedan.

As soon as Kai, Derrick and Emma approached, Austin Beck, the other agent she remembered as Derrick's partner from Lily's house, stood with a remote in his hand. He was dressed again more like a chic surfer boy than an agent—upscale knit hoodie in soft gray, black military-inspired jacket and a pair of orange pants, dark navy midtop deck shoes on his feet.

"I found the car just outside La Mesa, then picked it up again on the highway toward downtown. He stopped at a pharmacy before getting back in the car. I'm still looking for it after it left the pharmacy. The rendering from Ms. Baker was spot on. I'm running him through face-recognition right now."

The blonde woman came up alongside them and took the remote from Austin.

"This is Special Agent Amber Michaels," Derrick said.

Amber nodded to Emma and smiled encouragingly.

"I researched the tattoo with the information that Emma gave us. I found this." She clicked the remote and the tattoo came up on one side along with several men to the other. "These are the *Los Equis*, The Xs in English. It's considered a criminal syndicate by the Mexican government. The US has deemed it the most technically cutting-edge, sophisticated, brutal, callously vicious and dangerous cartel operating in Mexico."

The blood drained from Emma's face. This was much worse than she had imagined. The implications of this boggled her mind. Had her nephew been taken where it would be twice as hard to find him? How had these people come into her sister's life? She would never have consorted with criminals. Her job in the navy meant too much to her. Emma wanted to dismiss this avenue of the investigation because it was so far-fetched. Lily hadn't ever been to Mexico.

Amber was still talking. "They run their organization out of the state of Michoacán and came to power during the massive attacks by the government and DEA against the kingpins in the area. That left a big hole to fill. The seconds-in-command and all their soldiers needed leadership and they got it from this man." She put up a picture of a big, well-built, handsome man dressed impeccably in a blue suit. His tanned face was wreathed in a smile that crinkled his piercing blue eyes, a stunning contrast to his silver hair. "Gilberto Ortega, *Monte Diablo*— the Devil Mountain—as he's dubbed, because he's such a big man. His wife is deceased, killed in crossfire with a smaller rival cartel. Rumor has it he wiped them out, slaughtered everyone involved. But there is no proof and he was never charged," she said, her voice grim. "He has one son, Arturo." She put up another man's photo, tanned, fit and a younger version of his attractive father. "Arturo loves to live well and is somewhat of an international playboy." Amber switched to a close-up of the tattoo, a woman's eye with the big, red X. "Everyone in that organization has this tat. It's their calling card and it's symbolic of their oneness with death and their ability to mete it out as they see fit." She then put up the grainy picture of the man behind the sedan's wheel. "They are said to employ teen assassins, which fits perfectly with the rendering of the guy Lieutenant Baker described."

The blood came rushing back, flushing Emma's cheeks until they felt hot. She felt sickened and horrified, not only at the implications of her sister's fall, realizing that it could have been so much worse, but that these ruthless men could have Matty. "My sister would never get involved with a cartel!" Emma said, turning to face Amber. But the sickness and the horror was mixed in with the fact that Lily had been so damn trusting and sweet, so eager for love and affection, so eager to be in love. What had she done? What had she subjected Matty to without even realizing it? *Oh, Lily... So naive.*

Had the fight forced a rift between them? Had Lily been in trouble and felt as if she couldn't come to Emma for help? Had she alienated her sister because of her intense desire to protect her and this was the result—her sister in a coma in the hospital and her sweet Matty abducted?

Chapter 4

But it was Derrick who responded. "We're not saying she was involved with a cartel, but the evidence that it was this man who abducted your nephew is compelling. We aren't going to jump to conclusions until we have the full story."

"Amber, work up a profile on Ortega and his son. Austin, track that damn car down and see where it went. Derrick, check out the pharmacy. Take Ms. St. John with you."

He turned to protest, but his boss's eyes had their own hard, flinty look and he closed his mouth, the objections projecting out of his eyes like daggers.

He jammed the button for the elevator and when the doors opened, they stepped inside. She couldn't deal with his anger at having her tag along right now. She was caught up in the news that she had dropped the ball, and not a rubber one that would just bounce back, but a glass one that was smashed to smithereens, like her heart and her confidence. How could she have been unaware that her sister was in this kind of danger? An assassin? How had she missed this?

He beat her to his passenger door and she raised a brow when he opened it for her. She got inside and he closed the door, then settled in the driver's seat. After glancing at his phone's GPS, he started the car.

Once they were on the highway, he said, "Beating yourself up isn't going to help."

"I failed her so totally. As a former cop and a person who assessed threat for a living, I should have been aware that something was off."

"None of us are perfect, Emma. Hindsight is always clear and concise. All we can do now is get the people who did this and return her son to you both safe and sound."

She nodded.

"I guess you don't hold a grudge," she said, warmed by his words when she didn't want to be. She had only ever wanted to take care of herself, her sister and her own emotions. She had no illusions about how eager people were to stick around and care or make a difference. Part of her jaded outlook on life came from working the streets as a cop, but a large portion of it came from her grandmother who had been mostly absent from their lives, couldn't be bothered to take an interest in their daily activities, preferring to leave their rearing to a nanny. When she did focus on them, it was to criticize or make sure each of them knew how cruel the world could be and how important it was for them to be as strong, as resolute, as their formidable grandmother.

The world was a cruel and harsh place. Lily hadn't wanted to believe that, no matter how much Emma tried to force-feed her. She had ended up in the hospital. Love came with a price.

"No. This job is tough enough without judging people.

What happened to your sister is devastating, and I get that you're defensive and need to protect yourself right now. I know all about regrets and guilt and how it can tie you up into terrible knots."

"Don't be kind," she whispered. She wanted to touch his arm, but held back. Clasping her hands into fists, she eased in an unsteady breath. "Please, not now." It would have been better if he'd stayed in the enigmatic, hard-ass category. That would have been easier to handle, not this compassionate man. There was a tremendous pull in the tiny space between them, the kind of pull that made it almost impossible to ignore. Feeling unexpectedly close to tears—*again*, and this had to be a record for her—she kept her eyes straight ahead, her chest unbearably tight. She hadn't felt so alone or bereft like this since her parents died.

Nearly overcome by that feeling, she took a breath and asked, "So where are we going?"

Finally, she looked at him. He gripped the wheel and took a breath. His voice low and gruff, he said, "This pharmacy is in one of the busiest sections of La Mesa."

"He probably did that on purpose, so that he would be lost in a crowd," she responded and he turned admiring eyes on her.

"That's right. Good observation."

She tried to will away the ache, tried to collect a modicum of common sense. *Proximity*, her rational inner voice whispered. *He cares more than he should*, countered that other little voice. *Just two lonely people*, she mentally argued. *You're kidding yourself*, responded her conscience.

It didn't matter. Derrick in any proximity was potent enough. Up close and in person, he was downright irresistible. She wanted to get to know him better and see if that intensity and care transferred over into charm and humor. Even if Derrick wasn't an enemy to be wary of, he wasn't exactly an ally, either. If he'd had his way, she wouldn't be sitting here.

That thought gave her a spurt of anger she could use to ward off his intoxicating presence.

The rest of the trip was in silence while Emma nursed that spurt of anger into a barrier she could use against Derrick's sheer maleness. Once they'd parked and headed into the pharmacy, she followed him. Derrick said, "Let me take the lead."

She nodded, ready to lend any type of support or help she could.

One of the cashiers pointed them to the back where the clerk, Missy, had been on duty the day before. They found her behind the pharmacy counter and she smiled as they approached. Well, she smiled at Derrick, which irked Emma, but she wasn't going to acknowledge it. No damn way.

"Hello there, handsome," Missy said, "Can I help you with something?" She snapped her gum and smiled again.

He seemed unconcerned or not at all inclined to follow up her come-on with his own play-along. He flashed his badge, his face unsmiling. "We're here about a missing infant."

She gasped. "Someone was taken from the store?"

"No, the kidnapper was here yesterday." He pulled out the artist's rendering and the girl took it with wide eyes, studying it.

"Yes… I saw him in here. I remember he had scary eyes for such a young guy and this even scarier tattoo on his upper arm. The little boy I thought was his son was bundled up. He was in a huge hurry and not very talk-ative. Had an accent and I thought he was probably from Mexico, since we're so close to the border."

That statement immediately set panic off in Emma's chest. "Was the baby all right?"

"No, he was fussing up a storm. I could hear him all the way to the counter. He asked me for something to quiet him and I suggested some baby analgesic. He looked on edge and like the crying was getting to him."

"How did he pay?" Emma asked, hoping for some type of paper trail to follow.

"Cash. A hundred-dollar bill."

She didn't give Derrick a chance to speak, the urgency in her fueling her inquiries. "How long did he stay and did he give you any clue as to where he might be going?"

"Only the time it took to get his items and pay. Maybe fifteen minutes." She grimaced and her expression told Emma she wished she had more information. "He dropped this." She reached below the counter and pulled out a bootie. It was blue and Emma took it, her gut twist-ing with recognition and worry. "I tried to chase him down, but he didn't hear me. He got into a black sedan and headed south, toward the freeway."

Emma just stared at the bootie fitting in her palm, so soft, so small. She'd bought them after Matty had been born. They'd been a little too big then but he'd grown into them.

Even though Missy was looking at her, Derrick re-sponded, "Thank you for your time." She nodded and when Emma didn't move, Derrick nudged her. Pulling a plastic bag out of his pocket, he opened it so she could drop the booty inside.

Once they got back to the car, Derrick opened her door

again and she slid inside, feeling emotionally gutted. This was real. This was happening. Matty was gone, in the hands of the man who had injured his mother. They had no clue where they were, where they were going or why he had hurt Lily and taken her son.

"We'll head back to NCIS and regroup." He started the car, but when she didn't respond, he reached over and clasped her arm. "We'll find him. I promise you, Emma."

"You can't be sure of that," she whispered. The loss hitting her hard.

"I can guarantee you that I… We won't stop looking for him until we find him. That's a promise."

She nodded and said, her voice shaky, "He's fussy because he has an ear infection. My sister was giving him amoxicillin. We have to find him, Derrick."

He reached over and squeezed her arm in acknowledgement.

As they stepped off the elevator back at NCIS headquarters, Emma froze when she heard that cold, merciless voice demand, "Where is my granddaughter? I have a right to know."

Once she got her feet to move, everything shutting down inside her so she could deal with this new threat, Emma came face-to-face with her grandmother.

"There *you* are… you ungrateful wretch. I have to be *informed* of Lily's injury! You couldn't have the common decency to call me and let me know?"

Anger built inside Emma as she watched her grandmother do what she did best—grandstand with concern. But it was an act. Her grandmother was put out, like Lily's hospitalization had interrupted her life. Poor Bess; the granddaughter she never loved was hurt and the great-grandson she'd hardly acknowledged was gone.

Poor Bess, so cold and calculating, like a character out of Charles Dickens. There had never been the possibility of more in Emma and Lily's world. Bess saw to it that even the word *some* was meaningless.

"Really, Bess? I would have thought you'd find the interruption inconvenient."

Her grandmother's eyes narrowed. "How can you say such a thing to me?"

She shouldn't have. She knew she shouldn't have. Good girls didn't sass back. Ladies kept their opinions to themselves. But all the dictates from her upbringing couldn't hold back the rage she had stored inside her all these years. In her mind she could see Lily lying in that hospital bed, her face so pale, and she could hardly allow herself to imagine the way her sister had suffered. And here was Bess, playing the martyr. Never an ounce of compassion for anyone. Never mind who else might be in pain.

"Let's take this to the conference room," Derrick's boss, Kai, said, her voice ringing with authority. When Bess didn't move, Kai grabbed her arm and started to drag her down the hall. Derrick was right at Emma's elbow and she hadn't realized that he had been so close, and even though she barely knew him, his presence bolstered her.

With a deep breath, she followed them down the hall to the conference room.

Her grandmother had that stubborn set to her jaw, her eyes accusing and devoid of any compassion. "I have never been so insulted, Emma."

"Nothing ever changes, Bess," Emma said, uncaring that both Kai and Derrick were standing there. Neither one of them made any move to leave. "It was just the same when Mom and Dad were killed," she said, her voice trembling with the power of her emotions. "We were so little, so alone in the world. You could have made a difference, but you didn't. Instead you just have to turn it around to focus on you, so you got people's sympathy, so they all went around saying 'Poor Bess. She's such a good person for taking in her grandchildren.'"

"I was good to take you in!" Bess snarled. "I had lost my son. He meant everything to me!"

That was exactly what Emma had thought. Her grandmother had been so devastated by her son's death, the son she'd groomed in her image and doted on, that she'd taken out her grief on his children from the moment they stepped foot in her home. She'd never said it out loud, but the terrible knowledge was something Emma had never shared with Lily because she worried that it would have broken her heart. She was free to say it now and the weight of holding that knowledge was like a concrete block. It wouldn't bring Matty back. It wouldn't give them back their childhood. It could only prolong the pain and mire them more deeply in the muck of the past.

"I did what was best for all of us," Bess said imperiously. "Not that you or your sister ever showed a moment's appreciation. Both of you were spoiled. And Lily. She always had her head in the clouds. Not at all like your father."

"Exactly, and his children were the booby prize. We weren't him and you resented us for living."

"Emma! All the sacrifices I made for you and your sister, and all I get in return is this bitterness and criticism."

"You reap what you sow," Emma said.

Her grandmother just stared, then she looked away.

"Nevertheless. We can put our differences aside. I can contact people I know at the State Department."

Her grandmother rose when Austin burst into the conference room. "We got a hit on the BOLO."

She grasped Derrick's arm. "I want to go."

He looked to Kai and then sighed. "All right."

Her grandmother pulled out her cell phone as Emma left with Derrick, the door closing on her strained and pale face. She was shocked her grandmother was here and willing to help, but legally, it seemed a dead-end route to her for many reasons. Their best bet in getting Matty back was by going to where they had taken him and forcefully retrieving him. Her focus now had to be on finding Matty and nothing else.

Derrick watched Emma's confrontation with her grandmother and forced back his own memories of his childhood. Every brain cell needed to be focused on finding that baby. For his sake and Emma's.

Austin talked as they rushed down the hall. "It's right before the border. There's a California Highway Patrolman waiting for you."

As soon as they hit the pavement, he set the siren on his car and drove like hell to get to where the CHP officer had parked his motorcycle. Derrick came to a stop on the shoulder and he and Emma exited the car. Cars whizzed past and Derrick could see in the distance the line of cars slowing for the border crossing, and the booths and the signs at the border.

"It's off the road, back there buried behind some brush," the officer said as he pointed toward a clump of trees. "The sun was angled perfectly for me to see the reflection off the hood. I only got close enough to see the license plate."

"Thank you," Derrick said. He released his weapon and said, "Back me up."

"Yes, sir."

"Give me my weapon," Emma said, and Derrick pulled the gun out of his pocket and handed it to her. Emma was right behind him, the patrolman bringing up the rear as they approached the vehicle. Derrick flanked toward the rear, raising his weapon as the patrolman moved toward the front.

"This is NCIS! Step out of the vehicle with your hands up," he ordered, but there was no response. They moved in slowly, Derrick watching for any signs of threat or movement. As he rounded the back of the car, he saw that the driver's side was empty, but he didn't drop his guard. He approached the window and quickly looked inside, but the passenger seat and the floorboards were vacant.

He looked in the backseat and his gut tightened when Emma made a soft sound. An abandoned baby seat was empty.

Her nephew was gone. She reached out and captured a soft blue blanket with whimsical animals on it.

She brought the blanket to her face and stood there for a moment, lost in her pain. Then she dropped the blanket and looked toward the border crossing.

Derrick reached into the driver's side and pulled the trunk lever. It released with a popping sound. He walked to the back and raised the hood. The cop gasped, his gaze going to Emma. "Who is that?" he asked.

"George Douglas, I presume." Derrick searched the man and came up with his wallet. Sure enough, his ID confirmed it. "The abductor must have jumped him outside the rental office."

Derrick's cell rang. "Derrick, I have him on the walkway," Austin said.

"How long ago?" he said, the sleepless night catching up to him in the weariness in his voice, knowing they were too late even as he met Emma's stricken eyes.

"He's crossed into Mexico and has more than a day's start," Austin said grimly.

"We're going to need the ME again. We've got another dead body. It's George Douglas, the guy who rented the car from Crown."

Austin sighed. "This guy went through a lot to snatch this kid. It's got to be personal."

"Yeah, but why?"

"That is the question. I'll keep you posted if I find anything else."

Emma saw the answer in Derrick's eyes after he disconnected the call, her throat closing up. "When?" she said in a strangled tone.

"Emma—"

"When, dammit!"

"Twelve hours ago," he said, his voice gruff.

She clutched the blanket to her. One part of her brain knew panic wasn't going to help as she pressed the cloth to her mouth, trying to force some rationality past it. Her whole body trembling, she clenched her hands.

Matty's sweet baby scent left on the blanket filled her nose. Emma released a pent-up breath, turned and looked at the border crossing, her gaze desperate. "He's not going to get away with this." He was so little. *Please,*

Matty. Please be okay. "We should get over there and question as many people as we can," Emma said.

"NCIS will be by to impound this car and tow it to the lab. Please watch over it and wait for the ME and the technicians," Derrick instructed.

"Will do," the officer said. "Good luck with the search."

She headed for the car, but a strong hand gripped her arm. "We'll find him." He was relentless, his grip strong. Maintaining a hold on her, he caught her by the chin and forced her gaze away from the border crossing. "Look at me, Emma," he commanded firmly. She stared numbly at him, her chest heaving and hurting, her breathing still raw. "We're not at a dead end yet." He pulled her against him and she resisted for a moment, then relented. Her arms sliding around him, she gave in to the need to feel something solid and warm in her world right now.

"It's all right," he said. "It's going to be okay," he whispered. Pressing her head to his shoulder, he gathered her up in a tight embrace, his hand tangled in her hair. Shifting so she was flat against him, she closed her eyes, the rush of loneliness and panic subsiding into a dull ache. Derrick tightened his hold on her, her heart hammering, her breathing slowing to match his.

He released a shaky sigh, adjusting his hold on her, drawing her deeper into his embrace. She had never come apart like this, but losing Lily, Matty's uncertain future, the fight with her grandmother and not getting a wink of sleep the night before—all took their toll.

"Let's get going," she said, breaking away from him. Leaning time was over. She needed to get to work, and getting personal with the man she was planning on working with wasn't a smart idea.

They drove to the border and spent the next half an hour talking to everyone they could. She saw that Agent Gunn also spoke beautiful, fluent Spanish. He was impressing her all over the place.

Several of the border guards remembered seeing a young man meeting the abductor's description. They said he'd headed across the walkway and could have picked up a car on the other side or had one waiting. Then Emma and Agent Gunn watched footage between the time frame until Emma spied the kidnapper and Matty, who got into a white sedan and drove away. They captured his face so they'd have reference to the suspect when they caught up to him.

There was no way to know in what direction they had traveled after that. She worried that it would slow them down.

They went back to her office, both of them exhausted. "I know several government officials and could probably pave the way for us to enter Mexico," she said as she unlocked the door. Making her way to her office, she turned on the lights and he settled on her sofa. "I can order in." She threw him a menu.

"Coffee or tea?" she asked as she booted up her computer and paused in the doorway.

"Coffee. Black," he said, getting up and sitting in her desk chair. It gave her a little shiver down her spine, how good he looked there. She was gone and back in the time it took for her to use her one-shot coffeemaker that also boiled just plain water—a cup of steaming coffee for him, and calming tea for her.

She took a few sips and the hot liquid helped her to get her bearings. He leaned back in her chair, accepting the mug. "I've been thinking that maybe Lily hooked up with someone, maybe a fling, a one-night stand? Anything happen out of the ordinary eighteen months ago that could give us any clue as to how she came into the Ortegas' orbit?"

"No…" Wait. Eighteen months ago Lily had gone on a cruise. "The cruise. She went on a cruise eighteen months ago. That had to be when she conceived Matty."

"A cruise. Right." Derrick pulled out his cell and pressed in the number, setting it to speaker. "Austin, those pictures on Lily's phone."

"Yeah. I have them all in a file. Nothing there."

"How about you look for the pictures that aren't there."

"Aw, gotcha—in that she may have deleted some. Hang on."

After a few minutes Austin said, "Well, I'll be damned. Sending them now."

Derrick's phone beeped and he accessed the email.

Emma watched as numerous photos popped on his screen. "Oh, no," she whispered. "That's Gilberto and Arturo she's posing with." She closed her eyes and sat back. "Arturo's the father of her child. That's who took Matty. Oh, Lily…"

Derrick sat with her for a few minutes. He looked at her, then pressed a number into his phone. "Kai, Emma knows some officials that could get us into the country, maybe cut through some red tape. Can you conference us in with the director? Get Emma officially appointed to assist in the investigation."

They discussed the mission and Emma started working on getting in touch with the people she knew. When she looked over, Agent Gunn was stretched out on her couch, fast asleep. She rose and walked over to him and gazed into his face. She'd have to work with him. That was a given, but her insides jangled. She wasn't going to let this get personal—at least not as personal as it already was.

The Ortegas were a game changer. With the cartel involved, there was considerable danger. Emma knew that, but she also was capable of handling herself. It was good to know she'd have him backing her up. She reached down and shook his arm. "Agent Gunn, I have an update."

He opened those deep blue eyes and for a moment studied her. He was completely lucid and wide awake, when only moments ago he'd been deep in slumber. His big hand lay on his chest as it rose slowly with his even breathing. The light from the lamp on the table next to the sofa made his blue eyes appear lit from within. There was something oddly disconcerting about the way he scrutinized her, as if he was peeling away layer upon layer, looking for the person within. Emma didn't move a muscle, her heart suddenly laboring, her breath stuck in her chest. Awareness churned through her, making her heart labor even harder, and she was struck by a nearly overwhelming fascination with his hand, remembering the heat of his touch. "If we're going to work together, Emma, maybe you should call me Derrick." He didn't exactly say it with the kind of lazy, sleep-filled voice she expected. There was too much intensity in this man to ever label him languid.

He rose and she told him Mexican officials and the secretary of the navy had come to an agreement and they were both in. They should pack what they needed, get a good night's sleep. Then they could map out a plan and get the necessary paperwork. Derrick nodded and rose. Before she realized it, she was too close to him. Aware of the heat of his body. Resting his hand on her shoulder, he gave her a reassuring squeeze. Then walked toward the door. "Get some sleep, Emma. We're going to need it. We'll have to be on our toes in Mexico. Anything goes there, especially with a cartel involved."

She shivered as the door closed behind him. She stood there for a minute. She'd get some sleep, then find her passport. She was going into Mexico with gorgeous Special Agent Derrick Gunn. She was finding Matty no matter what and keeping her hands, heart and head in the right place.

Chapter 5

Santa Ana, Mexico

Luis Montoya rubbed his temple, his head close to bursting. Ever since he'd left the border yesterday, the kid wouldn't shut up, no matter what he did. Yet his *jefe's* request was nothing short of dire. If anything happened to the kid, he'd gut him and leave his entrails to the buzzards.

Luis wasn't going to take any chances with the boy. As the town of Santa Ana came up on his GPS, a small town in the state of Sonora, Luis made a quick decision. He pulled off and into town where he found a doctor, who diagnosed the infant with an ear infection and prescribed medicine for him. Luis went to the closest pharmacy and picked up what he needed. Carefully administering the dose recommended on the bottle, he decided that getting some much-needed sleep would be the best course of action. He had a long drive ahead of him and stopping for the night to rest would be prudent. Even if the Americans had figured out what had happened, they couldn't possibly find him. But precautions were required. Once he settled in for the night at a hotel out of town, he called the network of people associated with *Los Equis* and set up a welcoming committee.

Luckily, after eating, the baby went to sleep and Luis closed his eyes.

It had been bad luck for him, instead of the woman. She *had* heard him and when she'd turned around, he'd had no choice but to do what he was instructed, no matter his reluctance. Killing a mother just wasn't right. But she had some skills and she'd fought him, getting away. She'd rushed toward the stairs, screaming, and that's where he'd caught her. They had struggled some more and he'd pushed her. Her body had made a terrible noise going down the stairs. Worried that someone would overhear, he had gotten out of there as soon as possible.

He'd snatched the kid and, once he'd gotten to the bottom of the stairs, the mother had not moved. He thought about making sure she was dead, then heard voices. He couldn't risk it. He'd left as quickly as he could.

If the *jefe* found out the woman was still alive, it wouldn't be good for him, but he'd gotten the baby. *El jefe* would have to figure it out from there. Luis was just the tip of the boss's knife.

NCIS Headquarters
Camp Pendleton, California

They were all standing in the TacOps room, a specialized, secure area with a big screen on the far wall, and equipment and computers to the left. They were waiting for the Mexican secretariat of the interior and the attorney general to appear. Kai, Emma and Derrick were all waiting to get the go ahead. Derrick, who was chafing at the time it was taking to negotiate their entrance into Mexico, wanted to pace, but he held back his restless energy. The first twenty-four hours after an abduction were crucial. But he understood the need for the sovereign nation of Mexico to make sure about the agent and PI entering the country and the ability for them to carry firearms, and he was used to protocol.

Finally, the screen evened out and two men appeared, seated at a conference table. The director was shown on a split screen from his office in Washington, DC.

"Gentlemen, thank you for taking the time to hear our special request. Two American citizens were murdered and an infant boy has been taken from the United States and transported into Mexico."

"Yes," one man said. We have seen the footage and read the report. We understand PI Emma St. John is involved in this case."

The NCIS director nodded. "Yes, she is currently working with us in an official capacity."

"That is very fortuitous. We have worked with her in the past and have found her to be very competent. We have discussed this between us and wish to offer the courtesy of both Ms. St. John and Special Agent Derrick Gunn to carry concealed weapons in Mexico. We will produce the necessary paperwork and the permits that they should have with them once they cross the border to be presented to police or officials once in Mexico. We have also assigned two liaisons for them, Inspector Jorge Reyes and Agent Santiago Velasco, who is our drug enforcement liaison. He knows the cartels and the illegal activity in the area including details regarding Gilberto Ortega and the *Los Equis*. Inspector Reyes is a veteran *policia* and will have an office and equipment available for Agent Gunn and Ms. St. John in Caliche, Michoacán." Since the *Los Equis* were based out of this central state in Mexico and as their leader, it would follow that Gilberto Ortega ruled the area, Caliche would be the most likely place to base their search for Matthew St. John. "If there is any way we can assist you, please don't hesitate to contact us. Also, please give our regards to Ms. St. John."

Derrick looked over at Emma. She was thanking Kai for allowing her into the ops center and participating in the effort to get her nephew back.

Her hair was in a ponytail today, revealing the delicate bones of her face, the bangs making her look younger than she was. His eyes roamed over her; he was unable to curb his interest in the trim form, the generous breasts and her slim waist. He dragged his eyes away before someone noticed. What the hell was the matter with him? He couldn't initiate a thing with her. It wouldn't be professional or smart. But Derrick also knew that things happened when two people were thrown together and he made sure he had protection. He didn't want a repeat of what happened in Afghanistan with Afsana.

He tried to change gears. She obviously had some chops with the Mexican government and he was damned impressed. He shouldn't be surprised. She had wooed not only Kai over to her side, but the director, as well. He was outgunned and outvoted. He still felt it was better to exclude her from the trip into Mexico to locate and retrieve her nephew. It had nothing to do with her professionally and everything to do with her personally. He'd seen it enough what happened to people who got emotionally involved. Hell, he'd gotten involved with Afsana after working so closely with her and they had given into their desires. And dammit, Emma was very distracting.

She walked over and said, "Are you ready to go? The permits will be here in an hour."

"I've got my bags packed and my passport."

She nodded and looked at her watch. "I guess we could get some lunch before we have to go, map out a plan."

"We can go to the marine corps mess. It's not far."

"That sounds fine. I'm not sure how much I will eat."

There was a strained hesitation, then he said, his voice brusque. "Anxious?"

"No, I just don't eat much on car trips."

"Well, you might need to make an exception—this will be a long one. You'll need to keep your strength up."

"You handling me already, Agent Gunn?"

She stared at him, her expression unsmiling. "I thought I told you to call me Derrick." He forced a smile. "It wasn't an order, Emma. It was a suggestion."

Emma avoided his gaze, her voice not quite even when she said softly, "Right, you did. I forgot."

Sensing her abrupt withdrawal, as if walls had suddenly slammed shut between them, Derrick felt like he could breathe again. He watched her for a moment, wondering why she was avoiding looking at him. His expression fixed, he pulled open the passenger side of his vehicle and she slipped inside. After he got into the driver's side, he glanced at her. She sat there with her arms folded in front of her, exhaustion etched on her face. He tried to ease his own expression. She had heavy-duty stress and sorrow on her. Her sister in the hospital, her nephew gone. It wass no wonder she looked so beat. He really did wonder how much she'd slept last night. "So you weren't kidding. You do have some pull with the government."

She managed a small smile, and he stared at her a moment, then started the car.

He turned to look at her, the soft yellow fabric of her blouse clinging to her, making him think of a long, slender flower. "I have taken several high-profile cases, especially the release of Arthur Maddox, the CEO of TechCom, when he was kidnapped by extortionists in Mexico City. His family was terrified and felt the FBI wasn't doing all they could. They hired me and I worked with the Bureau. I have contacts there, too, if you ever need them."

Her smug tone made him chuckle. "Touché."

She met his gaze, her eyes steady. "We started off on the wrong foot. I went off the grid and investigated on my own when I should have contacted you." Her voice got softer. "I was worried and scared. I apologize for that."

It wasn't the danger he was worried about or the backup. He just didn't want to be in close proximity to this woman for weeks. He worried that her personal connection to the case would be what compromised her and…him.

"Apology accepted. I apologize for arresting you, but I was trying to prove a point."

"In a jerk move."

"Yeah, I'll admit. It was a jerk move," he said. He'd been pissed she had gone behind his back, seemingly hell-bent on her own agenda.

She heaved a sigh. "I know you don't want me on this trip, but I'm extremely competent in what I do. I hope that you don't feel I can't handle any situation that crops up."

He pulled out of the parking spot and drove out, turning right, heading toward Camp Pendleton North. "As

I said, I feel you're too close to the situation. When the time comes, it may take a cool head and nerves of steel to get your nephew back."

"His name is Matthew."

"I'm aware."

"But you haven't used his name. Is that your way of staying detached?"

He shrugged. "Maybe. When it comes to children and babies, I, like most law enforcement, find it a very difficult case."

She nodded and said in a subdued voice, "I could tell you horror stories about the homicides that involve children, especially in the LA area. Gruesome stuff."

"I'll pass." They were silent as he pulled up to the marine corps mess. He put the car in Park and glanced at her. "Is that why you left LAPD?"

"Yes. I was burned out, and I couldn't sleep at night anymore. The job was all-consuming. Also, Lily was here in San Diego and she wasn't doing well. Her love life was a complete mess. I wanted to be closer to her. So I opened a branch office here."

"It's pretty clear you don't get along with your grandmother. That must be pretty tough."

"It was. I'm sorry you had to witness that. It was embarrassing, but she pushes my buttons. Normally I can handle her, but with Lily hurt and in a coma, and Matty gone, I just lost my temper."

"It must be difficult for you to leave Lily and go on this trip."

"Yes, immensely. I've been battling my guilt, but it's necessary to get Matty back." She turned a hard gaze toward him. "We've got to get him back."

"We will." He exited the car and opened her door for her. She gave him a wan smile and stepped out.

Inside the mess, it was very busy, many uniforms milling about. It was a cafeteria-style venue and they each grabbed trays.

Derrick chose the spaghetti and meatballs and Emma opted for the veggie primavera with cream of broccoli soup. They settled down at a table.

"What is your best guess for the direction he headed?" Derrick said.

"There are several routes, but since we are almost certain it was either Arturo or Gilberto who took Matty, I would say we can rule out Routes One, Three and Five. They lead to a touristy peninsula. My guess is he will take Route Two to Route Fifteen. It runs into Route Fifteen-D, which is a toll road and goes all the way to Mexico City. It's better than the secondary roads that are filled with people, livestock crossings and *topes*, which are these horrible speed bumps that don't have signs and can ruin the undercarriage of your car. I would guess that Matty put up quite a ruckus with his ear infection, so that murdering thug would have had to stop." She looked at the map, then pointed, tapping a place south. "Santa Ana. It's a good-size town and would have doctors along with the cartel's network. He'd feel safe there. It is also a junction for Route Fifteen and is about a seven-to eight-hour trip."

Derrick nodded. "You do know Mexico."

"Have you ever been there?"

"No, but I've been to some of the worst places you can imagine on this earth, with hostile environments and people. I know how to work and survive there."

"You have?" Her eyes went speculative and her head tilted, the copper ponytail brushing her shoulder. "Military?"

"No."

She studied him for a moment. "Not a mercenary, that's for sure. You're too much of a hero for that." His heart jumped at what she said. Hero? He couldn't exactly agree. "And, I would say, not a contractor, either. Leaves only one possibility."

He took a bite of his spaghetti. No way was he confirming or denying anything. It was second nature.

"Spook."

He just kept eating. He expected her to get irritated with his nonanswer, but instead, her face softened. "You were a spy and that must have been a very lonely existence." She reached out and folded up the map and tucked it back into her purse. She set her forearms on the table; her soup had been barely touched and her pasta had only a few bites out of it. She silently met his eyes. Derrick was never one to flinch or give a thing away when people tried to find out what he had done before he'd joined NCIS. His upbringing had taught him about deception, lies, outright manipulation and living in the shadows, pretending to be something he wasn't. The strain of being interested in destroying what others had built took its toll. Derrick had lived the lie, knowing the moment he got control, he'd be the one to dismantle his adopted father's empire.

He'd been a CIA officer, a field agent, the kind that used lies and deception to his benefit. He was most definitely a master at manipulation and he lived in the shadows, often doing what was necessary to protect his country. He never batted an eyelash and had no remorse for anything he'd done to keep America safe.

"You are very good." She leaned forward, her beautiful blue eyes latched on to his. The noise of the room diminished, but his awareness of her blossomed, expanding his physical and mental knowledge of her. Appreciation, honed to a keen edge, sizzled along his nerve endings as Emma's eyes caressed his face, her eyes penetrating, mesmerizing. He instinctively knew she would have been a master in the spy game. Her marks wouldn't even know what had hit them. So he'd underestimated her, her competence masked by her emotional turmoil over her sister and nephew, but she was in hunter mode just like him, and in the crystalline depths he glimpsed the will of a predator.

Everything in him rose to that knowledge, a need to delve deeper into this woman and discover if she could actually understand him.

She let out a measured breath. "Many spies are not very heroic."

He stiffened and opened his mouth, but she was still talking. He wasn't sure what he would say. He had never admitted to another soul that he was a spy.

"The informants, assets or agents who do clandestine work are self-serving, money or the excitement driving them. Visions of James Bond dancing in their heads or the sense of being powerful, playing a dramatic role in historical events. Some just want revenge." Her voice dropped and Derrick found himself leaning toward her as she went on. "But heroic spies—entirely different people. They are set apart from those unheroic spies, not by the tradecraft they use, something completely general, but by their fundamental principles. They aren't self-serving individuals. The risks of espionage in the environment they chose to work in are too high to draw in selfish people. Add in the cost of secrecy and you get a solitary, lonely person. The detachment and isolation are keen where relationships are false, the real person buried under layers of deception. Maintaining cover is paramount, no matter the test."

He didn't give a thing away, but she was already seeing what he was so good at hiding.

"You have my admiration and gratitude, Derrick. The physical and psychological toll aside, heroic spies lie and manipulate, pretend to be what they're not, and they face terrible fates if unmasked. They carry out the most dangerous missions amongst the worst humanity has to offer and they do it without any public acknowledgement. Nothing but a star on the wall when fate turns against them. You saved anonymous lives, people who will never know they were saved, let alone who saved them. All of this in the shadows."

In all his life, he'd never ever had anyone describe him like this. He was working for his country and his government; never considered heroism at all. He wanted to find someplace private and…kiss the hell out of her, connect with that mouth, that brain, that freaking body that tantalized him even more now. She assaulted his senses, his mind. Hell, what part of him didn't she affect? She did things to him that no woman, not even Afsana, had done because he'd loved her deeply. But he'd given her up for his country, for his job, for his sanity, for the protection of her and of a son he would never get to know or be involved in his life, like a dad should. He lived with all of that alone, in the darkness with only one regret. He'd left the family he had craved his whole life behind in Afghanistan.

The biggest sacrifice he'd ever made in his life. He told her it was for her safety and for the boy's, but that had been a lie. The US wanted the intel she could provide and being compromised by an American CIA officer wasn't in their plans. He'd given up everything for his country and the mission that would save countless American lives.

There were weak moments when he wondered what it would have been like to be a dad, part terror and part pride to nurture someone. With his upbringing, he imagined he didn't know the first thing about it, but now he knew differently. If he'd been given the chance, it would have changed his life. It made everything real and put into perspective what love, real, unconditional love, was all about.

He hadn't gotten to hold him, be there when he woke up in the middle of the night, talk about his fears or the satisfaction of being there just for the random, everyday stuff. He knew he loved the kid, even if he wasn't in his life.

She reached out and covered his hand, squeezing it. He didn't move. He didn't want to give a thing away. "You done?" he said.

She smiled the kind of smile that wasn't at all offended, but one that was more…proud, and let go of him. "Yes, I'm done. Let's get this show on the road."

He grabbed her tray and his, needing a moment to turn away and compose himself. Being a spy was nothing compared to the danger Emma posed. She was working with him. He couldn't compromise this mission. Too much was at stake.

Soon, they were zooming along Route Two, their permits, passports, and his badge all locked up in belts they carried underneath their clothes. Each of them was armed and ready to run a killer to ground and take back a little boy who had somehow become a pawn.

About an hour into the trip, Emma fell asleep, but her

words continued to reverberate in him as the miles ran by under his tires.

When they hit Santa Ana, they were discreet, asking about the teen in the picture with the Santa Muerte tattoo who might have brought an infant in for treatment. Most people were happy to see them go, but a brave nurse told them in low tones that he'd been in the office. As far as she knew, he was instructed to let the infant rest. Perhaps they stopped for the night in one of the hotels on the outskirts of town.

Completely exhausted, Derrick and Emma got back into the car, stopped to pick up some food and headed for the hotels. There weren't many. When the proprietor of one gave them a terror-filled look and said they had left about eight hours ago, Derrick and Emma decided to eat and get a few hours of sleep, then get back on the road.

Emma was in full support of this plan. She had slept, but Derrick hadn't.

"How many rooms?" the hotel manager asked.

"One," Derrick said, and Emma looked at him, but didn't say anything in public. He took the key and they drove to the room and entered, each with a backpack, what Emma called a quick pack: change of clothes, water, first-aid kit, rain poncho, flashlight with batteries, nonperishable snacks and a lightweight blanket.

"One room?"

"Safer if we stay together." He didn't even wait for her to argue, but headed for the bathroom, dropping his pack near the door. "I'm going to take a shower."

"I can take the first watch."

He hesitated, then nodded. "All right, but we get on the road in a few."

* * *

He closed the door, and it took all of Emma's will-power not to imagine what that man looked like without those impeccable clothes. Earlier, he'd ditched the suit for more casual clothes, but anyone with a discerning eye could tell they were just as expensive as the suits. He had good taste and an amazing butt, his shoulders wide, tapering down to that trim waist. And those eyes, so dark, so deep, she used both hands to keep from falling into them. And when he smiled, really smiled, her knees got a bit weak.

The water came on and she went to the back of the room, not satisfied until she surveyed her surroundings. She peeked out to scrub grass, sage and brush, patches of red clay visible, the Sierra Madres in the background. The sun was setting, turning the sky purple, pink and orange. The distinct silhouette of saguaro cactus was black against the vibrant sky. Turning on the air conditioner, she dropped her bag.

She'd meant every word she'd said. He was a handsome, stoic son of a gun, that was for sure. But Emma had the kind of observation skills that were almost paranormal. Derrick was good, really good at that blank stare, giving nothing away. She would expect that of a skilled operative. The fact he neither confirmed nor denied her observations gave him away.

He hadn't admitted to anything, but she knew what he had been, even if she wasn't sure of the government acronym. She also was one hundred percent certain that he was a bona-fide hero.

She also recognized that lone-wolf way. She was guilty of the same damn thing. Sure, she'd worked closely with a partner, but Emma had kept herself separate. It felt safer that way. After what happened with her parents, and her emotionally bankrupt grandmother, keeping Lily safe was all about remaining strong and independent.

None of that really mattered. She wasn't here for Derrick; she was after Matty and that was her priority. Her sister, still in a coma in San Diego, was holding on and Emma had to be hopeful that she would pull through. She was confident her sister wouldn't want her hovering around a hospital when their precious Matty was in danger. Yet Emma couldn't quite escape the spurt of guilt for not being there.

Emma went back to the chair and checked her emails on her phone, handling some business while she waited.

After fifteen minutes he opened the door, steam wafting out. As he stepped out into the room in nothing but a towel around that ripped and cut waist, Emma's mouth went dry. He was still damp, water trailing over the impressive, roped muscles of his chest, his hair mussed from being towel-dried. In profile, the close-cropped beard that framed those gorgeous lips of his couldn't hide the strong angle of his jaw, the way it clenched as he grabbed his bag.

He dug in, turning his back to her, the smooth, powerful expanse rippling with his movement. Now she knew what swooning was all about. He tossed the bag next to hers in the back of the room.

When he turned with the clothes in his hands, she was still staring. He met her eyes and she couldn't help getting more of that body burned onto her retinas. The flat ridges of his abdomen, the trail of hair that disappeared beneath the terry-cloth were worth getting singed.

He set one hand on his hip. "Do you want to watch me get dressed? Or have your own shower?"

"Sure," she squeaked and that rare smile slipped across his face. She cleared her throat and rose. He was so close in the small room, she had to dance with him to get by, her body barely touching his, but so aware of him it hurt. He kept his eyes on hers, thickly lashed and heart-stopping blue.

He moved so effortlessly, fluidly graceful. A damp lock of hair fell over his forehead and it took everything she had not to smooth it back in place. His sultry gaze went darker, and man-oh-man did he have brooding down to a science. Still waters always ran deep.

"Emma? Shower? Don't forget your bag."

"You don't want to watch me get dressed?" she said breathlessly.

His jaw clenched and she realized just what she'd said. "I mean, of course you don't. I'll…ah…grab my stuff." She giggled and caught herself. She felt her face flame beet red and with her coloring there was no way to conceal her embarrassment. As she turned away, snagged her bag and entered the still steamy, moist bathroom, his scent lingered like a caress tingled along the skin. Shutting the door, she braced her back against it and took a deep, cleansing breath.

Boy, shoe leather wasn't at all tasty. She would pull her foot out of her mouth and get going.

Maybe she should make it a cold shower.

Chapter 6

When she came out, he was over by the window, peering out. He was dressed in worn jeans and a blue dress shirt, the sleeves rolled up his powerful forearms, the shoulder holster buckled across his chest, the weapon's butt protruding from the brown leather, the closure that held the gun in place unsnapped. He'd combed his hair, but that wayward lock wasn't cooperating, looking soft lying against his temple.

He glanced over his shoulder at her. "It's clear. Nothing stirring except some guys who got a bit rowdy. Sounds like they'd been drinking."

She nodded, noting that his shoulders were tense. She didn't blame him. They were in enemy territory. The room was steamy as she shoved her dirty clothes into the bag, dropping it near the chair by the window. Walking to the back of the room, she upped the setting on the air conditioner. "Let's eat, Derrick."

He came over to the bed and sat down. Emma grabbed her portion and went back to the chair she'd been sitting in. They dug into the food. Afterward, he stretched out on the bed and within moments he was asleep.

He let out a deep breath, sinking deeper into the mattress. She had opted for a clip-on holster situated in the middle of her back. She pulled out the semiautomatic, checking the magazine and racking the slide, chambering a round. Then she flipped on the safety and turned to peer out the window again. Emma checked out the immediate area. There wasn't anything out of the ordinary, but that edgy feeling wouldn't go away. It was a cop's intuition. A ripple of energy sliding down her spine, but she wasn't sure if it was intuition or Derrick's influence.

The air conditioner in the room was a joke and did little to take the edge off the heat. Instead, she rose and went to the back windows and peered out. It was dark, but she knew what was out there. The hottest desert in Mexico, the inhospitable Sonoran for as far as the eye could see, populated with bird, mammal, amphibian and reptile species. She shivered; it even had the only population of jaguars living in the US. Who knew if they had spilled over into Mexico? Suddenly, she heard the lone call of a coyote, or was that a wolf? Backing away from the window, she settled back in the chair after another look outside.

Focusing on Derrick, she watched him sleep. It was no hardship. His face softened in slumber, his jaw not so tense. Damn. He was beautiful. Watching him, a wave of heat built inside her, lovely and erotic—very forbidden—but compelling.

She heard voices, then the opening and closing of doors. There was something in the air, a tightness that transferred to the back of her neck and it prickled. She lunged forward, hitting Derrick and rolling them both across the bed to the floor. He groaned softly just as the windows exploded. The barrage of gunfire was ceaseless.

"What the hell," he growled. "How many?"

"Too many! We're outmanned and outgunned. He must have covered his tracks with his cartel brothers."

"We've got to get out of here." Derrick took his bag and shrugged into the straps. "The window." They reached for the window as voices in rapid Spanish sounded in the distance. *"Mata a los americanos."* Her Spanish was impeccable—it meant *kill the Americans.*

They punched out the screen and rolled out the window, crouching as the sound of running feet whipped through the grass. Derrick took her hand and staying low, they headed into the desert, using the darkness and vegetation for cover.

There was a shout and more explosions ripped through the night, the sound of bullets whizzing around them. Derrick made a strangled sound and she gasped. "Are you all right?" she whispered furiously.

"Just a nick. Keep moving," he said.

A nick? Of all the bull crap, macho man bravado— everything went out of her head as she tripped. Not just a stumble, but a full-out, face-planted-in-the-dirt, hand-scraping, bone-jarring collision with the hard-packed earth.

When she rolled to her back, she realized the enemy was on them. Derrick's semiautomatic discharged several times and dark shapes fell, but there were more. One guy's gun jammed and he used it as a bat, catching Derrick on the jaw and he reeled back. She went to pull her weapon, but in the fall, the holster had jarred loose and she reached for nothing but air. She surged up and charged the closest guy to her. With a quick grab-the-thumb, twist-his-arm move, she had him heading toward the ground and the hard blow of her knee as she brought it up into his face and dropped him like a stone. But Derrick was surrounded by three men.

She needed to even those odds. She jumped on the back of one of the men and jerked back. They fell, her back hitting the ground, knocking the air out of her, but she kept her hold on his throat until he wasn't moving anymore.

When she got out from under the guy and rose shakily to her knees, Derrick was whirling, nothing but a blur in the wan light of the moon with the sound of blows and grunts, cries of pain, until the only man left standing was him.

She dragged her eyes away from his solid form and frantically searched the ground. Her hand caught on her gun and she snatched it up.

"Come on, Emma," he growled. In moments she was up and racing after him.

Into the darkness.

Hunted.

A door slammed, and Derrick swore under his breath. Hell, no, they weren't out of this, not yet. Voices were coming from the back of the hotel, one yelling orders, another demanding answers, and in the middle of all the shouting, someone made a threat and backed it up with *Los Equis*'s name.

Dammit. It was time to get the hell out of this red zone.

His hand still firmly grasping Emma's, he went into a crouch and took off, keeping low. The profusion of vegetation, small trees and thick brush would have to do.

Doing his best to keep them out of sight and a firm grip on her hand, he ran past an outcropping and a cluster of small trees. He didn't stop and he didn't need to listen. There was no mistaking the sound of men in pursuit, the crunch of footfalls behind them enough to spur him on.

Running was their only option.

So they ran, and they kept running, Derrick dragging Emma with him through an endless chaparral and over arid, hard-packed earth. Supporting her when she stumbled. Down into a dry riverbed they slid, vegetation all around them, except for the long tract. Changing direction, the going easier, they bolted along the bank until they came to a small, tree-enclosed area.

As they came out of the depression, he slipped his gun into his shoulder holster. Taking in deep breaths, he released the death grip he had on her arm. His arm was hurting like a son of a bitch. He breathed around the pain. "You're doing great," he said, impressed as hell by her quick thinking in a battle and her survival instincts.

He tapped her shoulder and they moved back into the deeper cover of the small strand of trees. He had a round in the chamber of his 9mm and about seven left in the magazine, with a spare in his jeans pocket. The rest of his ammo, three magazines, was back at the hotel.

Under the best circumstances that was a damn short firefight. Under the worst circumstances it was a disaster waiting to happen. Going up against men armed with automatic weapons wasn't his idea of a good plan. Stealth always won out for him. If he had his sniper rifle, he might even the odds, but that wasn't something the Mexican government had approved. Thirty-eight rounds weren't enough for him to win a gun battle if *Los Equis* chased them down.

"How much ammo do you have?"

"All of it."

"That evens it up a bit." Even with her one hundred and twenty rounds, they were still woefully outgunned.

"There were at least ten of them. We downed four—that leaves six against two. Not bad odds."

"We're not going to engage them. We're getting to cover and getting out of the desert. We can't survive here for more than a few days, not with two bottles of water between us."

She nodded.

He froze. There was blood on her sleeve. He turned toward her, his grip inadvertently tightening on her hand, his gaze dropping to her arm. "Are you hurt?" he said gruffly.

"No... I—no." She sounded upset.

There was a bloody smear at her waist, but she couldn't have run the way she had, for as long as she had if she'd been hit. The material wasn't torn. It was just bloody.

"It's yours, Derrick. Are you all right?"

He must have gotten blood on his hand when he'd clutched his wounded arm. Relief rushed through him. The thought of her hurt, even a little, sent him into a tailspin.

"You're the one that needs attention. Let me look at your arm."

"Not yet. But damn, woman, you were badass." The words popped out of his mouth; the recognition of how well she'd followed his lead, covered his back and helped to get them out of that tight situation was warranted. He was incredibly grateful. It all could have gone so much worse—but he wasn't going to think about that.

Her gaze lifted to meet his, and he felt his heart beat triple time, even with the adrenaline still pumping into his system. Her eyes were steady, darkened by the low light and the shadows. She was panting slightly, her skin gleaming creamy white in the night.

"How many men have you killed?" he said, his voice rough and low.

"What? What kind of question is that?"

"A damn good one." He wished he hadn't been pressured to bring her along. He wished he was alone; risking his own life was…familiar, but working with her felt too much like working with an asset and he hated how that felt. She hadn't been exposed to this kind of danger, brutality, although an LAPD detective was no pushover. If she'd made it that far into their ranks, Emma really was a badass. He knew the score. He knew the playing field they were on, and he knew exactly what would have happened to the two of them if they were anything less than what they were: better than the bad guys out for their blood. "How many, Emma?"

"One, dead center, with no hesitation."

Better was right. Better than any of these monsters who were hunting them, smarter and faster. Derrick didn't have to be the best, but he knew with every cell in his body that he always had to be better, every single time, without fail. There was only one rule in warfare he'd been trained for: win or die. For many years, light years away from Emma's, it had been stark and dangerous and had no room for errors. "So none with your bare hands?"

Her voice shook a bit, then steadied. "No, that was a first."

"Yeah. May not be your last. Let's get going."

He scanned the area, listened intently, but heard nothing, sensed no movement. Checking again just to make sure, he grasped her hand again and pulled her out the other side of the copse.

They had to evade capture, get out of this desert and secure a vehicle. Then it was back on the road and in pursuit of that killer/kidnapper.

They ran for what seemed like miles, until the sun started to lighten the sky. He'd had his eye on a rocky outcropping in the distance. He picked up his pace and Emma matched his strides. She was quite the trouper.

He approached the rocks with caution, looking intently for snakes who liked this type of shade from the rising sun as much as he and Emma needed the shelter. He would be on the lookout for spiders and centipedes for their venom. Those creepy-crawlies would also like the shade of rocks to get out of the sun.

They couldn't travel by day. It was too damn hot and would deplete them much quicker than traveling at night.

He looked around and spied a stick. Picking one up, he began to probe the craggy depressions, displacing a few scorpions. Satisfied there were no more threats, he knelt down and pressed his back against the rock, exhausted.

Coyotes and bobcats were probably their biggest worries; they could smell blood on the air and the former ran in packs. He glanced down at his arm. His sleeve was torn and bloodied.

The sooner he covered the wound, the better. Last night they hadn't been able to stop running; the sound of four-wheel drives motoring in the distance told him they were being hunted. So far, so good. There hadn't been any dogs involved, but he wouldn't put it past the cartel to go that route.

He needed to get them out of here and back to the car. Trapped in the desert with very little water was dire. Food they could do without for weeks, but water… twenty-four hours was all it took for dehydration to occur.

"What's the plan?"

"We lay low until nightfall, then we hightail it parallel to the hotel. The hotel was in that direction." He used his thumb to indicate the general area behind him. "Hopefully we'll come across someplace where we can get some help or phone reception."

"You have your cell? That's a good break."

"In my back pocket. You have yours?"

"No. I left it in my bag back at the hotel. We're both armed, have your cell and some supplies. This won't be so bad."

He nodded, playing along.

"We make a good team."

He didn't respond. Truth be told, the last gig he'd had, pulling Rock Kaczewski and Neve Michaels, Amber's sister-in-law, out of the fire on a lone sniper trip to the Darién Gap in Latin America, was more his speed. Working with Austin and Amber had been an anomaly in his life. As an operative, he'd been alone most of the ten years he'd been with the company, except for that brief time with Afsana. He didn't like Butch and Sundancing it—going out with bullets flying. A loner by trade and training, compliments of The Farm, the CIA's boot camp, going solo was always Derrick's preferred modus operandi.

Emma cared only about three things: getting cool, hiding from the cartel and looking at Derrick's arm. She worried every step of the hours they'd run in the darkness about his arm, blood loss, his well-being. He was so in control: no panic, no headlong dash, just a steady movement. He grounded her and the sudden thought of being stranded out in this wasteland without him was a sobering thought. She shifted to take a look at his arm. "Can you take your shirt off? Let me see what I can do."

He reached for the buttons and Emma noticed the grimace on his face. "Let me do it," she said softly, gently nudging his hands away. She started to unbutton his shirt, her fingers nimble and fast.

"You all right?" he asked, closing his eyes and leaning his head back.

She pushed back the material, revealing the smooth skin, her fingers brushing his warm, damp chest. "Yeah, same since the last time you asked me, cuts and bruises. Apparently, I can duck better than you can, or is it that I make a much smaller target?"

He chuckled. "Duck better, probably."

When she pulled the shirt away from his skin, he sucked in a breath.

"I'm sorry," she murmured and braced herself. There was a nasty gash across the upper part of his arm, just above the elbow, and it clearly needed stitches. But it wasn't the ragged cut that made her stomach roil; it was the cloth caught in the wound. Her stomach dropped when she realized she'd have to extract it.

Knowing how much it must hurt, she carefully turned his arm around. There was no damage to the back. She rummaged around in his pack until she found the first-aid kit. She opened the box and grabbed one of the packs that held a sterile dressing. She ripped it open with her teeth, gently supporting his arm; her voice wasn't quite steady when she spoke. "This needs stitches, Derrick."

There was a brief pause, then he finally answered, his voice gruff. "I figured." He held her gaze for a minute, then looked away, the muscles in his face taut. "In this case, in this situation, it's best not to suture it. A bullet containing oil and gunpowder passing through cloth and dirty skin creates a contaminated wound. Closing it traps everything inside. Clean as best you can, pack it with gauze and antibiotic ointment. It's going to seep and will need to be changed frequently."

"All right. I have some anesthetic and painkiller." She reached for both, gave him the tablets and the water. Then she administered the anesthetic. While it worked to numb the area, she reached for the sealed antiseptic swabs and the forceps that went with them, her hands not quite steady as she broke open the seal. The thought of poking around in his wound to clean it of all debris made her stomach shrink to a hard, little knot.

He only made one sound initially, his mouth tightening, the muscles across his chest contracting when she went for every bit of cloth she could find. His face was pale by the time she finished. Then she was generous with the antibiotic ointment, packing the gash with gauze, then binding it securely with an elastic bandage to keep everything in place.

"Thank you," he said.

She met his dark eyes and hated causing him pain, but it had to be done. His features softened. Emma looked back down at the bandaged wound, feeling just a little too vulnerable. She nodded. "At least it missed the bone and there's no bullet to deal with."

A hint of amusement appeared in his eyes, and his expression relaxed a little. "Silver lining?"

She smiled slightly. "Usually there is one."

"Ah, glass half full."

Emma looked at him, caught off guard by the glimmer of humor in his eyes. She didn't know how to respond. The glimmer deepened, and suddenly the knots in her stomach relaxed. She gave him a warped smile, her tone dry when she responded. "Yeah, that's me."

It happened then, a disarming, sensual, intimate smile that did unbelievable things to his eyes and even more amazing things to her insides. The smile held, the creases around his eyes deepening, the glint in his eyes turning her heart to jelly. "Help me with my shirt," he murmured.

She got him back into it, so sensitized to him that she was conscious of every movement, every breath. "There you go, Mister Glass Half Empty."

Smiling back at him, she fell victim to the sparkle of amusement, to the glimmer of intimacy that she saw in his eyes. Oh, yes. She could care very easily for this man. So very easily. Flustered by that random thought, she dragged her gaze from his, her pulse erratic. She had to stop doing that—letting her mind wander—or she was going to end up in big trouble.

He held her gaze for a long, drawn-out moment; something…desolate…in his eyes made her heart contract, then he looked away, his profile tense.

Digging back in her bag, she grabbed another bottle of water and held it out to him, along with a nutrition bar. They consumed the food and water in silence.

"Let's get some rest. We'll have to be up and ready to move by nightfall," Derrick said.

Emma nodded and was surprised when he pulled her

flush to him with his good arm. His closeness overwhelmed her senses, and she swallowed hard, trying to struggle with the longing that surged through her, making her heart race even faster. She couldn't stop remembering his body after that shower and more important, the kind of man he was, which all drew her in.

His muscled arm went around her and he pressed her to him. "Sleep. We're safe for now. I'll take the first watch."

"Derrick—"

"No arguments, Emma."

They were two fiercely independent people, but right now, this minute, leaning on him felt so damn good. Along with the feeling of safety his arms offered, there was emotion filling her chest.

There was a line she couldn't cross. She couldn't. And it had everything to do with her sister and Matty. Everything to do with this man, who was doing something to her that no other man had been able to do.

They had a job to do, working together imperative.

Blurring the lines, getting romantically or physically involved with Derrick was a big no-no. Emma wasn't going to go down that road. The biggest reason really had nothing to do with her sister or this mission.

Derrick, stoic, brooding Derrick, scared the living daylights out of her.

Chapter 7

Emma rested heavily against him as he propped his back against the outcropping. The sun had been up for hours. They were resting in the depression in the earth he'd made to bring down their body temperatures, along with the cool, dark shadows that kept the increasing heat directly off them. But more important, it hid them from sight.

His arm tightened around her, both protective and impressed. Time to assess the damage. They were compromised here, stranded in the desert without adequate food and water, pursued by the cartel and he was wounded. But they had his cell, ammo, his wound wasn't that severe, and they both had their documents still around their waists.

He was under no illusions here. This was a serious situation and the Sonoran Desert was no joke. But he was a master at surviving in a large desert—in Afghanistan.

He shifted and winced as his arm protested. He flexed it; the pain was manageable. He'd been shot before, but grazes were the worst and the best. At least the bullet wasn't still in his body.

Taking a steadying breath, he looked down. Emma's thick, copper lashes lay on her cheeks and he caressed the fine bones of her beautiful face with his eyes. Her cheeks were flushed, her skin glistening. It was hotter than hell in the Sonoran Desert in mid-June, sometimes reaching 120 degrees. It was imperative they sleep in the day and travel at night. But Derrick didn't like the feeling of being pursued. He wasn't exactly the full-frontal assault guy. He liked to work from the shadows. Traversing the desert was dangerous enough without having a bunch of crazy, gun-toting killers after them. He also felt protective of this woman, even though she knew how to handle herself. He wanted her out of danger. He would put his mind to a plan.

She was asleep beside him, a disquieting feeling settling in his gut. She was lying with her head on his shoulder and her arm around his chest, the rhythm of her breathing indicating a very deep and heavy sleep. It wasn't a surprise. They had pushed themselves hard yesterday.

He focused on her mouth. He couldn't help it. Her lips were slightly parted, pink and inviting, looking soft and warm. All he had to do was move his head just a bit and he could press his mouth against them, take something he'd been thinking about since she'd eyed him coming out of the shower.

He wasn't oblivious to the kind of attention women paid him. He understood he was handsome. He'd used that to his advantage more than enough in the past. His looks aside, he was aroused by the way her eyes sort of… took him in. She wanted him, at least physically, but he wanted something more. Disturbed by that thought, he tightened his arm around her reflexively, the erection he'd woken up with hardening. The attraction between them was inescapable. He was a realist and Derrick wasn't going to waste his time or energy denying it. Emma might, but that was her prerogative.

She shifted and made a sleep-soft murmur, then settled deeper into his arms. Never in his wildest dreams had he expected something like this to happen. Not now. Not after so many years of keeping himself...separate. In the deepest part of his heart where he'd let go of his love for Afsana and the pain of not being able to claim his son, he acknowledged that getting involved with someone he worked with again was completely stupid.

And, he wanted to get involved.

Completely, with full-body contact involved.

His expression grew more somber. He was aware why that rock in the pit of his gut sat there heavy and undeniable, growing into a boulder. He was self-aware, analyzed his feelings as he was taught, looking for a work-around. He was heading for the kind of mistake that could really screw him up, screw up this mission, something he wasn't about to let happen.

The memory of the day his son was born took shape in his mind, and Derrick rested his free arm over his eyes and clenched his jaw, an old anger rushing up inside him. Anger over the last meeting with Afsana and how he'd sworn her to secrecy because her life and that of his unborn son depended on her silence, her heartache. He wasn't worried about his career like she'd accused him. He kept tabs on them through his web of contacts. He had to keep them safe because it had been him who'd put her and the baby she carried, his child, in danger in the first place.

Experiencing an acid rush to his belly, he stared out at the landscape as barren as his thoughts. He'd lost focus back then and it had almost led to disaster. If he gave in to this attraction, could he be making the same mistake here?

Emma stirred beside him, and Derrick glanced at her and rubbed his hand up her arm, wishing for more contact. Intimate contact. Tightening his arm around her, he watched her for a moment, then stared back out at the landscape, trying not to think at all. He felt as if everything was closing in on him.

She stirred again and murmured his name, and Derrick glanced down at her, realizing she was caught in that half-conscious state between sleeping and coming awake. He wondered why she'd said his name like that, breathless, with longing. The kind of longing that caused a hollow sensation in the pit of his stomach.

"That air conditioner is a joke. Hot, so hot," she whispered.

He looked down at her, a small twist of a smile working loose. He would have been happy to oblige, if only they were in a place that afforded them cool, refreshing air. His expression softened just a little as he watched her come awake. He got lost in thinking how easy it would be to arouse her when she was like this, how quickly she might respond, how soft and yielding she might be. But he shut that thought down almost immediately. He couldn't afford to slide into that trap again. He had made one mistake; he shouldn't compound that by making another. Assets...working partners...were best left alone.

That thought dissipated when she opened those crystal-blue eyes, still lost in some dream, unfocused and so warm when they met his. "Derrick," she said, the same breathless longing there. "You saved me."

He had no idea if she had been dreaming about him or if she was referring to yesterday. He just got lost in the way she looked at him as if he was her hero, the kind of man she needed. She reached up and smoothed her hand along his jaw as the desert temperature climbed another impossibly hot degree. Her fingers brushed over the bruise from the blow yesterday; concern filled her eyes and she pushed up so her mouth could press against his jaw.

He closed his eyes and breathed her in deep. The scent of heated woman, her mouth soft and aching as she kissed him. He'd been so lonely and his connection with Emma had been volatile from the beginning. Now he knew why. He'd been fighting something that seemed beyond him, no matter how much he fought against what he wanted.

He still wanted it.

His mind clouding over with desire, feeling raw, he cupped her jaw, then applied pressure with his thumb to get her to lift her head. Inhaling unevenly, he covered her mouth with a soft, searching kiss. Now that he had what he wanted, he tightened his hold on her jaw, his tone commanding as he whispered against her mouth, "Open up for me, babe."

Her breath caught, but she yielded to the pressure of his thumb, and Derrick adjusted the alignment of his mouth against hers, deepening the kiss with slow, lazy thoroughness. Working his lips softly, slowly against hers, he drank from her, probing the recesses, savoring the taste of her. Her breath caught again; then she finally responded, and he grasped the back of her head, her hair tangling like silk around his fingers. His chest tightening, he softened his mouth even more, and her muscles went slack, as if all the fight, all the common sense, just drained out of her.

Slipping her arm around his neck, she devoured his mouth, meeting his lips with heated and moist caresses. Derrick let his breath go in a rush, an electrifying weakness radiating through his lower body. She did it again, and he tightened his hold on her hair as his erection grew even harder.

The buzz in the distance froze them both as they listened, then broke apart. Her startled eyes fixed on his.

"Helicopter," he whispered. But he was sure it had nothing to do with their rescue. The cartel had taken to the air.

"Stay here," he ordered and inched his way to the edge of the outcropping, still in the shadow of the massive rock. He peered out at the sky and spotted the "bird" coming directly toward them. Of course, the cartel members might be cold-blooded killers, but they weren't stupid. They would be searching rocky areas looking for them. They knew as well as Derrick did that it was their only chance of survival to find shade in the heat of the day.

The chopper hovered along the ridge of rock, obviously searching for any sign of them, but Derrick was adept at hiding. His whole life had been about being invisible.

Finally, after a few more minutes of searching, they buzzed off and Derrick relaxed. The sun was low on the horizon. It would be nightfall in a few hours. Their priority here was finding a source of water and filling the bottles they had.

But with the appearance and disappearance of the helicopter, he'd smiled, a predatory gleam in his eyes. He'd just gotten a germ of an idea. It was time to turn the tables.

The hunted would become the hunters.

When he turned around, Emma was watching him, and even though the danger had passed for now, she hadn't relaxed. She was sitting on the ground, staring up at him with concern in her eyes, but it didn't have anything to do with being exposed to the cartel searching for them.

And everything to do with that damn kiss.

He cleared his throat. "We can deny it as much as we want, but we both know there's something here. It's not smart and we should... I should be better at resisting."

"But you're..." She bit her lip. "We're not."

"We should focus on getting out of here and back to civilization in one piece. I can't promise what we're feeling will go away. We just have to process it separately for now. Can we agree on that?"

"Don't," she whispered. "Just don't."

His expression sobering, Derrick stepped forward and caught her along the jaw, turning her head so she had to look at him. "Don't what?" he commanded quietly. She hesitated, her expression stark, wariness dilating her eyes. He gave her head a small shake, prodding her to answer. "Don't what?"

She took a deep, unsteady breath, then looked away, her face pensive. "Don't diminish it." She paused, obviously struggling; then she looked up at him, pleading with her eyes. "I liked kissing you," she whispered. "But I get it. We have to soldier on. We don't have time for this." She frowned and looked away, as if her emotions were too raw to hold his gaze. Finally, she looked up at him again, her face drawn and anxious. "I'm not sure I can keep everything in perspective."

No matter how unbelievable it had been kissing her, wanting her, it was no quick fix. Sex was a bodily need, but even as they stared at each other, he was well aware this…thing…with Emma was more than just his body wanting something, more than just stirred up hormones. It was all about Emma and wanting to see her in every nuance, every experience, that was jacking him up. Not just her beauty or her delectable body.

Before he thought better of it, he hauled her up and pulled her tight against him. He whispered in her ear. "I liked kissing you, too." She hugged him, hard and brief, staring deep in his eyes for an instant, then she pulled away.

She released a breath and they started to prepare to leave, packing up the blanket they'd been resting on, cleaning up any sign they were there, and slathering on generous coatings of sunscreen.

"Let me change your bandage," she said when the sun was almost gone. He nodded and sat down while she unwound the bandage, her touch anything but impersonal. She was so gentle when she reapplied the gauze and antibiotic ointment and then wrapped it again. He thanked her and she nodded.

They buried all the debris and started off toward the west, still keeping parallel to the hotel. Trudging through the spotty underbrush, Derrick headed steadily toward more shelter for their second day in the desert.

When they came to a dry riverbed, Derrick stopped

and set down the pack. He took the flashlight and searched the ground. Sure enough, there was green vegetation, an indication there was water just under the soil. "Emma, find me a bunch of small rocks." While she went off looking for them, he searched the area for something to dig with and found a flat, hollowed-out rock. He shoveled two feet across and about a foot deep. As he scooped, he noticed that the soil was getting moister. He redoubled his efforts until water started to fill the small well.

"Emma," he said and she dumped a bunch of rocks near him. He lined the hole as the water inside rose. The stones would help reduce the amount of dirt stirred up by movement in the liquid. She pulled out the bottles and they filled them, using his T-shirt to filter out the sediment. Then he dropped in purification tablets.

They sat down and rested. Moonlight cast long, faint shadows across the ground, and off in the distance, a lone coyote yipped. The call was answered, then answered again, until a discordant yodel resonated along the length of the shallow valley, the sounds carrying for miles on the cool, clear air.

Emma inched closer to him, and without thinking about it, he wrapped his arm around her. "They are some ways away. It's okay."

"If you say so. You were pretty good at finding water. I'm so impressed by you, Derrick. If I'm ever in a wilderness situation, I'd always want you by my side."

He leaned back against the wall of the creek bed. "We'll rest here and drink our fill, then pack the bottles with us to travel."

"I'm looking for good places we can hide."

"That's good, but that chopper gave me an idea."

"Oh, I'm all ears."

"We still have my clothes in the backpack. I think we can use them to our advantage."

"How do you propose to do that?"

"Lure the chopper into landing."

"What? And how are you going to do that? Signal them. They could take us out from the air."

"No, by giving them our...dead bodies."

Trying to stay detached from the emotions rolling inside her, Emma lay perfectly still on the sweltering ground, the cloth of Derrick's shirt visible in her line of sight. Her weapon was tucked neatly underneath her. This was going to be tricky, but she had confidence in Derrick's plan.

What she didn't have confidence in was her own stupid proclivity to melt whenever that man looked at her or touched her. These weren't the kind of thoughts she should be having right now. But she couldn't seem to help reliving that kiss over and over all night long. Even as the sun of the new day beat down on her, the heat from the kiss stirred her deeply.

Get a freaking grip!

She took some deep breaths and tried to tell herself that getting involved with him would be too scary. He was too virile, much too alpha. They would most likely butt heads when they weren't in bed together. Although, so far, since the initial tug of war between them just after Matty had been kidnapped, they seemed to be working together just fine. But they were caught up in survival mode. Who knew what it would be like when they got back to chasing down the kidnapper and got more involved in the case? That should be her priority and was another really good reason to forget how good his mouth tasted, how good his muscles felt beneath her hands. Derrick was the kind of man who liked to be in charge and Emma hadn't released her hold on her independence since she'd gotten free of her grandmother's house.

All her thoughts scattered when she heard the sound of the helicopter in the distance. She focused on one thing: remaining calm.

She didn't move a muscle when it hovered above her, the wind from the rotors beating the ground, dirt and debris blowing across her body. She kept her eyes closed, her muscles loose. The chopper buzzed away and she heard the sound of it getting closer and closer. It was landing. She worked at staying calm. Derrick was depending on her and she couldn't let him down.

She heard the crunch of boots getting closer and closer, then stop. *"Chica?"* the man said, his voice wary. She didn't respond. He kicked her with his boot tip and she groaned softly. She pushed up on her hands, but his foot came down in the middle of her back. "Don't move," he ordered. When he flipped her over, she shifted so her gun was under her hip. There were only two men, but Derrick was most likely right; they were in communication with the others. He looked over to where Derrick's shirt could be seen above a depression in the ground.

"Get up!"

"He's dead," she whispered brokenly. "He died from the gunshot wound." He looked down at her and an appreciative gleam came into his eyes.

"Well, his troubles are over. Don't fight me and your death will be painless and quick. Weapon?"

"I lost it when you chased us out of the hotel."

"I don't believe you."

"Search me, then."

He smirked. "Take off your clothes."

She reached for the buttons of her shirt just as a shot rang out from behind the cartel member. He whirled, bringing his gun up, but it was too late. Derrick had already gotten the drop on the pilot and he was dead, slumped in the seat. Emma went for hers and Derrick fired just as she pulled the trigger. The guy dropped to the ground.

Then she was up and running, rushing over to his clothes stuffed with brush. The ploy had worked perfectly. Derrick had concealed himself beneath their blanket, disguised it with rubbed-on mud, while Emma had placed brush around it. He'd looked like a rock mixed into the desert landscape. Then she'd assumed her "I'm unconscious" position on the ground. She gathered the clothes up with a relieved breath and shook them out. Then she turned and raced for the chopper. Derrick had already pulled the pilot out of the seat and was ready to take off.

She climbed into the passenger's seat and the chopper lifted into the air. "So you can fly, too?"

"Yeah, and in a pinch, I can make a mean lasagna."

"I might hold you to that."

They flew for about twenty minutes until Derrick spied a dilapidated gas station below them with access to the highway beyond. He landed and when they got out, the owner, clutching his old, beat-up hat, came up to them. In Spanish, Derrick offered him the helicopter for a vehicle.

He gave them a toothy grin and led them over to a pickup truck. After shaking on the deal, they exchanged keys and Emma and Derrick were soon tooling down the road. As the truck let out a belch of noxious black smoke and backfired, Derrick shifted and said, "I think, even with the cartel connection, he got the better part of the deal."

Emma laughed.

They drove back to the hotel and Derrick parked the truck behind some vegetation off the side of the road. They walked back on foot and when they reached the manager's office, Emma had to hold back her bile. There was dried blood splattered against the back wall with no one in sight.

They must have killed him for giving them shelter and information. "Poor old guy," she murmured. Derrick didn't even pause. Under the cover of darkness, he made his way to where they had parked their first vehicle. It was gone.

"Looks like we're going to the next city in the pickup. Nothing here to salvage."

"I would love to get my cell phone. It was in my bag."

"Let's check inside."

They entered the hotel room and Emma was glad to see her bag was there, the contents ransacked, but her phone was in amongst the debris. She snatched it up and they hightailed it back to the truck.

Derrick called the office and, from the one-sided conversation, she could tell he was touched by his boss's concern. When he hung up, he turned to her and said, "She wants us to head to Hermosillo, a much larger city located almost two hours from Santa Ana, where we can blend in and lie low. Our original plan to catch up to the kidnapper took a direct hit, as he now has a much larger lead. We need to recover and restock. She'll be in touch with instructions."

"I bet everyone was relieved to hear from you."

"They were glad we were both alive and well. They feared the worst when we didn't check in."

"I bet." She was aware of every move he made and ever since she'd met him, she couldn't shake it. He was so masculine, the heavy growth of facial hair only adding to that rugged quality he exuded without even trying. "That was a great idea. Risky, but it paid off."

"Yeah, it was lucky we grabbed my bag instead of yours. I think he would have just put a bullet into me. But with your beauty, that guy didn't have a chance."

She turned to look at him. His profile was tense, but she was sure he was quite aware of what he had said about her being beautiful. This could so easily get out of control with this man.

"Derrick?"

He looked at her and she said, "I was right about you."

"Oh yeah? That I'm a crazy son of a bitch?" he said roughly.

"Well, that and…you're one of the heroic ones."

He slipped his hand over hers where it rested on her thigh, squeezing. She tightened her hold on him. He said nothing, just held her gaze for the longest moment. Then he brought her hand to his mouth, all the while holding her gaze. He closed his eyes and placed a soft, quick kiss on her knuckles. Wrapping his hand around hers, he looked up into her eyes, his an almost impossible indigo blue through a thick fringe of dark lashes.

Experiencing a flurry of emotions, a thickness in her chest, he gave them both a minute then eased his hold, but didn't let go.

Knowing she had to maintain a balancing act, Emma managed a smile.

"Considering it's late and we're both completely exhausted, I say we get some food and sleep in the truck. Safer."

Pleasantly full and hydrated for the first time in two days, Emma watched as Derrick dropped off immediately. Her knuckles still tingled from his mouth and she thought immediately about that disrupted kiss, wondering where it would have gone if they hadn't been interrupted. That thought sent a flood of tingles sizzling through her.

There was something building between them, but even more still left unsaid. And if she couldn't get her mind around what exactly *this* was, then it was going to spell disaster for both of them. A fling wasn't out of the realm of possibility, but would be so damn stupid on her part. To get involved with a man she was working with, who was her ticket to this venture in the first place, seemed even dumber. If things went south or didn't…she couldn't even contemplate that. Best to keep her mind on what they were here to accomplish.

She closed her eyes, absorbing his closeness. She thought his appeal would diminish once they were safe, but it was clear that her attraction to Derrick was much more grounded than hero worship. Much more connected than hormones. When she was this close to him, all she could feel was safe, and that only seemed as dangerous as hell.

NCIS Headquarters
Camp Pendleton, California

"It's late, Austin and Amber. Go on home," Kai said from her desk.

Austin's relief after Derrick's call was subsiding as he looked over at Amber. She nodded and they rose together. Derrick might be a pain in his ass, might be hard as nails and twice as wily, but the thought of losing him made Austin's throat contract. He'd been with Derrick on most of their cases and dammit, they'd bonded. As much as Derrick would allow them to bond, that is. He was one tough son of a bitch.

Austin turned back, then he and Amber said in unison, "We could back up Derrick down in Mexico."

Austin smiled and Amber laughed.

"It's not like we aren't all thinking this," Kai said. "We can serve him better here, giving him backup. He can handle himself. He's already proven that by being resourceful. Go home, get some sleep."

Amber grabbed her bag and Austin jingled his car keys. They headed for the elevator. "Thanks for offering. Both of you," Kai said as she turned off her desk lamp.

Austin and Amber entered the elevator. They rode down to the lobby in silence. Amber said as they exited the elevator, "He is smart as hell."

"He is," Austin agreed. "Brilliant and slick." He squeezed her shoulder. "He'll be fine. I'll see you tomorrow." Amber smiled and waved as she walked away.

As Austin got into his car, his cell phone rang. When he looked at the display, he activated the call. "Derrick. You all right?"

Derrick's soft puff of air on a laugh eased Austin's nerves. "Yeah, worrywort. I'm fine."

"And the PI?"

Derrick's voice softened. "She does have a name. Emma's asleep."

Oh, that was new. They hadn't been the best of friends when they'd left to go on this mission. Now, it was Emma. Interesting, that inflection of affection in his voice. Derrick was usually more guarded than that, so did that mean he wasn't aware of it? Hard to believe, the man was so self-possessed. "Why aren't you?"

"I was, but I woke up. It's occurred to me that we are probably compromised. The Ortegas probably know we're coming. I don't know what that means for the kid. It's got my gut tied up in knots just thinking about it. What's going on there?"

"Kai is talking with the Mexican government. They aren't very happy about what happened to you. *Los Equis* is considered the most dangerous of the cartels in the area. They would like to see Gilberto Ortega, his son and the rest of that drug outfit eradicated."

There was the sound of crunching as if Derrick was walking on gravel. "Yeah, and why haven't they accomplished that?"

"Corruption." Austin started his car. "So watch your back and don't trust anyone."

"I never do."

"Derrick—"

"Except you guys. You know that, right? I know you've got my back."

That eased some tension in Austin's gut. "You going soft, Derrick?"

"No, I'm going to kick your ass when I get home."

Austin chuckled. "You can try. Hey, be careful, huh? Amber and I don't want to have to break in a new guy."

"Yeah? All right. I'll talk to you later."

Somewhere near Caliche, Mexico

Gilberto Ortega took one last drag off the Cuban Montecristo cigar. It had a marvelous fragrance, fruity, the smoke curling above his head. He sat on his balcony overlooking the beautiful valley. His domain. He'd fought and bled for his business. Suffered untold loss.

He crushed the stub of the cigar into the ashtray sitting on the small table, his heart heavy. It always was when he thought of his beautiful and fiery Maria. She'd been gone for three years, but his love for her had never diminished and his revenge had been both brutal and bloody. Not even when he'd met Arturo's beautiful Americana, who looked more like a tiny, blonde fairy.

And now Matthew St. John, Mateo, had been born, and that little fairy had proven to have a spine of steel when it came to her son. But Gilberto wasn't about to let her keep him. He had plans for the boy, plans for Arturo, as well.

A car rushed down through the compound gates, the sound of the powerful engine purring like a cat in the night. It came to a squealing halt in front of the hacienda. Drunken laughter filtered up to him on the balcony and disgust twisted his gut.

Arturo.

The sound of a female's laughter mixed in with the deeper sounds of his son's amusement traveled from the driveway into the house, where it reverberated in the downstairs hall. Then up the stairs. Gilberto didn't move.

This was a nightly occurrence: different female giggles each time. The laughter and murmurs were cut off as a door opened, then closed.

Yes, he had plans for Mateo and Arturo.

He rose and stood at the banister. He wasn't about to let some American cops disrupt those carefully laid plans. No matter. Santa Muerte would answer his prayers in both blood and design.

He was certain of it.

Chapter 8

Just outside Santa Ana, Mexico

After waking, getting some *chilaquiles*—eggs, pulled chicken, and salsa over quartered corn tortillas—and using a gas station's questionable facilities, they drove in companionable silence. It was amazing to him how luminous Emma was first thing in the morning. They both still looked a bit worse for wear with their dirty and ripped clothes. Derrick had switched out his bloody shirt for the still dirty, but blood-free one that they'd used to lure the chopper in. He itched a bit and his arm still hurt, but both had lessened quite a bit. He was thankful for Emma's quick thinking in grabbing their bag of supplies. It could have ended a lot differently without the water and much needed first-aid supplies.

When they got to the outskirts of Hermosillo, the capital city of the state of Sonora, Derrick drove to the nearest junkyard and sold the truck for scrap. On his way out of the facility, he dropped the plates into a metal shredder.

"You think that's enough to make sure they don't fol-

low us? I'm starting to get a twinge of remorse for dup-
ing that gas station owner. What if the cartel takes out
their frustration on him like they did with that poor hotel
owner?"

Derrick snorted. "He looked like he knew the score.
He'll probably sell both the helicopter and information
back to the cartel. Who do you think tattled on us?"

She sighed, tidying her hair and without a mirror,
pulled that mass of red hair into a ponytail. "You're
probably right."

It was hard to believe she looked so good after two
days in the same clothes and after being chased through
the desert by murderous thugs. A closer inspection would
reveal the wrinkled cargo pants, the smudged shirt, the
tiny lines of fatigue feathering the corners of her eyes
and tugging at the edges of her mouth. But all he could
see was how pink and inviting those lips were and the
rosy glow flushing her cheeks. "I know you want to think
the best of people. But it's easier to think the worst. At
least, that's kept me alive."

It was a cynical way to look at the world, but Derrick really hadn't had a different view. "I'm not naive,
Derrick. I just like to think there are good people in this
world."

"There may be, but there are also plenty of baddies."

She gave him a look that said she couldn't argue with
that. "Let's grab a cab. Find a nice hotel. Rest and re-
charge a little."

She lifted one eyebrow but said nothing as she took
his hand, making Derrick smile. "I wasn't implying anything…physical," he said.

The corner of her mouth curved. "It has been more

than physical enough for me. Thank you very much." But her rebuttal came out in a breathless rush of air.

It's never been...whatever this is, he wanted to say. Not this overwhelming attraction. He'd fallen for Afsana, but it had been in a more subdued, understated way. Emma made him feel...reckless. But when she looked down and dusted at the tails of her shirt, as if suddenly thinking about that, as well, he opted to leave it alone.

"A hot shower, a hot meal—"

"Oh, yes. Please," she said instantly, her blue eyes sparking to life.

"Let's go, then." He took her hand, and they went around to the front of the building, grabbing the next cab. "I'll check in with Kai and from there, we'll figure out our next move. I'm sure she's had time to confer with the government agents assigned to us."

"I do realize that we've probably tipped them off that we're searching for Matty. But they don't really know that for sure. There were two murders in La Mesa, after all."

"All that is true, Emma. Doesn't mean we're going to stop just because we have targets on our backs." He got them both settled in the backseat. "The nearest hotel, please," he instructed the driver. "A good one," he amended.

The driver smiled as he glanced back at them.

"Plenty of stars?"

"Sí," Emma piped in.

He nodded and pulled into traffic.

"What time does the mall open?" she asked the cabbie. When he told her ten o'clock, she said, "Change of plans," as she glanced at her watch. "Take us there."

Derrick groaned and the cabbie laughed.

She nudged him with her elbow. "I want clean clothes

to go along with that shower. We don't have a stitch left. I had some expensive clothes in my luggage. Not to mention my sister gave me that suitcase for Christmas."

He did, too, but it was the cost of finding her nephew.

He dropped them in front of the Galerias, a typical mall. "We should split up. It will be faster. You get what you need, and I'll do the same. We can meet back at this information kiosk," Emma said.

He hesitated. The idea of them separating didn't appeal to him. And he had to admit to himself it had more to do with personal reasons than anything to do with her safety. He doubted the cartel had trailed them here. But that did nothing to diminish his need to keep her close.

"Derrick?"

Emma wasn't exactly fragile or helpless. Which was a great part of why he was drawn to her. But that didn't make him feel any less conflicted. He wasn't used to feeling so proprietary or giving so much thought to a woman of late.

Partnerships could be tricky at times; he knew that from working with Austin and Amber, discovering their boundaries and limits, as well as developing trust and faith, especially for a former spook who didn't really trust a soul. But with Emma there was the added emotional element, which was as huge as it was confusing. It was the part that wasn't rational or reasonable, more like a primal directive to protect and defend. He snorted at himself. Had he just gone back in time millions of years? Neanderthal.

"Sure," he responded. "Good idea." He stared after her as she disappeared among the racks of clothing, thinking about that, which led him to think about what would likely happen if they were in the same hotel room. Realizing he was wasting time, he headed for the closest upscale men's store and started shopping.

Two hours later all the new clothes, underthings and toiletries were stashed in their newly purchased luggage—a suitcase for Emma and an easy to carry bag for Derrick. The cab eased into a circular drive in front of a modern-looking hotel. It stopped at the entrance, and several bellmen immediately moved in their direction. "I can't decide whether I want food or a shower first. Maybe I'll just eat in the shower," she said as she took the bellman's hand and slid out of the vehicle.

He smiled at Emma as his door was opened. He could see the fatigue etched on her face quite clearly now, and knew he didn't look much better. He put his hand on her lower back as the bellman held the lobby door for them. Once inside they headed for the registration desk, the clerk looking askance at their dirty and sweaty appearance.

To explain their state, Derrick had a story ready about their car breaking down and how they had to walk for miles. When it came time to decide on the room, he didn't hesitate. "One room, please." Emma glanced at him, but like in Santa Ana, she didn't say anything. It was probably "safer" for them to get separate rooms, but Derrick decided it was better to be together. They were mature adults. They could handle this.

With room keys in hand, they headed for the elevator, the bellman trailing behind. Emma leaned in and said, "That was so convincing I almost believed it."

He chuckled as they stepped inside for the brief ride up. Once inside their room with their luggage and the bellman handled, Derrick indicated the bathroom with his hand. "You go first. I'll order. Just decide what you would like."

"The menu."

He walked over to the table in the room and picked up the menu. "No," she said with a smile. "The whole menu."

He chuckled as she took it out of his hands, her stomach growling. "Breakfast didn't go far enough."

"We were in survival mode for a couple of days. We need to refuel."

She nodded absently as she looked at the menu, then told him her order, disappearing into the bathroom.

With one lingering look at the closed bathroom door and his imagination at what she was doing right about now, he turned away and pressed the numbers on his phone.

"Naval Medical Center, ICU, Lieutenant Keenan speaking."

"Lieutenant Keenan, this is Special Agent Derrick Gunn inquiring as to the status of Petty Officer Lily St. John."

"I'm afraid she's still in a coma and unresponsive. But she's stable," she said in a no-nonsense voice.

"Thank you, Lieutenant."

He hung up and then sent a call to Austin. He picked up on the first ring. "Hey, we were just about to call you. Here's Kai."

A moment passed and Kai's voice came on the line. "Did you make it okay?"

"Yes, We're in the hotel now. We weren't followed."

"Good. So, I've consulted with Inspector Reyes and Agent Velasco and they both say you should stay put and they'll come to you. Once you've had a chance to touch base, they'll escort you to Caliche by plane. They can smooth your way through security with your side-arms. So take time to rest and regroup. They will be there first thing tomorrow morning. Don't worry about the government-issued car."

"Yes, boss lady," he replied. "About the car…yeah, that was taken along with our luggage. I managed to salvage my bag, tablet, and we both have our cells. We still both have our documents and money along with my badge."

"Well, you're going to have to submit paperwork for the car."

"Will do."

"And Derrick, stay alert once you get to Caliche." His eyes snagged on Emma's bag open on the bed, lacy and frilly things visible. He closed his eyes and turned away. "It's stable, but lawless. The cartel runs roughshod over a lot of the local law enforcement."

"I've been in worse places," he murmured.

"Well, now you're working for me, and that's an order."

"Copy that. Can I speak to Austin?"

"Of course, touch base when you get to Caliche. Bye, Derrick."

There was another short silence, then Austin said, "Yeah, what's up?"

"Delve deeper into the Ortegas and get me anything you find on them. I like to know who I'm going up against in detail. Especially weaknesses." Derrick sat on the bed. "And, find out who that teen killer is, Austin. Like yesterday," he growled.

"I'm working on it. Okay? Cool your jets. I know what's at stake," Austin said defensively. "How are you and Emma holding up?"

"We're making do," Derrick said, unable to lose the edge to his words.

Austin lowered his voice and Derrick could imagine him at his desk, swiveling around so his back was to the office. "I couldn't help overhearing that tone in your voice or miss the way you looked at her...ah, when you weren't glaring at her." He lowered his voice even more. "You getting along with this woman?"

"Yeah, she's special. Very professional. I think I did her an injustice by generalizing her job."

The water shut off and Derrick focused desperately on the conversation, trying to keep his mind completely off clean, damp skin as the terry-cloth slid over it, soaking up every drop. "Oh, okay, it's like that."

Austin and Amber were the two people closest to him, knew him the best and that was saying something. Along with Kai, they were the longest long-term coworkers/ friendships he'd ever had, except for a few CIA officers he still had contact with. "Uh, Austin. It's not like anything." *Anything I've ever known, anyway.*

"Sure it isn't. You're too suave and slick to get snagged by a beautiful, smart and savvy woman."

Derrick remained silent, still reluctant to even engage in this type of banter with his coworker. He was still struggling with their connection. He'd never experienced anything like the laid-back surfer, but Austin's mind was as ridiculously agile as his hands. The most evolved technology, along with mechanical objects of all sizes and complexity, bowed before his amazing, inborn talents.

The blow-dryer sounded. "Stay loose, surfer boy, and wipe that damn, smug-ass grin off your face."

His voice was filled with that smug-ass grin. "I'll be

in touch when I come up with more information." Then he clicked off.

The door opened and Emma stepped out, her hair straight and loose, her bangs fluffed from the blow-dryer. She looked…pensive, but when she passed him, she gave him a smile. "All yours." She smelled deliciously female and he wanted to bury his nose in her hair.

Instead, he watched as she opened the sliding glass door and went onto the balcony. Ten minutes later he stepped out of the hottest shower he'd taken in a long time, happy to be clean, but not feeling as rejuvenated as he'd hoped. He was worried and probably overanalyzing everything.

He didn't need any more distraction after having been through the emotional roller coaster of the past couple of days. He came out of the bedroom and she was still standing on the balcony. Grabbing a pair of boxer briefs, he put them on under the towel. Then a pair of khaki shorts. He rubbed the towel over his hair and threw it on the bed as he passed. Slipping onto the balcony, he saw the city stretch off into urban sprawl below them. He said, "I called the medical center. Your sister is the same, but the nurse said she was stable."

She looked at him over her shoulder. "Thank you." Her shoulders were a little curved, arms folded across her middle, her gaze on the city below. "Do you think we messed up, Derrick? Showed our hand and it's going to be doubly hard to find Matty?"

He knew it was fatigue and worry talking, but it still made him wish he had a better handle on the situation, and better options available. He wished he could find her nephew and return him to her. "We'll find him, Emma. I swear it. Let's not give up before we've even begun."

Her arms tightened around herself and he could barely stand the pain on her face. She was unraveling and, if he was being honest, he'd expected it to happen either in private or before now. Exhaustion broke down the defenses faster than anything. He knew that from his training and from experience, had been taught ways to contain his emotions, finish the mission, no matter what horrible thing or personal catastrophe had happened.

But he wasn't a spy anymore. That hit him like a ton of bricks. He didn't have to be secretive or guarded. He didn't have to hide the fact that he wanted to comfort this woman.

"I'm not giving up. I'm just so afraid for him," she whispered.

He stepped up behind her and wrapped his arms around her, pulling her against his chest. For a moment he just held her, fortifying her and giving her a shoulder to lean on for now. Until she was strong again.

He bent down and kissed her hair, wanting to connect with her like never in his life.

When he kissed her head, the tenderness, the comfort from that gesture, rushed through her. It was tantalizing for a woman who had been alone for a long time, fiercely independent and determined not to give in to weakness. She'd had to be strong for Lily her whole life. Emma had told herself over and over in the shower everything was going to be all right. Yet anxiety churned in her gut anyway. If they had tipped off the cartel they were after Matty, what repercussions would follow? That was what she couldn't seem to shake. That somehow they had made things worse. But what was the alternative?

She turned in his arms, and he hugged her hard. Achingly moved by the hug, even more moved by the protective way he tucked her head against his shoulder, Emma shut her eyes and struggled against the sudden threat of tears.

Resting his cheek against her hair, Derrick rubbed her back, and Emma turned her face against his neck, saturating herself in his touch.

"Emma, there was no other course of action. The Ortegas were going to find out sooner or later. We have to move forward."

She looked up at him, his gaze troubled. He lifted a wisp of hair off her face and carefully tucked it behind her ear. It was then that Emma understood that her attraction to Derrick was more than she could handle, cosmic, gigantic and overwhelming.

She took his face between her hands, then stretched up and gave him a soft kiss.

He stopped breathing and went very still. Emma could feel the need in him, the lonely, lonely need, and she put her heart and soul into that kiss, wordlessly telling him things she couldn't say aloud. A shudder coursed through him, and he drew a ragged breath, catching her by the back of the head, his jaw flexing beneath her hand as he responded. He moved his mouth slowly against hers, tasting her, savoring her, drawing her breath from her and leaving her weak.

It went on and on until Emma felt as if she were suffocating from all the sensation pouring in on her, and she flattened her hand against his chest. Derrick tensed and dragged his mouth away from hers. His heart was slamming, and his breathing was harsh and uneven, but he gathered her up in a cuddling embrace, and Emma hung on to him, needing him—needing his strength around her. Finally, Derrick ran his hand up her back, pressing her to him. He turned his head, placing an unsteady kiss against the curve of her neck, then nestled her closer. "Together we'll get him back."

Emma closed her eyes and hugged him hard, moved by his husky admission. "Promise."

"I promise," he murmured as the knock sounded against the door. "The food," he said, easing away from her.

She was in big trouble with Derrick. Big, big trouble.

Chapter 9

Derrick had the bellman set up the table in the middle of the room. Derrick tipped him and closed the door after he left.

She moved over to the table, still feeling a bit shaky. It had been sweet of him to find out about her sister for her, but she experienced a stab of guilt that she was indulging in kissy-face with Derrick when she should be working to track down who had Matty and had thrown her sister down the stairs.

She hoped that Lily would come out of her coma. Hoped that she would be all right and when she got Matty back, they could all be a family again. Emma felt so petty about their fight now that she knew Commander Ward was part of Lily's life. Maybe she had been jealous that Lily was getting on with her life, or maybe she had been afraid of her sister leaving her alone. Maybe Emma was afraid to get on with her own life?

She closed her eyes at that realization.

The scent of the food made her stomach growl and her mouth water. Derrick took the top off her burger and his, setting them aside. Emma dragged one of the chairs over to the table and settled into the seat. This wasn't exactly the best setup to get involved with a man. Part of it was all that adrenaline jacking them up and the other part was the forced proximity to a man she was attracted to, but was seeing in something more intense than a normal dating situation. Not that she was dating Derrick or would date him. She ran her hands through her hair, deciding that thinking about anything but food was going to be counterproductive until she got some sleep and was able to think in a rational manner.

She set the napkin against her lap and picked up the burger, taking a bite. Chewing, she glanced at Derrick. He was focusing on his meal. "Thank you again for checking up on my sister. It was going to be my first call after the shower."

He nodded. "I'm sure it's heavy on your mind. But you have your grandmother to stop in and visit."

Emma snorted, setting down the burger without biting into it again. "I'm sure she's much too busy to worry about Lily," she bit out, then took an uneven breath. Picking up her burger, she didn't encourage Derrick to ask any questions. Her volatile relationship with Bess as dinner conversation would only cause her indigestion.

They continued in silence for several surprisingly comfortable minutes, comfortable enough that she ate the rest of her burger and sat back to enjoy the coffee.

"Inspector Reyes and Agent Velasco are going to be landing here tomorrow and escorting us to Caliche. We've lost any advantage we would have had trailing your nephew by car, but could possibly beat him to Caliche."

"Escort us?" she said with a bit of an edge to her voice.

"Just as a courtesy. I don't think it was meant as an insult, Emma."

She set the napkin on the small table and rose, while Derrick wheeled the remnants of their lunch into the hall. "You're probably right. I'm just on edge. If it'll get us to Matty faster, I'm all for it."

She walked to the TV and grabbed up the remote, turning it on. Flipping through the channels, she found their news station. Derrick came up to her and turned her around. "Emma, this isn't a slight against us. They are here to help."

She breathed a huff of breath. "I'm just tired, Derrick. I'm sure they don't mean any disrespect."

"They don't want anything to happen to us out on the open road. I don't want that, either."

The way he'd said it, the look on his face, made her heart squeeze. She tried to ignore that and focus on business, even though she knew there was some subtext there. "I can handle myself, Derrick. Just to make sure you know that."

"No, of course you can. You proved me wrong there. This is the best course of action. I agree with Kai. If I didn't, I would have said so."

He hadn't removed his hands from her arms and his touch was strong and warm, thoroughly distracting. "You don't want anything to happen to me."

"I didn't say it was logical, or even rational. It's…caveman." He smiled. "And, trust me, it's not something I'm entirely comfortable with, either. Especially since I was so vocal you shouldn't be allowed to accompany me. But if I'd been alone, Emma, it would have been much more difficult to get out of that situation. Not that I couldn't."

"I have no doubt about that," she said, even as her

insides were melting a little. No one had cared for her. She'd always cared for others and this felt strange. "Worry about the cartel. Worry about finding Matty. Don't worry about me."

"I will," he said, looking down into her eyes. "But that doesn't stop me from worrying about you."

"Are you going soft on me?" she said, tilting her head.

He smiled slightly. "Maybe. You're making me eat my words, lady. I don't often have to do that."

"Oh, so you're usually right?"

"Usually, except when I'm wrong."

She laughed softly. "Oh, Derrick, there aren't any guarantees. In anything."

"I'm aware of that." Those intense eyes captured hers. "I can't guarantee a thing, your safety included. I just feel that if we stick together, we have a better chance of dealing with whatever is out there." His smile returned, but there was something tender, almost vulnerable in it. "We make a good team, Emma. I don't say that easily because I'm not the best team member."

She couldn't manage to look away, couldn't seem to find whatever it was she had left that would keep her mind strictly on business. "I think we do, too," she said, being completely honest.

She couldn't seem to stop her wayward hands as they slid up his hard torso to wrap around his neck. His hands fell away from her upper arms in the movement, snaking around her waist. "Emma," he warned, swallowing hard. "We could complicate things."

"I know," she whispered.

He closed his eyes, his hands flattening out and grasping her hips, dragging her against his thick arousal.

She gasped and he groaned softly, deep in his throat.

Then his mouth was finally, blessedly on hers again. And there was nothing tentative about his kiss, regardless of his doubts. He was confident, a warrior. She had no doubts about that. But he was also beautiful, seductive and so very male.

For the first time in her life, she wanted to be with a man who was so responsive to her needs, who pushed her to reach for more, no matter how spent she'd thought herself, but also someone from whom she'd learned the depths of pleasure to be gained from satisfying their needs. She felt aggressive, discovering a confidence that being successful in her other endeavors had never given her. She had no idea if Derrick knew the myriad gifts he was giving her.

Her heart squeezed, engaged despite her own misgivings and her own fears, as he tenderly drew his fingers along the side of her neck, moving his mouth to the delicate line of her jaw, then following the trail of his fingers.

He was so gentle, this warrior who had subdued several men. So much more of her than her body was at risk of being seduced.

Instinctively she eased away from him, pushed on his shoulders. It wasn't a shove; she wasn't strong enough for that, still wanting—craving—what he was giving her, but knowing she hadn't the control needed to protect herself. And she wasn't ready to surrender. Not fully.

She wore her independence like armor.

How much would she have to give up? Compromise? How vulnerable would he make her?

He allowed her to shift back, then framed her hips in his wide palms when she stepped back unsteadily. He balanced her, kept his hands there firmly, but nothing more.

He did balance her, in so many ways, she thought, struggling for clarity of mind she so desperately needed.

"Maybe you're right," she breathed, willing her head to stop spinning, her legs to stop trembling and her heart to stop pounding. "But if I don't have you, all of you, I might just lose my mind."

He took her mouth this time like a man starved. There was nothing tender about it and it was what she needed. She could only let herself feel…whatever he made her feel. Then deal with it later.

Even as he started walking her backward, even as the back of her knees hit the bed, she was aware this was the biggest mistake she'd ever made. And the point was moot. She was making it with her eyes wide open. Because he made her feel so good, and telling herself she was strong enough to resist him was laughable.

"Emma," he murmured, his voice huskier, his body already harder. "Protection."

"I'm safe on birth control."

He spun her around, held her close with one arm. He kissed the nape of her neck, sending sensation quivering down to her breasts and into the aching tips of her nipples. His free hand slipped beneath the waistband of her shorts and the panel of her silky underwear, delving to her core. The arm around her waist moved upward until his warm hand pushed aside her bra and cupped her breast, pinching her throbbing nipple at the same time he stroked over her.

She arched into his hand, gasping. She was lost. Lost to the hunger. Lost to the sensations pumping through her. Lost to the urgency of his questing fingers. She moved her hips involuntarily to the pressure of his fingers. An explosion detonated inside her, and a chain of convulsions ripped through her as she came apart.

She was still shuddering, still jerking against his hand and the oh-so-clever fingers he'd slid inside her, when he was already slipping them out and shifting her around so she faced him, taking her mouth with his, even as he slid his hand between them to unbuckle and unzip.

She craved him, needed him filling her up, as she'd never craved anything before. She would have pushed his hands away and torn at his pants herself if she'd thought it would get him inside her any faster.

He was freeing her, getting his shorts off, and just as he bared her, he was pushing her back onto the bed. He pushed inside and she pushed back, grinding on him, glorying in the long groan of satisfaction she wrenched from him as she clenched her still-twitching muscles tightly around him and accepted him into her body, needing so much more.

He was on his knees, his arm around her back, his mouth on hers, his tongue deep inside, thrusting. She took both as fast and deep as she could. She felt him gather as his climax built. She bit his bottom lip, causing him to growl and his hips bucked higher, which compelled her to cry out as he found a sweet spot that almost made her mindless with pleasure.

His masterful movement shot sparks everywhere, and she arched beneath him, trying to release the building electricity between them. Her movement took him over the edge, groaning, growling, as he pistoned inside her while coming in a shuddering fury. She clung to him tightly, clutching him to her, even as she struggled to breathe around the sheer mind-blowing pleasure.

Fighting for breath, she cradled his head against the

curve of her neck, a fierce, almost frantic protectiveness welling up in her. She was sure the only thing holding her together was the savage strength of his arms.

It took a while for her to get her bearings, for the storm of emotion to ease, but when she could at last collect her senses, she hugged him and stroked his hair, profoundly moved by the care he'd taken with her.

His expression was more serious than she'd ever seen it, his gaze locked on hers so intently it was as physical a connection as his warm body on hers. There was a stunned silence between them, the power and essence of which she saw reflected in the depth of those striking eyes.

It was nice to know she wasn't alone in discovering the intensity of what she'd felt had happened just now, even if she couldn't define it, and common sense just completely deserted her. This had been life-altering. She just wasn't sure how much it would hurt, change her life or affect her heart. She could barely think straight.

Closing her eyes against the feelings he invoked, she stroked his head, needing to give him comfort, so full of feeling for him that she could barely stand it.

Derrick stirred in her arms, and she lifted her head and found his mouth, kissing him with infinite gentleness and desire.

Brushing the hair back from her temple with his thumb, he released an uneven sigh and kissed her back, his mouth warm and moist and seductive still.

He exhaled raggedly, then tucked her face against the curve of his shoulder. Emma rubbed the back of his neck, wishing he was totally naked against her. Derrick tightened his hold on her, his chest expanding as he took a deep, unsteady breath. Fingering the soft silk of his hair, she kissed his temple, tenderness filling her. "Now things are complicated," she whispered unevenly against his cheek. "Boy, are they ever."

Bracing his weight on one arm, he lifted his head, his touch leaving her breathless as he kissed her mouth again. "I'm thinking it was worth it," he said, his tone husky and intimate. "Boy, was it ever."

Suppressing a grin, she parted her lips and kissed him, the caress gentle and searching. Inhaling unevenly, Derrick slid his arms around her in a warm embrace, deepening the kiss as she smoothed her hand up the center of his back.

It was as if he couldn't get enough of that soft, caressing intimacy and it was a long time later when he reluctantly eased away. Brushing back her hair with his knuckles, he lifted her chin and gave her another light kiss, then released his breath in an unsteady sigh. "Let's get some real sleep," he whispered gruffly.

She wrapped her arms around his neck and kissed his jaw. He turned his face and found her lips as he slid his hand up the back of her head, deepening the contact, molding her against him with the weight of his body. Finally, he eased away and gave her one final kiss, then rolled free. His profile was outlined by the bright sunlight coming through the wide window; she watched him shed his shirt, longing to caress every inch of his muscled body. He turned toward the window and pulled the drapes against the bright day. Back at the bed he lifted her into a sitting position and pulled off her shirt and undid her bra. "Beautiful," he whispered, running his hands over her breasts, kissing and tonguing her nipples as he pushed her onto her back.

"I thought you wanted to sleep."

"I'm a little busy right now," he said, sucking her hard nipple. She sent her hands into his hair as he switched to the other, his hands molding over her waist and hips. "Derrick," she whispered and he moaned as he moved down her body—making her come again with his mouth, then his hands and his mouth again, until she was mindless.

Then he snuggled up against her as Emma turned into his embrace, his kiss intensifying when her naked breasts grazed his chest. Slipping his hand up her hip and across her back, he separated his legs and settled her between his thighs, and Emma's breath caught at the feel of his naked body molded fully against hers. Raking her hair back, Derrick drew away from the kiss, then firmly nestled her head again in the curve of his shoulder. "Now go to sleep, babe," he whispered gruffly.

Emma closed her eyes, loving the feel of his arms around her, feeling again safe and secure for the first time in a very long time.

The room was dark when Emma woke up, the silence only broken by Derrick's even breathing. She glanced at the clock to see it was late evening. They'd slept for a long time, refilling their wells. It had been a trying two days fighting for their lives.

She was suddenly starving again. When she moved, a strong, muscled arm snagged her around the waist and drew her against him. "What time is it?"

"Nine," she whispered against his silky jaw.

"I'm—"

"Starving?"

He chuckled.

"Yeah, me, too." He rose and scooped her up and

headed for the bathroom, where they enjoyed touching and caressing each other in the shower while the warm water washed away their lovemaking. Once they were dry and back out into the room, Emma dressed in a pair of gray shorts and a soft, shapeless top that did nothing to hide her full breasts, while Derrick donned a pair of black shorts, leaving his chest bare. Emma couldn't protest that. They ordered room service, then after their meal went for a quick walk around the grounds.

In a lighted courtyard, they settled onto a bench. A nighttime stillness had settled outside, and a breeze rustled through the fronds on the palms, filling the air with a soft whispering sound. They were holding hands, not something Emma usually did with a man she'd first met and, in this case, something as unexpected as getting involved with someone she was working with, not to mention someone with his alpha tendencies. Her independent nature balked at it, but with Derrick, it just seemed to work. "What we're doing here…" Derrick said.

"Is crazy," Emma added.

He looked away. "To say the least. I was drawn to you from the get-go. You took me by surprise. The way you hold yourself, the way you stood up to your grandmother, your confidence, your ease with yourself and everyone else. You're a natural and draw attention just by being yourself." He reached up and tucked a loose strand of hair behind her ear, then very lightly ran his fingertip along her cheekbone and down along her chin.

The brief contact made her shiver, but in a damn good way. He talked about commanding attention. He had no idea.

"I could say the same thing about you," she said,

which caused his gaze to intensify, so many shades of Derrick.

"I was against bringing you and my reasons were sound. The emotional attachment was only the tip of the iceberg."

"You thought we'd end up in bed together? That's pretty presumptuous."

He shrugged, looking rugged and unapologetic. She rather liked that. "I don't waste energy fighting against the inevitable. That's not exactly true. I wasted some energy wrestling with it."

She smiled and shook her head.

"What?" She raised a brow and he huffed out a short laugh. "Oh, that sounded so arrogant. Okay, maybe I'm sure of myself, too."

"Ya think?" She nudged him and he laughed again.

"I don't know where we're going or how this is going to pan out, but my life has been *different*, Emma. Maybe *too* different for me to be in any kind of a relationship. I'm a loner."

"Maybe that's because you've always been alone. Engineered it that way?"

He swallowed and looked away. "Talking about my past isn't something I normally do. To anyone."

She nodded. It was no surprise this man had some scars. It was there in his eyes and in his voice. Curiosity and a deep-seated need to know fueled her craving for more details. If Derrick couldn't share with her, that was something she could accept, understood even. Hell, her childhood and adult life were also rife with scars. It wasn't lost on her that she was also very good at deflecting interest and keeping things on a superficial level, but she found with Derrick that was nigh impossible.

She wanted more. That thought scared her more than anything had in her life. She was the one who dictated how a relationship would go. She was the one who called the shots. Was that because she *needed* to call the shots to keep herself on top in a relationship, to keep herself from getting hurt?

She craved an equal partnership, but was always demanding control. How would that work with a man who had the same kind of need for control as she did?

"Derrick, you don't have to—"

"I want to, that's the crazy thing about all this. The strength of the attraction between us isn't something to be easily dismissed. I'm certain what we shared goes both ways. If I'm wrong, let me know and we'll just keep this simple."

"I think simple went out the window from the moment I pointed my gun at your impossibly broad shoulders and you blindsided me with those cobalt blue eyes."

"Yeah, helluva way to meet."

She laughed. "That's a good story. Mommy pointed a gun at Daddy—"

His sharp intake of air wiped the smile off her face. "Derrick, it was just a joke."

He closed his eyes, resting his head on her shoulder. Moved beyond measure, she slipped her hand into his hair. "I'm sorry. I didn't mean anything by it."

"I know you didn't, Emma. It's my own stuff." He took a deep breath.

She cupped his face and raised his head. Kissing him softly on the mouth, she said, "Talk to me if you want to. But if you're not ready…"

"I've never had a family." He leaned back against the bench seat, the breeze ruffling his hair so dark against his forehead. He looked down, more pensive than she'd ever seen him. "My parents either died a long time ago, when I was a baby, or something else happened. I didn't even know them. I don't remember them at all. I lost all ties to the people who do remember. No one tells a kid anything, so the circumstances are just…lost."

She closed her eyes and took a breath of her own. Boy, did she know exactly what he was talking about. "When I lost my parents, everyone acted like it was okay. Part of it, I'm sure, was to lessen the trauma. But there's no minimizing that kind of pain."

He turned tormented eyes toward her with a look she was sure he'd never shown to another living soul. If he hadn't stolen her heart, this would have done her in. "Oh, Derrick. You don't have to do this—"

Derrick stiffened. "No… I need to tell you. I want to tell you." His voice was strained. "I don't want to be alone anymore. You do that to me."

She waited until he gathered his composure. "I was in the foster system and in and out of homes until I was about ten. I knew the score even then. I wasn't some lost boy pickpocket, but I was a thief. It made me feel good to slip inside a home and take something personal. I'd never been caught until Jerome Thompson III caught me. But instead of turning me over to the police, he adopted me."

He shifted to look at her. "I thought it was cool to be taken in by this rich guy. But adopting me had nothing to do with me at all. It had to do with him preserving his legacy and his money. He groomed me to take over from the minute I stepped foot in that house. He liked that I was a thief."

She smoothed her hand over his warm forearm, and he entwined his fingers with hers. "I've always been good about blending in, taking on roles because they amused me or by necessity. It was the same with Thompson. He was cold, cruel, and indifferent to my needs. The moment he kicked, I liquidated everything down to the last nail. Gave half to charity and banked the other half. The only thing I kept was some property."

He stopped speaking and Emma slipped her arms around him and they sat in silence. It was a long, long time before Emma could ease her hold. Her heart was crushed by the memories that flooded her and the empathy she felt for Derrick. They did have that in common.

Rubbing the back of his neck, she turned her face against his. "If things had been different, you wouldn't have turned out to be this amazing guy that you are."

His chest expanded sharply; then he hugged her so hard she couldn't breathe, and she hugged him back. She'd like to think that, in this moment, he didn't feel alone.

Letting down barriers took a lot of courage. She wasn't sure she had the same kind of courage he did.

Back in the room, Derrick booted up his tablet and they pored over information about Caliche, the cartels in power there. When it got late, they curled up together and fell back to sleep in each other's arms.

It felt so natural. So right. So real.

But Emma never took anything for granted. They still had a job to do, their budding relationship aside. Sleeping with him was something she couldn't seem to resist. But was she ready to release her secrets?

Only time would tell.

Chapter 10

Derrick woke at dawn with Emma tucked into the curve of his body, his arm secure around her waist, her breath warm against his neck.

His eyes drifted shut, loving the feel of waking up with her in his arms. He couldn't have had more than three hours' sleep, but he was feeling surprisingly rested. They had ended up talking into the night—not about his childhood or what had happened to him afterward, things he was still holding back because he didn't want to…scare her off.

But now it was morning, and the sun was coming up. Softly rubbing her arm, Derrick shifted and looked at the clock. Deciding it was too risky to stay this way any longer, he lifted his arm and eased away from her. As soon as he moved, Emma rolled over on her stomach. Smiling down at her, he pulled the sheet up to cover her.

They were going to have company soon, and it was time to resume the pursuit of her nephew now that they had fully recovered from the desert. He was under no illusions that going to Caliche, their base of operations to comb the *Los Equis* infested area and find Matthew, would give them any sense of safety. They were going to the devil's door and Derrick was ready for any kind of hell he unleashed. He was getting Emma's Matty back.

He leaned down and kissed her temple. Letting go last night, about who he was and where he'd come from, might have been his way of warning her that he had baggage. He wasn't sure where this relationship was going. After all, they'd been thrown together here and he was still reeling at his feelings for Emma. Even now he'd rather slip back into bed with her and make love to her again instead of facing reality.

But he'd never shirked his responsibilities, even when it came as a great personal sacrifice for him. She had gotten under his skin, but he was certain it would be better that they kept on their game faces when in public, especially with these agents sent by the Mexican government.

They needed to remain professional.

He ordered room service before he went into the bathroom, taking a hot shower. As he came out of the steamy interior into the room with nothing but a towel around his hips, there was a knock at the door. He walked over and opened it, expecting it to be room service.

Instead two men stood there. He didn't react, giving nothing away. One of them was older, with gray hair, bushy brows and a wide mouth. His dark eyes were warm and open. The other one was young, handsome, had the kind of looks that would turn women's heads. He on the other hand had a cocky look about him that Derrick recognized immediately. Macho.

The older man reached out his hand. "Agent Gunn, I'm Inspector Jorge Reyes and this is my colleague—"

"Agent Santiago Velasco," he said with a wide, sharp

smile. His grip was harder than it needed to be. Derrick didn't react to the guy setting up some boundaries.

"Nice to meet you. Sorry it has to be under these conditions."

"Where is Ms. St. John? We did text that we were coming," Agent Velasco said, his voice full of his interest in Emma. Derrick didn't like it, but he didn't react.

"She's in her room, and I'll notify her you're here." Derrick lied smoothly. "Let me get dressed and Ms. St. John and I will meet you downstairs for breakfast."

"Our flight isn't for several hours, so that will be fine," Inspector Reyes said.

Without waiting for an answer, he closed the door. Turning he found Emma sitting up in bed, the sheet pressed to her breasts, looking mussed and tantalizing.

"I missed the text," she said sheepishly. "I'm sorry."

"It's all right. I covered."

She frowned. "Covered?"

"I think we should be quiet about…us. This."

"Oh, why?"

"It's more professional, Emma." He wasn't ready to fully deal with his relationship with Emma, let alone anyone else who might scrutinize it.

"Is that it, or is it your need for secrecy taking over here? We don't have to be overt, but I don't see a need to cover up anything."

That caught him off guard and he was rarely ever blindsided. He took a step toward the bed, frustrated and annoyed and turned on and…a whole lot of complicated things he didn't want to be. Why was she being so contrary when he was also working to protect her reputation, her privacy? "It's none of their business."

She gave him her best steely-eyed glare, something

he realized a PI had likely perfected as a matter of survival. "Is this a problem with NCIS?"

"No, I'm not crossing any professional lines by getting involved with you." He wasn't. It was his own ingrained principles that were in question here. He couldn't shake it, feeling raw after telling her something so personal. "Morally, it's iffy."

"Morally?"

At her strident tone, he wondered what kind of nerve he just hit. "You've had a serious shock with your sister in the hospital and your nephew taken by a cartel, Emma. That makes you more vulnerable than you would be in normal circumstances." He was more irritated with himself than with the conversation and her reaction.

She rose up, her eyes narrowing. "As in you taking advantage of me in my weakened state?"

"No, that's not what I meant."

"Maybe you should just be quiet," she bit out and threw the sheet aside. "We don't have time for this conversation. Fine. Mum's the word." She brushed past him and went into the bathroom and closed the door. Somehow he'd gotten her back up and he wasn't exactly sure how he'd done that. Normally, he read people like an open book, but with Emma, the pages seemed to be blurred. He spent the time she was in the shower packing up his suitcase and checking out of the room.

When she came out of the bathroom, she dressed and packed her bag; her tight shoulders and expression didn't invite him to continue the conversation. He had to agree. They didn't have time to go into this now.

When she was ready, he followed her out of the room. Down in the lobby, she headed toward the dining room. When he spotted the two Mexican officials, he went to steer Emma in that direction, but she shook off his attention. Smiling, she greeted both men. Agent Velasco's eyes lit up at the sight of her.

"Ms. St. John. My superior couldn't say enough wonderful things about you. It's a distinct pleasure meeting such a beautiful woman."

Derrick gritted his teeth, but kept his emotions bottled up and safely under wraps. He was going to act neutral if it killed him. During the breakfast, Velasco flirted with Emma, but she was a master at engaging, but not encouraging.

A couple of hours later they were in the air heading to Caliche, an almost eight-hour flight. Through the window, he watched the wispy clouds over the dark land below. It was better than watching Velasco talking to Emma, as he'd done almost nonstop since he'd commandeered the seat next to her.

Derrick couldn't say anything about it. He'd wordlessly met her eyes and moved to the seat across the aisle. Reyes settled down next to him. He looked over at the animated Velasco and shook his head.

"Such a ladies' man," he murmured, then he turned to Derrick. "Have you been to Mexico before, senor?"

Derrick had with the company, but he smiled and said, "No, my first time."

"You been with NCIS long?"

"Five years. How about you?" Velasco leaned in and Emma did this subtle block with her shoulder that put a slight smile on Derrick's face and a frown on the younger man's. She was something else. He couldn't quite believe that he had told her anything about himself. It felt...alien, but good. He hadn't told her everything. He was still getting used to this partner/lover thing.

"Oh, came up in the ranks. I guess you get to a certain age and survive, they give you a prestigious position."

Derrick chuckled, eyeing Emma, who was smiling at something Velasco said. He'd never felt jealousy before. With Afsana it was more about pain, but with Emma, he was confident in her.

He wanted to shout, to startle the son of a bitch into giving up any hope, to tell him he would never touch Emma.

Every cell in his body echoed with the need. She ran through his blood, entered with his breath and would not leave him, no matter how much logic or common sense he used trying to bend the need to his will.

He turned toward the window and decided that it was best to ignore Velasco's antics and focus on his plan of action when they landed in Caliche. Emma had it under control.

"Agent Gunn." Velasco's subdued voice reached him and he turned to find him standing in the aisle. "The lovely Emma has requested you sit with her. She wants to discuss something with you."

Derrick rose, keeping his face neutral. He slid past Reyes and moved away so Velasco could slide into his vacated seat. He sat down next to Emma and she turned to look at him. Her snapping eyes told him she was still in a snit, but all he could do was smile. He'd take facing a pissed off Emma any day over her sitting next to that hormone laden guy.

"You think this is funny?"

"No. I think you're amazing."

For a moment she stared at him as if he'd just caught her off guard. She leaned toward him like she couldn't help herself, and he knew exactly how that felt. "I can take care of myself, Derrick. You don't have to worry about that. If I thought you were crossing a line with me, I would make sure you tripped over it hard."

"I don't have any doubt about it."

"Then let me decide if you're taking advantage of me. I'm not weak. I've never been weak."

He captured her gaze and made sure she heard every word. "I didn't say you were weak. I said you were vulnerable. It's not the same. I don't want to mess up here. I want to be honest with you about how I feel. I've kept way too much to myself when it mattered. I'm not going to do that with you. If it pisses you off, too damn bad. We'll hash it out." She blinked a couple of times and then looked away as if she was trying to regain her composure. He leaned over. "I really wish I could kiss you right now."

She took a quick breath and let it out. "You really are something else, Derrick."

"Is that a good thing?"

"I'm not sure, but you're never boring."

"And for all your gentleness, you have a surprisingly direct way of dealing with people."

"Some respond to gentle. People, at least those in my line of work, tend to respond better to direct and to the point."

"Even more important, given the gender inequity in your line of work, I would imagine." If his sensitivity to her plight surprised her, she didn't show it. "I'm sorry if I offended you, Emma. I'm not sorry for what I said. I'd like to shout it to the rooftops that we're together, but it will put us at a disadvantage here. You do see that. Especially with the cartel and the Ortegas."

"I still don't see the need for it, but I will defer to you."

She'd said it calmly enough, but he noticed, in his peripheral vision, that she was fidgeting a bit as if unable to get comfortable.

"You can do anything you want to me in private," he said huskily and that stopped the fidgeting completely.

His direct answer, coupled with his very direct gaze, seemed to catch her off guard. He wasn't flirting now. And she knew it.

"I don't know what to do with that or what to do with you."

"That's okay, babe. I have enough ideas for both of us," he replied, a hint of the teasing smile coming back, but still keeping his gaze focused tightly on her.

She took a breath and let it go. "Now I want to kiss you."

"Keep that thought. We've got seven hours before we touch down."

"What are your plans for when we get there?"

"I'm going to see if anyone in the area knows the teen. We may be ahead of him unless he had the same idea and got on a plane. He may have already delivered Matty to the Ortegas. We don't know for sure, but if we can get a bead on the guy who kidnapped him, we might have a case to question the father and son on not only the murders, but more important on Matty's abduction. Maybe we can get some negotiations going."

"I would certainly prefer to get Matty back without violence."

"We'll do what it takes to get him back." Within or without the letter of the law. They were dealing with lawless thugs here and Derrick wasn't about to play by the rules when he was certain Gilberto and Arturo had no intention of doing so.

When the plane landed it was early evening. They stopped for a bite to eat at a cantina and the two Mexican officials drove them to a compound.

"This once belonged to the Medianoche Cartel. *Los Equis* took them out, so the local police took over as a fortified place to have their base of operations," Reyes said. "This is where you'll be staying. You can use it as your base of operations. The Ortegas don't often bother the residents of Caliche. Their beef is with two other cartels in the area and their focus is on them. But we can talk about that in the morning."

They drove up to a metal gate, which swung open after Reyes talked to someone. They entered a large yard with a fresh-cut lawn, more palm trees and a circular pool in the middle.

Derrick liked the idea they were in a fortified area. But he agreed with Reyes that any information would be better absorbed in the morning. He nodded. "Let me show you to your rooms."

The house itself was a two-story dwelling, also painted in bright yellow with white accents and double-paned windows with arched tops and a red tile roof.

In any large American city, this house would be a suburban, upper-middle-class home—but in this city in the area of Michoacán, it seemed much grander, certainly in stark contrast to the adobe houses next door.

The entrance opened into a decorative foyer and into a hallway that connected to the living area with a large sofa and coffee table, and a fully operating kitchen. "There are four bedrooms upstairs. We brief down here. It's been a long day. We can meet you down here tomorrow morning at eight. There will be guards at the gate twenty-four/seven. So sleep easy."

Derrick never slept easy, except for the two nights in Emma's arms. But here, they would have to be more careful and much more discreet. He grabbed her bag and carried the suitcases up the stairs. Emma followed. He opened one of the doors to find an opulent bedroom. Going inside, he set her case on the bed.

"I'll be right next door if you need me." She nodded, looking weary. Unable to stop himself, he pulled her against him. "I wish I could stay."

"I know. I wish you could, too. But I've got to check in on my sister and I'm sure you want to touch base with your team."

He tugged her mouth close and kissed her. "We're both full of crap," he whispered, catching the door with his foot and nudging it closed.

She laughed a bit breathlessly as he pinned her against the wall. His grin felt lazy, and he knew his gaze was just a touch more than a little proprietary as he stroked the side of her face, tucking a stray hair behind her ear. "I'll be taking a very long, very lonely cold shower one room over."

"Brr," she said with a mock shiver.

He laughed. "I've survived worse."

"You are my hero."

"Yeah, I am," he said, his voice gruff.

She smiled up into his eyes. "I have no business getting sidetracked by you, you know, much less letting you get sidetracked by me."

"I know. It's sidetrack city where you're concerned."

"Are you sure you won't stay?" She grinned without a hint of remorse.

"You're killing me here, Emma."

"That's the plan."

"I'm getting that." He wrapped his arms around her waist and pulled her snug between his legs. "And I'm enjoying this."

She swatted at him, but she wasn't making any move whatsoever to disengage his tight hold. Which only had him drawing her closer still. "I do want you, Emma." He moved his hips. "Hard to deny that one. But I'll want more than just that."

"Maybe if you only wanted me for my body, this would be easier."

"Ha, not likely. Nothing is easy with you."

She smiled. "Wear your heart on your sleeve, do you?"

"Typically, never. With you? It's fast becoming something of a struggle."

She closed her eyes and pressed her face into his neck. "Geez, you smell good."

"Emma—" She moved her head and tugged his face down to hers and kissed him. Then she broke the kiss. When he tried to resume it, she pressed her fingers across his mouth and stopped him. "I want to. That much is obvious but—"

He moved his mouth a little and nibbled on the end of her fingers.

"You're incorrigible."

"Unrepentantly."

She slipped from his hold, and reached out her hand. When he took hold of it, she pulled him over to the door. "I won't sleep if you stay. We're both almost giddy with exhaustion. I think maybe we'd best get at least a little rest. We're in a war zone now."

He wanted to argue, but clearly, as she was yawning, she had a point.

"We are in a war zone," he said with a sigh.

She laughed. "Go before I change my mind."

He stepped out of the room and paused at her open door. "Good night, babe."

"Good night, Derrick." She paused, looked up at him. "Thank you for what you said about me not being weak. That means a lot to me."

He nodded. "I meant it."

She smiled. He stood there, long after she'd closed the door. He listened to the creak of the floorboards overhead as she readied herself for bed. Stood there while she checked in with the hospital and until the creaking stopped and the light splintering through the door went out.

"Good night," he murmured, and walked to the room next door, opening the door and going inside. Getting involved with this woman had a profound influence in his life. In him.

He wondered, really wondered, if a leopard could change his spots…wondered if he could really acclimate himself, or was he doomed to be alone forever?

She was making him think and feel differently about everything. Especially about getting her nephew back, making him think about his own kid, and even though he wasn't in the boy's life, he felt protective of him just as much as Emma was feeling protective of her nephew. He'd promised that he would work with her, but he vowed he'd break that promise if he had to—all tied up in knots about his own son. He couldn't imagine Emma and her sister Lily having to go through what he was going through. His son was also in a war zone and if he could get him out of it, he would in a heartbeat. His hands were tied there, but not with Emma's nephew. He would never leave that innocent boy to the Ortegas. It was inconceivable.

He really meant it. He'd get the boy back no matter what it took.

With or without her.

Promise or no promise.

Chapter 11

Somewhere near Caliche, Mexico

Luis drove through the compound gates. It had been the worst trip he'd ever driven in his life. With the crying baby, stopping for changes, feeding and administering the medication prescribed by the doctor in Santa Ana, he was frazzled. Being only sixteen, he wasn't used to handling a baby. Yet *Jefe* had sent him and that made him proud that his boss trusted him with this job. He only wished he'd done better, killed the baby's mother like he'd been instructed and neutralized the American threat to them back in Santa Ana.

He pulled up outside the kitchen in the back where he'd been instructed to go. He'd had to duck several roadblocks by the local cops. Word must have gotten out, since the Americans had escaped their execution in the desert outside Santa Ana. Formidable opponents in this battle for the baby boy.

The back door opened and a small, heavyset woman peered out. Luis opened his door and stepped out of the car. He went to the back and clicked the latch to remove the car seat from its base and transform it into a carrier.

The boy didn't stir as Luis had just fed him a half an hour ago. He was so tiny, so unaware of his plight. But if Gilberto wanted him, Luis was sure he would treat him well. After all, what would he want with a baby anyway? He grabbed up the infant's bag and slung it over his shoulder. The woman held the door wide as he entered the house, her dark eyes troubled. She touched his arm, but he shrugged her off. Luis didn't question what he was asked to do. He did it, but deep down he couldn't be sorry the boy's mother hadn't died.

"Follow me," she said, her voice quiet.

"The medicine must go into the refrigerator," he said, holding out the plastic bag to her. She took the bottle of pink liquid from the portable cooler Luis had purchased at the pharmacy and the light from the fridge flashed in the dimness, then winked out as the door closed. She walked back and they ascended the stairs and entered a fully furnished and stocked nursery.

"How is the baby?" she whispered.

"He is well. Much less fussy since he has received several doses of the amoxicillin. I fed him, changed him and he should be fine. She unbuckled the straps that held the boy inside and with the ease of a mother lifted him out of the seat. For a moment she stared down into his little face, the fat cheeks, the downy hair, his pink, pursed lips. He reached out and nudged her. "It must be done. We don't have a choice in that matter. You know that." She set him in the crib on his back and covered him with a blanket. Even though the night was warm, the air-conditioning kept the house chilled. He stirred and made soft noises, but settled down again into slumber. Luis breathed a sigh of relief. This was finally over.

They left the room and went back downstairs. "He will see you in the study. Please be careful, my boy."

"Ah, Mama, you know I do this for you."

She wiped at her eyes with her apron. "This is wrong and we both know it. What you have had to do in his employ is…monstrous. What we both have had to do has marked our souls."

"We survive, Mama. That is what we do. You've worked for him for most of your life. I was practically raised here. He's provided everything for us. He is our *jefe* and it must be done."

He left and walked through the house and knocked at the carved wooden door.

"Enter."

Luis pushed open the door to an opulent study done in dark green and gold, an expensive rug under his feet, covering the wooden floor of the same dark oak as the big desk. He moved forward and was soon in front of Gilberto Ortega, who reclined in a tall leather chair, the fruity smell of smoke from the Cuban cigar he was fond of scenting the air.

"He is here?" Gilberto's voice was melodious and deep. He took a drag on the cigar and breathed out smoke.

"Yes, Mr. Ortega. Upstairs. Safe and sound. He has an ear infection, but I've given him the medicine as I was instructed." Luis's gut was tied up in knots. If Gilberto wasn't pleased, he'd never leave this estate alive.

"You have performed…adequately. The Americans are in Caliche. That is unfortunate they have discovered the connection between the baby's mother and us. But they have no proof. No concrete evidence. So it's of no matter. If they get bothersome, I will neutralize the threat. The boy is now mine. It would have complicated matters for the American government if their agents had gone missing. I'm displeased about that turn of events."

"One is an NCIS agent and the other one, the woman, is a private investigator."

"NCIS?"

"Naval Criminal Investigative Service. They are involved because the boy's mother was in the navy."

Gilberto huffed out a laugh. "Not even the FBI. Ha, these people are of no consequence."

"Our contacts in Santa Ana took heavy damages. They would like the two Americans' heads."

"Hmmm, good to know. I'll keep that under advisement." He took a drag of the cigar and blew out the fragrant smoke. "The mother still lives."

He nodded, wiping his palms on his pant legs. "She is in a coma. That is true. But she fought me and she fell down the stairs. I'm sorry I didn't finish her off, but I didn't want to attract undue attention, and getting the boy out was my number one concern." He swallowed. Mr. Ortega sounded calm and cool. But Luis knew that wasn't an indication of the man's state of mind. He gave nothing away when he was pleased, when he was sad and when he was homicidal.

Mr. Ortega leaned forward and tapped his cigar against a beautiful marble ashtray. "Get something to eat, then lay low. The authorities don't know who you are and that is good. Let's keep it that way. For your sake and my competent and resourceful Gabriela, your mama, I will send someone to handle the situation you botched."

"Yes, sir," Luis said, his heart pounding. It was a subtle threat. Mr. Ortega would kill his mother without a second thought. But not today, it seemed.

"Send in Mr. Flores."

That was his dismissal and Luis backed toward the door. "Thank you, Mr. Ortega." He ducked outside and found Mr. Ortega's right-hand man cleaning his fingernails with the tip of the knife he carried. It was slim and wicked-looking, the kind of weapon that killed quietly before the victim even knew it was coming. Luis should know; Francisco had taught him everything he knew.

If Mr. Ortega was threatening in a neutral way, Francisco Flores was an overt, stone-cold blunt instrument. It was in his dead black eyes, in the square jaw and the big, but surprisingly elegant, hands. Violence was etched into every line in his face.

Francisco didn't look up even when Luis called his name, then cleared his throat. When Luis went to reach out to shake him, he exploded out of the chair, knocking it back against the wall. The sharp knife was against Luis's throat before he could take his next breath. "Don't ever touch me," he rasped out as the razor-sharp knife nicked him.

"No, sir." Luis's words wobbled. "Mr. Ortega would like to see you. He doesn't like to be kept waiting."

Flores smiled, but it never reached his eyes. "Does he? Probably to clean up your damn mess." He removed the knife, spun it in his hand and sheathed it in a leather case on his belt. "Get the hell out of here."

The moment the Montoya boy left, Gilberto's mind started to spin. It was true the Americans might have a clue that Gilberto and his son Arturo had been on the same cruise as Lily St. John, but there was no proof that either he or his son had harmed her or taken the baby. All he had to do was tie up any loose ends and put his plan into motion. When Francisco walked into the room, Gilberto said, "Close the door. We have much to discuss."

Hermosillo, Mexico

Emma woke up and in that place between waking and sleeping, she felt as if something important was missing. She opened her eyes to the unfamiliar room, then recollection flooded back to her. Derrick. She was missing his warmth. She was on the way to Caliche, one step closer to Matty. She could almost feel the little boy's presence. Could Gilberto have brought him someplace nearby?

She slipped out of bed and took a shower, then got dressed. It was early, but Emma was ready to take the next steps to get Matty back.

She exited her room and paused in the hallway. She could already hear Derrick's voice from downstairs, the fluid, deep tones that sent shivers over her skin. She wanted to wake up to him in the morning, and she felt out of sorts still that he wouldn't stay with her.

At the bottom of the stairs, she almost ran into Velasco. He reached out to steady her and smiled. She stepped back, enough so that his hands fell away. "Excuse me," she said.

"No problem, Emma."

"I would love some coffee," she said to get him to move out of the way. Derrick and Inspector Reyes were seated at the table with a map of the area spread out before them.

She walked across the room, her eyes on Derrick. He looked good, rested at least. So he had slept. She wished she could just touch him. Even a caress along his broad shoulders would be good, but she adhered to his wishes. He rose and grabbed a mug from a cupboard and poured her a cup, grabbing the half-and-half from the fridge.

Coming back to the table, he set the mug down.

She took a sip and sighed. She looked at Derrick and got a little lost in his eyes for a moment as his greeting was wordless and private.

He looked down then over to Reyes. "Jorge was just talking about the town and the lay of the land around here. I'll let him finish."

"As I told your colleague, Caliche is located about twenty-eight miles from the capital city of Morelia. It's an aristocratic colonial city, whereas Caliche is a colonial town, which still remains true to its roots. For the most part it's peaceful, except for drug lords who might like to set up their compound just outside the city's limits. People around here are very friendly and don't mix with the cartels. *Los Equis* likes it that way and makes sure to keep the people around here in line with violence. For the most part the town is peaceful and safe. That's why they get plenty of tourists and even some retired Americans."

"Let's go get some breakfast, then talk to the local police. They might have some information on the Ortegas we can use. But just as a warning, the moment we start asking questions, it could get rough. So we need to be very careful who we talk to."

"As in, corruption runs rampant?" Derrick said.

"Very much so. They have an endless flow of cash at their disposal, that and intimidation. The threat of violence is real not only to the individual but also their whole families. Some people find it safer and easier to give in to the demands of the cartel."

They left the house, got into one of the two sedans and drove into town. Emma could easily understand why this area of Mexico was considered the most beautiful country in the state with its panoramas of mountains and lush valleys of trees. "This is very beautiful," Emma said.

Velasco turned and said, "We'll get some breakfast at the Grand Hotel, then head to the station where you can ask your questions."

At brunch, amongst a sizable crowd, Derrick got into a discussion with Reyes, which left her with Velasco once again. "So, Emma, I understand that you are a private investigator in the United States."

"Yes, I handle many standard cases."

"How is it that you are involved in this case? It seems a dangerous mission for a beautiful woman."

"I'm quite capable of handling myself, Agent Velasco."

"Ah, no, I have requested that you call me Santiago. We will be working close together. This I believe is true. You are capable. Is this because you have been to Mexico before and are good at kidnapping cases?"

"That, and the infant that was taken is my nephew."

His brows rose. "Oh, that is very personal. It must be a difficult time for you."

"It is. My sister was injured in the abduction of my nephew."

"That also is very unfortunate, but the cartel doesn't care much for life. They are indiscriminate when it comes to protecting their business and keeping their stranglehold over their drug routes into the United States. What could they possibly want with your nephew?"

"I wish I knew. It's something we are looking to discover." His personal interest in her might stem from his overt romantic advances, but could also be a way to gather information. Derrick said to trust no one. How could they be sure either of these officials was trustworthy? Just because they were assigned by the government didn't mean they had been uncorrupted by the cartels.

After they finished breakfast, Emma joined Derrick in the backseat of the sedan. "What was that all about?" he said, keeping his voice low.

"The game of Twenty Questions? I don't know. Maybe he just likes me. Is that so far-fetched?"

"No," he said warmly, brushing the back of her hand briefly and out of sight of the two officials in the front seat. "It's not from where I'm sitting."

Just the touch of his hand made her heart falter.

"We have to keep our guard up."

"Believe me. I have no interest in Velasco. He's much too pretty," she whispered for his ears only.

Derrick chuckled. "Is that so?"

She gave him a cheeky grin. Even with Velasco's looks, it was Derrick her eyes got snagged on; Derrick who completely swamped her senses whenever he was near her. She worked at getting her composure back. "Don't worry. I think you're pretty, too."

"Well, one of us has to be, in this partnership."

That made her laugh, and she swiped at his shoulder. They both sobered as they approached the police station. It was on one of the main highways leaving Caliche, an adobe structure with a red tiled roof. Marked cars were parked out front and in the parking lot adjacent to the building.

Once inside and after checking at the front desk, they were ushered deeper inside and into the office of the police commissioner.

He greeted them, and when they asked about the Ortegas, his eyes narrowed. But he gave them a name of a person who might help them. He was one of the stall owners in the marketplace. They thanked him and headed toward the central plaza.

"Stay close," Reyes said as they exited the car and headed into the dense crowd. In the main square, called La Plaza Grande, there were places to buy ice cream, fresh fruit, vegetables, fish and meats as well as herbal medicines and local crafts. Just on the fringes, street performers played instruments and some juggled.

The place was packed, vendors lining the square. Their guy was in the back, hawking Catrina dolls, figurines that depicted a woman with a skeleton head and boney hands. One of the dolls was holding a bouquet of marigolds, a Mexican symbol for death. It seemed they had come to the right place.

In Spanish, Reyes said, "Antonio Guzman?"

The man stiffened and said, "Yes, I am Antonio. What is it you want?"

"A few words," Reyes said. He turned to a woman behind him and said, "Watch the booth. I will be right back."

Antonio moved off to the side, the crowd still thick. "What is it I can do for you? You smell like Federales."

"We are officials from the government, but these are Americans. They want to ask you a few questions about the Ortegas."

Antonio's eyes widened. "The Ortegas? Are you out of your mind? Why would you go anywhere near them? They will kill you as soon as look at you."

"We're looking for an infant boy. Dark hair, nine months old. He would have arrived sometime within the last day or two," Emma said, her heart in her throat. If he had any knowledge about the baby, it would give them a head start at where to begin looking.

"An infant boy? One of Arturo's? Hard to believe he'd want anything to do with a baby. He is too busy partying."

"The boy was kidnapped and taken from the US. These agents are here to recover him. If you have any information, it would be helpful if you tell us now. We wouldn't want your permit to come under scrutiny."

The shop owner sighed. "I have heard of the arrival of a baby boy. It's been hushed up, but I have ears everywhere."

"Where is he?" Emma said, taking a step forward.

A gunshot exploded and the man stopped talking as blood blossomed on his forehead, and he fell backward. People started screaming and Emma turned to find a man who looked like her sister's attacker standing there in plain sight. He smiled, turned and ran.

She couldn't let him get away. He was the key they needed to lock up Gilberto for good. He would also have information on Matty. She sprinted after him. Derrick called out her name, but Emma didn't slow down. She chased him across the plaza, bumping into people in general panic. Her eyes on his fleeing form, she cut across the manicured bushes and splashed through a fountain.

He fired at her and missed. She continued after him until he disappeared around a bend. She pursued him and then skidded to a halt. A pickup truck filled with men toting automatic weapons halted at the curb.

Derrick reached her and said, "Come on." She had no choice, and deep-seated anger settled in her. He gripped her hand tightly. The warmth of it seeped into her, and she banked her anger. They would have another shot at them.

He guided her around a group. Her gaze moved rapidly over the crowd, her senses jumping, and then she glanced at Derrick. His attention was far ahead. She followed it. Men were coming this way, ignoring the festivities, the people. They stood out easily with their Santa Muerte tats on their forearms.

Derrick spun her and had her against the wall in a heartbeat, his body covering hers as he drew his weapon and turned. He fired just as the wall above his head splintered. They dropped, chips of stucco sprinkling over them. He didn't waste a moment, pulling her along with him, past storefronts and cafés, his pistol tucked to his stomach.

"It was a trap?"

"Maybe? Not sure who ratted us out."

He barely flinched when a bullet shattered the wood near his shoulder. He didn't return fire. There were too many civilians. Derrick pulled her with him, his steps so wide she was forced to run hard. They made it to the end of the alley. People were just figuring out that the noise wasn't firecrackers and were running in all directions as bullets sliced through the air. Sirens sounded in the distance.

"Here comes the cavalry," Derrick said from between gritted teeth.

A man stepped out in the open, firing straight at them.

Derrick dove to the ground, taking her with him. The impact nearly knocked her out and Derrick rolled, his back against the wall. He aimed, pulling Emma close. They leaned out to return fire and Emma heard a scream, then the thump of the man going down.

"Not a moment to spare," she murmured, then saw a shadow flicker. "Derrick," she shouted and shoved him down, firing off four fast rounds. Bullets shredded the other man's body and he fell facedown onto the cobblestones.

The sirens got louder and another bullet whizzed past her, hitting the adobe wall; a chip struck her cheek, stinging. Derrick clutched her.

"Are you all right?"

"Felt the wind on that one," she said with a shaky tone.

Derrick swore viciously and hauled her back the way they had come. It was as if the shooters had disappeared into the woodwork. Nothing remained except blood and spent shell casings. When Derrick got back to the square, the police were there, taking control and soothing the crowd.

Reyes broke away from the chief inspector, the one who had given them Antonio's name. Antonio was still lying where he'd fallen, a pool of blood around his head. The woman in the booth was sobbing.

He eyed Emma's face and reached in and pulled out a handkerchief. Offering it to her, he said, "Are you two all right?"

"Yes, we're fine."

"Looks like this might have been an ambush," Reyes said, looking over his shoulder at Velasco as he conversed with the chief inspector. Emma wasn't sure which man Reyes was scrutinizing. "There are many corrupt cops. Hard to know who might have set us up. Everyone knows this man is a snitch."

Emma ran her eyes over the crowd, looking for him, but he wasn't there. She squeezed her eyes closed, her fear for Matty escalating. He was in the hands of murderers and Emma could barely handle the pain and frustration climbing in her.

She broke away from Derrick and closed the gap between her, Velasco and the chief inspector. "If you sold us out, so help me!" she said to him.

Valesco's eyes widened and he stepped back. The chief inspector scowled at her, then said, "Neither of us had any dealings with the cartel," he said stiffly.

Of course they would deny it. "Someone set us up," she replied just as stiffly, anger lining each word. She didn't say anything else as they went to the police station and gave them a statement. Each of them was taken to different rooms. The injury to her face was superficial, but it bled a lot. When they were released, Emma pulled out the rendition of Matty's abductor.

She held it up to the chief inspector and said, "Do you know this man?"

His eyes widened. "Come with me," he said.

With Derrick following, he took her to a set of stairs that led down into the basement. It was colder down here and Emma shivered. He led them into a room and closed the door. It was like a meat locker. She could see her breath.

He pulled a sheet from a prone body on the table. The man they'd been hunting lay on the table. His eyes were closed, but it was clear he was dead. "We found him at the edge of the plaza."

Emma covered her face and took a moment to compose herself. Their best lead had died in the battle. When she looked at him again, she realized there wasn't a mark on him.

"How did he die?"

The chief inspector indicated to two white-coated men to turn him over. "A thin knife was inserted at the base of his skull."

Chapter 12

Derrick watched her startled expression as she stared at the body, pain and anger flickering in her eyes, then she turned to walk away. Outside the cold room, he clasped her arm as the other three men continued up the stairs.

He caught her by the jaw and forced her to look at him, something dark and painful breaking loose in him when he saw how pale her face had gone, when he saw the fear in her eyes. The small, raw wound made him realize how close that bullet had come to her face. "We're going to find him," Derrick said roughly. He looked away, his temper cresting at the drug lord for putting Emma through this. Then he looked back at her, a thick ache unfolding in his chest.

"He knew where Matty is. He knew how he is. I'm trying with all my might to keep it together, but I just want to scream."

He turned to look at the door, the dead teenager behind it now beyond anyone's reach, including the law and decency. "I know. We've got to keep it together. Can't let the emotion rule us, Emma. Matty's future rests in our hands."

Inhaling deeply, he shifted his gaze and looked at her, his stomach dropping like a rock when he saw the stark, distressed expression in her eyes. He stared at her, then exhaled heavily, his anger settling into a heavy, resigned feeling. It was a culmination of how he felt about his own son being just as effectively taken from him. Except, in his case, under the current circumstances, he might never get to know him.

He caught her behind the neck and pulled her hard against him, locking her up in a tight embrace. "Derrick," she whispered.

"Just shut up and let me hold you."

She remained rigid in his arms for an instant, then the tension went out of her, and she slid one arm around his back and pressed her face against his neck. As soon as she wrapped both arms around him, he let go of her.

Back upstairs, Emma asked, "What is his name?" She was pacing and Derrick wanted to reach out and gather her close again. But that wouldn't be appropriate now. At this moment he almost didn't give a damn. Her voice was strained, and she was hurting. To be so close to the man who had abducted her nephew, hurt her sister and to have him silenced… It was cruel and difficult to control emotions. But he admired her courage as she kept herself together.

"Luis Montoya."

Derrick was pulling out his cell and texting the information to Austin. The reply was short and to the point.

I'm on it.

"Does he have family?" Her hopeful tone was almost too hard for him to hear.

"Yes, his mother, Gabriela Montoya. She's been notified."

"There's nothing to do at this point," Reyes said. "Let's get back to the compound and regroup."

She glanced at Derrick, but then turned and directed her comment to Reyes. "We can talk to his mother," Emma said, a stubborn slant to her jaw.

"Not right now. We need to let her pick up the body and prepare it for burial," Reyes countered. "They have sacred rites to perform and disrupting this will not be conducive to your investigation. If she's our best lead, then we need to be patient."

She turned, facing him dead on, her mouth compressing into a hard line. "And in that time, the Ortegas could take Matty anywhere. He's here. I can feel it. We need to dig."

"Digging now would net you nothing. The mother isn't going to talk. Not many people in this area will want to talk. They're terrified of *Los Equis*. We need to give her some time to grieve. Then maybe we can make a case for her to talk to us. But storming in now and demanding answers isn't going to help your case."

"I disagree. I understand your customs, especially the ones about death. She just lost her son. We can recover Matty alive. That has to mean something to a mother. Just give me a chance to talk to her."

Derrick said, "Emma. He's right. Let's give it some time. Let's give her a chance to grieve." She folded her arms across her chest and Derrick walked up to her and murmured. "This is going to get us nowhere. Let's go back to the compound and we can talk."

She gave him a disgruntled look, but nodded. He could tell she wasn't convinced, but he completely understood Emma's need to charge in and get answers. He worried that her judgment was clouding because of her closeness to Matty. It had been his main concern letting her in on this case. "We have to maintain perspective, Emma."

She didn't say anything at first, then she gave him a curt nod and they exited the police station, cautiously checking around the area before getting in their sedan.

Once back at the compound, Emma wasn't happy. She argued some more, then finally gave up and went upstairs.

"Are you sure she's up to this investigation?" Reyes said, pouring himself a cup of coffee. "Women can be irrational when it comes to corralling their emotions regarding a family member."

"She's my partner and I stand by her. She's partly right. Standing around isn't going to get us any closer to finding her nephew," Derrick growled.

Reyes tipped his head, his expression thoughtful. "All right, point taken. We can ask around, but it could all come to nothing."

"I understand. I'll stay here with Emma."

Reyes nodded and he and Velasco left.

Derrick climbed the stairs and at Emma's door, he knocked. "Come in." When he opened the panel, she was seated on the bed, her phone in her hand.

"I just checked on Lily," she said, her voice trembling, an edge of anxiety in her tone. "She's still the same. I'm worried about her." She raised her eyes to his. "If they killed the kidnapper, what's to stop them from going after my sister again? She's a loose end. They have to know that if she recovers, she will never stop looking for her son."

A twinge of guilt tightened in his gut. He didn't have to look for his son. Derrick knew exactly where he was. But he might as well be on the moon. "I think that has merit. I'll text Austin to be vigilant. We already have guards on her now."

Emma nodded. "Nothing is guaranteed. We can only do the best we can to protect the ones we love."

He closed his eyes, reliving that moment when the bullet had whizzed past her head. He wanted her out of here. Back in San Diego, where there was nothing but traffic clogging the expressways, coffee shops on every corner and the grind of everyday life. He wanted her back there, with her family whole and together. He could give that to her. He was alone, had no family, only his ties to his job.

That wasn't exactly true. He'd struggled with it, but NCIS was his family. But they would understand him putting himself in harm's way to finish out this case. "Emma. Maybe it would be best if you headed back home. Help from afar."

She sat up straighter. "Is this because I wanted to go after Luis's mother right away? You see that as irrational?" Her eyes narrowed. "Or is this about protecting me?"

The tension that had been riding him since the shootout let go in a rush, and he rested his hands on his hips and wearily tipped his head back, long days of exhaustion piling up on him. "My biggest argument against your involvement was about how close you are to this case. We're in a dangerous position here. We don't know who we can trust. Maybe not even the good guys."

With a choked sound, she came up off the bed and into his arms. "Then you need me here to watch your back." He gathered her up into a tight hold, roughly tucking her face against the curve of his neck. "I'm not going to let you cowboy this by yourself." Derrick felt her take a deep, tremulous breath, then she pressed her face tighter against him as she slid her arms around his waist. He could feel her trembling—she cared so much—and he pressed a kiss to her temple, then slid his fingers along her scalp, cradling her head in a firm grip. "I can't be completely neutral. That's true. Matty is part of me, my family. I've taken care of them for so long and I don't intend to give up. It's worthwhile, isn't it, Derrick?"

His fingers tangled in her copper hair, soft like satin, and he closed his eyes and hugged her hard, a swell of emotion making his chest tighten. This woman filled him up inside. "Yes," he whispered gruffly. "It's worthwhile."

He felt her take another tremulous breath, and he smoothed one hand across her hips and up her back, molding her tightly against him. Easing in a tight breath of his own, he brushed a kiss against her temple. "I don't want anything to happen to you," he said unevenly, drawing her hips flush against him.

A tremor coursed through her, and Emma dragged her arms free and slipped them around his neck, the shift intimately and fully aligning her body against his. Derrick drew in an unsteady breath and angled her head back, making a low, indistinguishable sound as he covered her mouth in a kiss that was raw with desire, governed by a need to comfort and reassure. Emma went still. Then, with a soft exhalation, she clutched at him and yielded to his deep, comforting kiss.

Derrick slid his hand along her jaw, his callused fingers snagging in her silky strands as he altered the angle of her head. She moved against him, and Derrick shuddered, tightening his hold, a fever of emotion sluicing through him, wishing this woman was his forever.

Dragging his mouth away, he trailed a string of kisses down her neck, then caught her head again and gave her another hot, wet kiss. His breathing ragged, he tightened his hold on her face and drew back, cuddling her against his chest. He held her like that, his hand cupping the back of her neck, until his breathing evened out.

He held her tight, trying to get a grip on the wild clamor rising up inside him. He clenched his jaw and rubbed his cheek against the softness of her hair. She reached for his shirt, undoing the buttons and pushing it off his shoulders, then unbucked his belt, and shoved his pants off his hips. He stepped out of them.

She reached for her own shirt buttons, but he'd already grasped the hem and pulled it off over her head, the bra unsnapped and removed, her pants stripped off her. He lifted her onto the bed, then followed her down, dragging her beneath him. He felt as if his heart would explode, as if his lungs would seize up, if he didn't get inside her, if he didn't get as close to her as he could possibly get. She made a small, desperate sound and rolled her hips, urging him with her hands. Derrick clenched his jaw and closed his eyes, burying himself deep inside her. So deep and tight.

He locked his arms around her, a shudder coursing through him, and he ground his teeth together, the sensory onslaught nearly ripping him apart, the intensity of the physical connection more important than the sex. They fused into one dynamic whole.

Braced against the mind-shattering sensation, Derrick remained rigid in her arms, waiting for the heated, electrifying rush to ease. Releasing a shaky sigh, he braced his weight on his forearms and bracketed her face in his hands, his heart trapped in his chest as he covered her mouth in a slow, wet, aching kiss.

Emma sobbed into his mouth, her hands clutching at him, and she lifted her hips, rolling her pelvis hard against him. Derrick roughly slid his hand under her head and locked his other arm around her buttocks, working his mouth hungrily against hers as he lifted her higher, then rolled his hips against hers. Emma made a choked sound, and Derrick drank it in, his mind blurring with a red haze when Emma countered his thrust, her body moving convulsively beneath him.

Aware of how desperately she needed this kind of comfort, Derrick dragged his mouth away and gritted his teeth, a fine sheen of sweat dampening his skin as he moved against her, trying to give her the maximum contact, trying to exert the right amount of pressure where she needed it the most, trying to hang on until she came apart in his arms. She made another wild sound, and her counterthrusts turned desperate and erratic, and Derrick tightened his hold. His senses on overdrive, he roughly buried his face against her neck and thrust into her, fighting to go the distance, the red haze governing him.

Emma arched stiffly beneath him, and Derrick's face contorted with an agony of pleasure as her body convulsed around him, pulling, pulling at him. Then, with a ragged groan, he went rigid in her arms and let go, emptying himself deep inside her. Holding on to her with grasping strength, he held her against him, her face wet against his neck. Feeling as if he had been turned inside out, he pressed his mouth against her temple and closed his eyes, his pulse choppy and erratic, the feelings in his chest almost too much to handle.

She filled him up and made him feel indestructible.

He drew a deep, shaky breath and pressed another kiss on the corner of her mouth, his touch slow and comforting as he softly stroked the angle of her jaw with his thumb. He braced his weight on one arm and hip, lifting her against him and rolling to his back.

She smelled like flowers and sunshine; he inhaled deeply. Taking another deep breath, he bracketed her face with his hands, shifting his weight so her legs entwined with his.

He tipped her head back and brushed a light kiss against her mouth, the rawness of his feelings for her swamping him.

"I think we have something going here, Gunn," she whispered against his mouth. "You can't dispute it. I'm a private investigator after all."

"Is that so?" he murmured, taking a slow, savoring kiss. He felt her smile against his mouth; then she tightened her arms around his back and slid one hand back and forth across his shoulders.

"Thank you for listening to me, for supporting me. This is so difficult."

He caressed her wrist, then lowered his head and slowly moistened her bottom lip; he took her mouth again, taking great care to do it well. He released a soft sigh, and she slid her free hand up his torso. "You've got some serious gorgeous going on here. Did I tell you that muscle—" she bumped her fingers over his abdomen "—turns me on?"

"Hmm, that's going to make those sit-ups and work-outs much easier, except for the hard-on I might get just thinking about how my body affects you," he said. Cupping the back of her head, he kissed her, deepening the contact. Emma yielded fully to his questing tongue. Finally, Derrick let go of her wrist and slid his arm under her, holding her with infinite care. After a long and satisfying kiss, he reluctantly drew away, gazing down at her as he caressed her bottom lip with his thumb. He stroked her face, tracing her cheekbones, the arch of her brows, then gave her another quick kiss.

Cradling her head against him, he ran his hand up her naked back, then tucked his head and kissed her brow. "You know I'm on your side, Emma. I want to recover Matty as much as you do."

"I know that." She sighed and her hand slipped into his hair. She toyed with a lock for a few minutes. "I need to trust my instincts." Emma lay still in his arms for a split second, then she went up on one elbow and looked down at him, her hair brushing his jaw as she rose. She stared at him, the light from outside washing across her face and revealing the determination in her expression. A glimmer of urgency appeared in her eyes. "I usually don't question them and they've never steered me wrong. There are just some things women are better at than men. Dealing with a grieving mother falls into that category. Reyes and Velasco are not only men, but they can't see how to question her and get answers."

He stared up at her a moment, then shifted his focus. Avoiding her gaze, he painstakingly hooked his thumb under a thick swath of hair and drew it back, tucking it carefully behind her ear. "How about my manliness?" he asked quietly.

She took a quick breath, closing her eyes. "Potent, but you're an American male and an investigator. I've got the feeling you'd know how to get blood from a stone." She lightly ran her fingertips along his jaw. Her gaze direct, she stroked along the hair there, and Derrick waited, sensing her urgency. "Trust me, Derrick. If we wait too long, it might be too late."

Derrick grasped her face and stared into her eyes. "You're absolutely sure about this?"

She stared right back at him, her eyes hardening. "Completely." She gazed at him and swallowed hard, looking away, her hand caressing his shoulder, running up and down over the swell of his biceps.

He rose up on his elbow and stared at her, knowing that he was falling for her and not being able to help himself, wondering if, once again, his judgment was skewed. He couldn't afford to make any mistakes here. Was he giving in to her because he was reacting to his own emotions or was her argument sound?

He decided that it was both. He also had good instincts. For some reason, Derrick felt as if he'd just been released out of a tight, dark prison, and he closed his eyes and hugged her hard, feeling as if he could take his first deep breath in his life. He pressed a kiss against her brow, then hugged her again. He trusted her, really trusted her. His chest expanding, he said, "Get dressed. I know where the keys are to the second sedan."

Her eyes lit up and softened. "But we don't know where she lives."

"Leave that to me."

Derrick reached for his pants and his cell. He texted Austin. Then he got dressed.

Naval Medical Center
San Diego, California

Austin was heading over to the hospital to supervise the additional guards on Lily St. John. It was important for him to make sure Emma's sister was safe. He knew he was being paranoid, but he couldn't seem to help it. He needed to be proactive when dealing with a cartel, especially one as brutal as *Los Equis*. When he got Derrick's text, he was pulling up to a parking spot. He opened his tablet and accessed the information he'd already compiled on the Montoyas. It wasn't much; neither the son nor the family had much of an electronic footprint. Luis certainly didn't show up in any database for any kind of crime, including international. He texted all that information back to Derrick as he exited his vehicle.

He entered the hospital and went up to the ICU. When he got there, he saw that four MPs were there. One at the end of the hall, one inside her room, and two outside.

He entered the room and walked to the bed. She seemed like she was resting peacefully. She was a pretty little thing with soft blond hair, delicate features, her small figure looking so vulnerable in the bed. It made him angry to think that Luis Montoya had planned on killing her instead of shoving her down the stairs. The bruises on her face were fading. Hopefully, they would be gone by the time she woke up.

His cell buzzed and a passing nurse frowned at him

and shook her head. As soon as she was safely past, he answered. "Beck."

"Austin, I want you back here as soon as possible. Is everything secure there?" Kai's weary voice came through loud and clear.

Austin rubbed his eyes. He'd caught a twenty-minute cat nap about an hour ago. All of them were running on fumes. "Yes, four guards, and Lily is resting well. I can head back now."

"All right."

He left the room and walked down the hall. Pushing the button for the elevator, he spied an orderly coming down the hall with a gurney. The guy had the kind of stare that moved people out of the way without words, a sense of presence that made the hair on the back of Austin's neck rise and prickle. The guy passed him without a glance and turned down the hall that led to ICU and Lily St. John's room.

He had to adjust the gurney to avoid a wheelchair in the hall, and Austin saw ink on his arm. His heart started to pound when he realized it was a sewn mouth, just like the tattoo on Luis's arm. Austin reached for his gun and shouted, "You there with the gurney! Stop! NCIS!"

The guy exploded into movement and from beneath the gurney sheets pulled out an automatic weapon. Austin dropped as the man opened fire, the sound of the bullets hitting the elevator doors with metallic thuds.

He turned and took out the hall guard, rushing around the corner of the hallway. Austin scrambled to his feet and rushed down the hall as more automatic fire ripped through the quiet hospital. As he rounded the corner, he saw the gunman and the downed guards. The weapon was pointed directly at Lily St. John, lying prone and totally helpless in her hospital bed.

Austin opened fire and his bullets hit the man in the shoulder and the leg. The gun jerked and the bullets went wild. The guy turned to fire at Austin again, but Austin threw himself out of the line of fire. Without hesitation, he was up again, but the man was gone. With his heart in his throat he raced toward Lily's room, breathing a sigh of relief when one of the guards was already up, bleeding from his shoulder.

"She's alive. Go."

Austin gave chase, catching sight of the gunman as he fled through the exit door and into the stairwell. As he hit the door, MPs were racing up the stairs. He heard footsteps above him, then the guy leaned over the railing and a burst of gunfire rained into the stairwell. Everyone took cover.

Austin took the stairs two at a time, his heart pounding. He was determined this man wouldn't get away. When he reached the top, his breathing ragged, he took a few breaths and carefully peered out the door. When he saw nothing, he cautiously stepped onto the roof, several MPs following him. He indicated he was going right, his gun held in front of him in a two-handed grip. He searched the roof until he had to quickly take cover when automatic gunfire erupted just ahead of him. The guy ran and Austin chased him.

But the gunman was trapped between a long fall and four determined men with guns.

"Drop the weapon, get flat on your stomach and interlock your hands."

"We'll get to her. There's nothing you can do to stop us."

Austin shouted. "Drop the weapon!"

But the guy brought it up and Austin pulled the trigger three times.

The enemy dropped, the gun falling out of his lax fingers.

Austin approached him and kicked the weapon away. He looked down at him and said, "That's where you're wrong. You have no idea what we're capable of, mister."

His lips thinned and he put in a call to Kai.

Chapter 13

Caliche, Mexico

It was simple for them to grab the car keys, fire up the sedan and leave the compound with no problem. Emma had never experienced anything like what she had with Derrick. She was used to being independent, and no man had supported her like he had so far. Trusting her. She'd proven herself over and over again with clients, her other stints in Mexico, but nothing had ever felt like this. It was an understatement to say Derrick was special. Unique.

Yet there was still something wild about him. Not in the reckless sense of the word, but something nagging at her, making the fear inside her come into play. He was such a loner, had been all his life. There was more of his story he hadn't shared, a sadness about him when he spoke about Matty, a sense of intent purpose to get the boy back for her and Lily. She was keen on discovering why, but now was not the time to ask him personal questions. They had to be vigilant.

The warmth and lushness of this area of Mexico

showed her there were still places on earth that were definitely off the beaten track. Yet this is where people lived, drug lords flourished and murder happened often. There was no concrete for miles. She breathed a sigh as the warm breeze slipped through the sedan's window, tugging at her hair. Emma actually felt relieved that Reyes and Velasco were not present. She felt their judgment constantly. Whether that had to do with her being a woman, she wasn't sure. But she couldn't quite shake the fact that she and Derrick were being corralled. Boxed in and fed the information someone wanted them to swallow and say it was delicious.

She wondered if Derrick had the same feeling. He had to downshift to navigate an especially steep decline. Off in the distance Lake Caliche glittered in the moonlight. The rest of the forest was like a blanket of rolling green, the air thin and the trees so dense she could barely see a few feet beyond the road.

"What do you think about our two official escorts?" Emma said.

He glanced at her. "In terms of?"

"I get the feeling we're being led around by our noses. One or both could be in the cartel's pocket for all we know. They could be working for the Ortegas." They passed a small village, the lights the only indication there was life out here.

"The ambush? The fact they didn't want you talking to Luis's mother?"

"Yeah, it was a good argument, but my nephew's abduction should matter. He's alive and Luis is dead. I'm sympathetic to his mother's grief. I truly am, but Matty's welfare should count for a disruption in ritual. I've got a bad feeling about this, Derrick."

His expression was set, his eyes calm, his hands lightly gripping the wheel, his attention now tightly focused on her. "It's been a nagging thought for me, as well. But if it's one or both on the take, we're going to have to discover which one."

Something shifted inside her as she continued to watch him. It was that focus, that intensity, that she couldn't help but respond to. There was no doubt she was physically attracted to Derrick. The man was gorgeous, but as she shivered, she knew the depth of the connection she was forming with him was head and shoulders above anything in her life, except maybe her sister. "I know this environment," Emma said. "Velasco is young, more susceptible to money or even addictions the cartel can play on. Hell, they could even be threatening his family." She hoped not for his sake, but expected it was mostly greed. "As for Reyes, he's been a good guy from the first day I met him. But still, *Los Equis* is ruthless, and Gilberto has run the organization like a well-oiled machine. He wouldn't leave anything to chance when it comes to Matty. If he's Arturo's son, that means he's Gilberto's grandson." She paused and she could feel Derrick's interest in the short distance that separated them. He was alert, always, to every nuance, every word, every sound, breath, scent and texture of the world around him. No wonder he scared the living hell out of her. It was intimidating to be on the receiving end of such focused attention.

But she also identified with it. She was much the same, only she'd felt hers was a more intuitive connection. Maybe that was why everything with Derrick seemed so gut-deep intensive, because so much of her was tied up in him.

"Maybe Lily wanted nothing to do with them, which is understandable," he said as they bumped over some ruts in the road, the suspension bouncing back as the tires hit smooth road again. "Maybe she cut off all ties and that angered both of them?" He shook his head and glanced at her, his eyes hard. "They feel they had a right to see Matty. Being the ruthless thugs they are, they decided that kidnapping him was their only course of action. Murdering your sister would take her out of the equation. What I don't understand is why they didn't come after you, as well."

"Maybe that was something they planned on doing later on in the game. Especially if I caused a stink. Contacting the State Department about Matty, since I am his aunt, was a good move. There's a legal precedence here called The Hague Convention that states no child under sixteen may be removed from their habitual residence or wrongfully removed or retained. Mexico is part of that treaty and my grandmother already got that legal ball rolling."

Derrick nodded. "Too bad it turned out to be a dead end—even my buddy said so. Making the choice to go after him, the director and SECNAV made the stand that no US Military child would be subjected to abduction. It was a coordinated effort."

"One I'm grateful for, but you're probably right. As it stands right now, Lily is incapacitated. I don't believe she has made any stipulation for Matty in that case. Even my grandmother, who is working with the State Department, could kick up a lot of dust. Maybe Gilberto just expects to disappear with Matty. Change his name, hide him God knows where and time will make the difference."

Derrick frowned, his voice clipped. "He thinks he's

above the law and he has the right because Matty is of his blood. It doesn't make it right."

She looked over to find Derrick giving her quick glances. "But does Arturo have rights where Matty is concerned?"

Derrick reached over and squeezed her hand as if to soften his words. "Yes, he does, but if he wanted to exercise those rights, he's gone about it the wrong way."

She looked over at him, but his attention was back on the road. She worked at shoving aside the panic fluttering in her stomach. It had all been compartmentalized until now, when they might be close to finding out where Matty was. Jumbled-up nervousness and how much she wanted, needed, Matty back spiked over and over. "I'm horrified that Matty is connected to these people by blood and family, Derrick." She looked out the window at the dark night. "I know the right course of action. Matty needs to be protected from them, for both his physical and psychological safety. Gilberto has to know that no judge in the US will ever give him visitation rights. He really didn't have a legal recourse."

"No, he didn't."

"It makes him extremely dangerous. He's already killed two people and tried to murder my sister. It boggles my mind that my sister, my sweet, head-in-the-clouds sister, stood up to a drug lord's son." Her voice was full of the pride she felt.

"Why is that surprising? You said she changed her life."

"Yes, she did, but now that I think about it, I realize that Matty was the fulcrum that brought her around. It was that tiny, happy, precious boy that had pushed her forward. She wanted to be the kind of mother Matty would be proud of—and that had nothing to do with career or a profession, although I believe the navy played a role in her transformation. It had to do with Lily's self-esteem and inner strength. The navy gave her self-respect, but Matty gave her what she'd always been searching for—unconditional love. Motherhood was what really changed her."

"Didn't she have unconditional love with you?"

Emma looked at him, his profile so handsome even in the dim light of the car. "No. I was judgmental and always pushed her to be more responsible. I was more worried about protecting her than seeing her grow, even with our argument about her going to Japan." Remorse thick in her voice, she murmured. "I was stubborn and ugly. I said some things I wish I could take back. She was so… strong, so sure of what she wanted. I couldn't see that because I was too busy remembering Lily as she was in the past and not recognizing how much she'd changed. If I hadn't been so…difficult, so judgmental, maybe she would have come to the agent with this problem instead of trying to handle it on her own. She was so sweet, she probably truly expected Arturo to just back off and bend to her wishes." Her voice filled with affection. "She was naive when it came to harsher parts of life. Something I always tried to shield her from. It breaks my heart, Derrick. I truly regret treating her like a child and dismissing her ideas and plans."

He clasped her hand and squeezed. "You understand now. It was out of love that you acted the way that you did. Give yourself some credit and cut yourself some slack. You're not an ogre."

"I feel like one and I so hope I don't lose my sister. I

hope I get the chance to tell her how much she means to me and how sorry I am."

"You will."

"Look at you, Mister Glass Half Full."

He chuckled.

"We're almost there. I'm going to give you lead on this one. I think you're right. Woman to woman. Mother to aunt is the way to handle Mrs. Montoya. I'll hang back."

"Thank you, Derrick, for trusting me on this."

They came around a bend and she said, "Turn here."

He made the left, which put them in a very small village. One house was lit up. Candles and people everywhere—it had to be the Montoya residence.

Derrick pulled the car over far enough from the house, he didn't garner any interest. He shut off the engine.

"The Mexican people share a depth of obligation toward family members that extends beyond death to burial. Funeral homes are pretty much nonexistent, so the body is returned to the family." She reached for the door handle just as Derrick's cell chimed. He looked at the display and his mouth tightened.

"What is it?"

"There's been an attempt on your sister's life. It was something that a cartel member got onto a naval facility. They believe he entered illegally."

Her heart sank at the same time her stomach tightened. "Is she all right?"

"Yes, she's fine. They've doubled the guards and everyone is being searched before they enter the hospital."

She sagged against the seat, her heart pounding from the adrenaline. "I'm so relieved." He leaned over and kissed her on the temple, then gently hugged her, before settling back behind the wheel. She pushed the door open. "We have to resolve this now, but Matty and Lily are always going to be in danger, even if we do rescue him." She got nauseated thinking about the implications and the disruption to both their lives. How were they going to handle this threat hanging over them? She would have to think about that once they got Matty back. Right now she had to talk to the grieving mother of the man who had taken her nephew and almost killed her sister. The same man—teenager, really—who, God help her, had tried to kill them.

Derrick started texting as she closed the door behind her, trying to breathe around her fear for her sister and their precarious future. Focus. This moment, this desperate, heart-rending moment, was about Matty.

She walked up the street. Glancing back, she saw Derrick get out of the car and follow her at a safe distance. She took a deep breath. People were filing through the home; condolences to the family were part of every funeral.

Emma got in the line, many of the women openly weeping, others stony-faced; there were even children present. Once Emma was in the house, she found Luis's mother accepting condolences from people, seated in a chair near the altar. Luis's body was in the center on the floor, covered with a white sheet and surrounded by four lighted candles.

The Montoyas' loved ones and friends were sharing in a prayer vigil, or *velario*.

Emma moved forward as an elderly woman who cried and squeezed Mrs. Montoya's hands moved off, wiping her eyes. Gabriela Montoya's eyes were red-rimmed and her cheeks rosy from crying. When Emma reached her, she looked up and her features froze. "You should not be here," she whispered.

"I know this is a terrible breach of conduct, but it is imperative that I speak with you privately. Please, Mrs. Montoya. We both have lost so much," Emma said in Spanish.

Gabriela heaved a huge sigh and Emma waited, her gut in knots, anticipating her response. If she turned her away, it would be the last best chance to find Matty.

The woman closed her eyes, then she rose. "Come with me." Emma followed her into a small room and she closed the door.

"What is it you wish to speak with me about?"

"You know why I'm here. You know what your son has done."

She brought a tissue up to her nose and blew, wiping vigorously. "Yes, I know all of it. He had no choice. I have no choice."

"Yes, you do have a choice. You can choose to do the right thing." She reached into her jacket and pulled out a photo of Lily and Matty. "This is my sister, Lily. She's in a coma in the hospital. That's my nephew, Matthew, but we call him Matty. He was kidnapped and I think you know where he is."

A sob caught in her throat as shame and remorse filled her eyes. She clutched the tissue to her mouth, gasping around the sorrow, pain and tears. "Mateo."

Emma's eyes burned, her throat thick as tears welled and slid down her cheeks. "Yes, Matthew. Will you tell me where he is? Please… Gabriela, from a terrified and loving aunt, to a grieving and loving mother. I'm begging you."

"He is not far from here," she whispered and Emma let out a soft, relieved sound.

"Where?"

"A hacienda in the forest, one that used to belong to the Sanchez family. They were wealthy and prosperous before the cartels took over. Murdered and buried now. That place is the home of a monster. But Gilberto took it over. I work for him and have for many years. He is a bad, bad man, but he is death to those who refuse to do as he says. We couldn't go against him, but he's killed my boy anyway. Loose ends, I overheard him say. He ordered that…monster with no heart… Flores to kill him and leave his body for the police to find. He wants you and your friend dead."

"We aren't going to give up. Will you help us?"

"He plans to replace his son Arturo with your nephew. He will make it look like a rival cartel has killed Arturo. But he's tired of Arturo's party boy ways."

"He's going to kill Matty's father?"

She looked at Emma with a startled expression. "Arturo? No, he isn't the boy's father. It's Gilberto. He is the one."

Shock coursed through Emma and she had to take a moment to absorb the information. All this time she thought it was his son who had gotten Lily pregnant, but it hadn't been. Gilberto wanted a new family legacy. He was going to make Matty in his image, a monster, a dealer in death and addiction. A greedy, ruthless drug lord. *Oh, no!*

Emma reached out and clasped the woman's shoulders. "Where is he? Where? Please tell me."

Gabriela sobbed for a few minutes, the sympathy in her eyes thick with her grief. Then she took a breath, her eyes hardening. "I will give you directions, but you will have to be very careful. If he catches you, he will kill you. I will draw a map of the house and where the nursery is. I have already packed a bag for him in case of emergency. It's in the closet. Don't forget his medicine in the fridge. He has an ear infection, but he is doing very well."

Emma hugged her hard and the woman hugged her back. "I'm sorry for what my son has done. Maybe my actions can redeem him in God's eyes. I can only pray." She wrote out the directions, then drew a quick map. "There are guards, but you can avoid them. Go through this path."

Emma reached for the door, but Gabriela stopped her with a hand to her arm. "Good luck and may God go with you."

Emma covered her hand, then reached into her pocket and pressed some bills into Gabriela's palm. "Take this for your son as a gift from one he's wronged. I hope you find peace."

She nodded, closing her fist over the money as Emma slipped out the door and made her way past the altar. Derrick was standing just outside the house.

"I know where he is," she said, brushing at her tears.

"That's great news."

"There's more, Derrick. So much more," she said grimly.

Derrick absorbed all the information that Emma told him as they raced through the night toward the Ortegas' place, located at the edge of the forest, according to the map. It was several miles past the Montoyas' village.

They would have to be quick and silent to get in and

then get the infant out. If he cried, made any noise whatsoever, they were going to be toast.

When he stopped the sedan, they were far enough away from the hacienda to stay out of sight, but close enough to go through the woods and take the path Gabriela had outlined for them. They exited the vehicle. "Let's take another look at the map."

"Derrick, we need to hurry." She took a step, and he hauled her around and into his arms.

He wrapped her tightly against him, stilling her for the moment. "We have to be strategic about this. Let me get our ducks in a row."

She tore her gaze away from the path and the lighted house beyond and looked at him. "He's so close, Derrick."

He tightened his hold on her again when she renewed her struggle. "I know. Give me a few more minutes. Trust me, Emma."

She relaxed then gave him a nod. "All right."

He took the paper from her and studied Gabriela's drawing, memorizing it, then he handed it back to her. "This is the way we're handling this. I will go first, neutralize any threat."

"What about getting into the house?"

"We'll go in through the kitchen. Everyone should be asleep except the guards. Gilberto and Arturo's rooms aren't near the nursery, but the nanny's room is, so we'll have to be very careful not to wake her. We'll go up the back staircase—it'll bring us close to the baby. We'll get him and then we'll hightail it out of there."

He pulled out his cell and texted.

We need extraction thirty minutes from now. We should have the boy. Will advise if not.

Austin texted back:

Copy that. Helo inbound. Stay safe.

The chopper was on standby and would meet them at a small airfield only ten minutes from here.

Derrick reached back and pulled out a wicked-looking knife. He was in his element, here in the shadows. No one would stand in his way.

With Emma behind him, they started through the trees. After going a few steps, Derrick spied a man taking a leak near one of the trees. He signaled Emma to stop and Derrick melted into the shadows, his steps so quiet it was as if he'd transformed into a ghost.

He came up behind the man, and he died without a sound.

He motioned Emma forward. They walked the rest of the way to the kitchen door without incident, avoiding two patrols. "Keep watch," he whispered as Emma turned her back to his and he picked the lock.

He opened the door and stepped inside. Emma went directly to the fridge, opened the door wide enough to grab Matty's medicine. She tucked it into her jeans pocket. Then in the dim light Derrick, using the memorized map in his head, found the stairs.

Taking it slow, they climbed to the top. Derrick could hear light snoring coming from the room across from what Gabriela had marked as the nursery. On quiet feet they eased the baby's door open and quickly ducked inside. Trembling, Emma went directly over to the crib, and she clutched the bars, her face alight with joy, and Derrick held back his own fierce triumph. They weren't out of the woods yet.

"Matty, oh my little love." She reached down and came up with a bundle of blankets and sleepy infant. He looked up at her, his eyes blinking owlishly in the dim light, then he smiled softly and drifted off to sleep.

"Get the bag in the closet while I get him strapped in," she whispered low and urgently. As she navigated the confusion of the carrier, snuggling Matty up close to her chest, he didn't stir. Derrick pulled open the closet door and grabbed the fully stocked bag inside, slinging it over his shoulder.

At the door, he listened intently, then opened it a crack. Nothing moved; the snoring was still buzzing in the quiet of the house. They slipped out, closing the door behind them, then made their way down the stairs.

They crept silently across the kitchen and out the door, crouching until Derrick was certain the area was clear.

"Move and don't stop for anything," he said in a gruff whisper. "If I'm not there in five minutes, head to the airfield."

"Derrick—"

"Don't argue with me, Emma."

She ran her hand over Matty's head, then she leaned over and kissed Derrick, her mouth soft and warm. He closed his eyes, absorbing the aching press of her lips. "Thank you," she whispered fiercely.

He cupped her face for a moment, then his hand dropped to her upper back. He gave her a little nudge. "Go." Her gaze lingered on his for a few more seconds, telling him how much he meant to her in that short moment. His throat got tight.

She rose and cautiously covered the open ground. He watched her disappear into the trees and he straightened, pulling out the knife. He started to follow, covering her back. There was no way he was going to let her down now. No matter the cost.

Guard Duty

She rose the mountains revolted Matthew around the quiet to begin to ease. "Not he's on it," came Hash putting out the road, if he knew it down, they so staff knew... configure up acquire looking up to its recumbent now recovering road.

Chapter 14

Emma clutched Matty as she ran. He opened his eyes a couple of times, but the rocking of her body seemed to soothe him. She looked over her shoulder several times, but couldn't see Derrick.

Her emotions were running wild at this point. She was elated to have her nephew back, but terrified about getting them all safely out of Mexico. When she reached the car, she pulled out the keys and stood there, searching the trees for Derrick. She was praying with all her might that he would show up and they could go to the airfield together, her insides twisting with fear. There wasn't a moment to spare and anything could go wrong.

A few minutes passed and sweat trickled down her temple, her muscles held in such tense awareness, her body starting to tremble. It was in such contrast to the sweet-cheeked, peacefully sleeping baby in her arms. She held on to the belief that Derrick would show up any minute. How could she leave him behind?

Her breathing harsh, she paced back and forth, looking down at her nephew. Looking at her watch, a sob caught in her throat.

It had been six minutes. She couldn't wait. Torn in two, her heart feeling like it was being ripped from her chest, she started to unstrap the carrier, fear and dread coursing through her.

"Emma," Derrick whispered as he broke from the trees, "get in the car."

Almost collapsing from the relief, she threw him the keys, which he caught on the run. Jumping inside, she strapped both her and the baby in. Drenched in sweat, Derrick started the car and was soon going back the way they had come.

They flew over the road and turned down a dirt track to the hidden airstrip. Derrick's contacts and network had revealed this remote runway was often used by drug runners. It was out of the way, but close enough to Caliche to make it the prime spot for them to catch the Blackhawk.

When they drove up, Emma was overjoyed to see that the chopper was already on the ground. Without waiting, she threw her door open and started to run for the vehicle.

A car engine rumbled behind them. She whirled and took cover behind the hood of her car. Derrick was already out and pulling his weapon. He trained his gun on the driver as he stepped out.

"Hey, what is going on with you two?" Velasco said, his voice confused.

He stepped forward, but stopped dead when Derrick pointed his gun at him and said, "How did you find us?"

"We were notified by our government that you had secured the boy and were headed to this airstrip. Reyes called me. He came on ahead." Velasco's gaze went to a point behind them. "Hey, there he—"

A gunshot cracked across the forest, sending birds fluttering into the sky with frightened shrieks. The faint light of dawn was just brightening the horizon. Velasco clutched his chest, a shocked look on his face, betrayal in his eyes as he crumpled to the dirt and lay still.

They whirled and Emma's heart climbed into her throat when Inspector Reyes, Arturo Ortega and another man stepped from the cover of the chopper. Arturo looked like the playboy he was, not someone who'd be involved in kidnapping, the ugly world of drug dealing or murder. On the other hand, the man with the coldest, deadest eyes she'd ever seen looked like he fit right in. Her attention shifted to the man who had betrayed them, his oath and his country. Reyes said, "You two are very resourceful. I knew that old woman would give everything up. I should have just taken you out when you were sleeping."

"Why didn't you?" Derrick said, his voice glacial.

Reyes shrugged and smiled as if they were having a pleasant conversation. "I have a reputation to uphold. I didn't want you dead in my custody, so many messy explanations." He chuckled and swept the gun toward Velasco's prone body. "Now, I'll just blame everything on Velasco. It'll look like he was the traitor."

"Why?" Emma said, desperate to save her nephew, but seeing no way around this cold, calculating man.

"Well, the money. Gilberto pays so damn well." Arturo laughed, while the silent man's eyes glittered. "I've been working for him for quite some time." He shifted and focused on Derrick, his brow furrowing. "Remember I told you I'd gotten where I am by surviving. You've got to play the game. That's how you continue to breathe."

She could see both pilots slumped over in their seats.

Emma started to back up, but before she could take another step, Reyes said, "Uh-uh, Emma. I'll take your nephew. Hand him over to my colleague and your deaths will be quick and painless. The boy will not be harmed. If you don't…" He shrugged again. "Well, a stray bullet might cut short the boy's promising future."

She squeezed her eyes briefly closed as the man approached her. His blank eyes meeting hers, he smiled and said, "Give me the boy."

She looked at Derrick with an anguished expression. He sighed heavily and she could see he was calculating his odds. With a resigned but furious nod, he told Emma they had no choice.

Awash with a whole storm of emotion, she uttered a broken cry and convulsively tightened her hold on Matty. She trembled from head to toe, leaving her emotionally suspended: *Oh, no. Oh, God, no.* Something broke loose in her. The man grasped the baby and it was all Emma could do not to fight him. He ripped the boy out of the carrier and from her arms. Then the man shoved her back against the car. Her nephew woke up with a start. He took one look at the man's face, burst into tears as he twisted his body and reached for her. Derrick caught her against him, watching the man with eyes that promised retribution. He laughed and walked around them, casually stepping over Velasco's body. The sound of an engine broke the dawn's stillness as a Lincoln pulled up and the man with the empty eyes set Matty into the backseat.

Arturo passed her and Derrick caught his arm. Arturo looked at him as if he wasn't clean enough to touch his shirtsleeve. "Your father's going to kill you, Arturo," Derrick said. Reyes backhanded Derrick with the gun and he was knocked back into the car.

"That's a lie," Reyes said, giving Arturo a smile. "He's just trying to manipulate you."

Emma clutched at Derrick as he glared at Reyes. "No," she said brokenly. Feeling as if she was trapped in a nightmare, Emma stared in horror at the back of the man who had Matty, whose wails were deep and urgent, tearing at her heart. Transfixed in shock, her numb reaction turning to a chilling sense of helplessness as she watched Velasco smile again, form his finger into a gun and point it at her. "Pow," he said. His laughter cut off as he got into the backseat with Matty. Arturo, his expression haughty and smug, got into the front passenger seat.

"Now that wasn't so hard, was it?" Reyes purred. Derrick punched him and Reyes reeled backward. "I'll give you that one," Reyes said. Scowling, he wiped blood off the corner of his mouth, all humor gone from his face. "Hand over your weapons, two fingers only, and let's take a walk into the trees. I don't have time to deal with dragging bodies into the woods."

"I'm going to kill you with my bare hands," Derrick said, the promise of mayhem in his eyes so potent, Emma shivered.

His scowl darkened, winging his brows low over his dark eyes. He extended his hand toward Emma. "Your weapon."

Emma pulled out her gun and handed it to Reyes, who tossed it, and when Derrick followed suit, he repeated the action. Derrick put his arm around her waist and leaned in as if he was comforting her. "When I tell you to run, run," he whispered in her ear.

She nodded imperceptibly.

Without comment, Derrick took her hand and did as

they were told, the other one palming the knife. Emma understood.

As soon as they cleared the trees, Derrick stumbled and Reyes stepped forward to shove him hard, but instead, Derrick twisted and sunk the knife into Reyes's shoulder, then punched him in the face. He stumbled away. "Run, Emma!"

He didn't have to tell her twice. She bolted. Moving targets were difficult to hit, especially after the shooter had been stabbed and punched.

Several shots went off, but Emma kept her legs pumping. The sound of anger broke the silence a few moments later. "I'm coming for you!" the man shouted. "This time there won't be any hope of a quick death."

Neither of them slowed. They rushed through the underbrush, jumping over logs and muscling through bushes, heading deeper into the forest.

There were only two thoughts streaking through her head: kill him and go for Matty. But to do that, she had to stay alive.

Her lungs burned, the heat and humidity cutting into her strength as she slipped over more logs and down a ravine. They had to do a kind of careful jog to control their forward momentum down the steep incline. Trees towered above them. Derrick grabbed her shoulder and together they dove into the brush for cover, hitting the ground hard.

Instantly he rolled to his feet at the same time she did. They concealed themselves behind a thick tree trunk.

Breathing hard, she managed, "Plan?"

"I'm going to circle around, take him from behind. He's a cocky son of a bitch, but I don't want to give him an opportunity to call for backup. He's not leaving here alive."

"Agreed," she said, sweating freely. "I guess that leaves me as bait again?"

"You play that role so well."

She shoved him and he grinned. "Be careful," she whispered.

His eyes narrowed and a look came over his face that chilled her to the bone. "Don't worry about me, babe."

He flicked the knife around, offering her the handle. She stared at it wordlessly, then looked up at him. "Won't you need it?"

Another chill went down her spine. "No. I won't."

As soon as Derrick melted out of sight—*how did he do that?*—she started to thrash around in the bushes, making enough noise, Reyes couldn't possibly miss it. She heard him approach and as he came into view, she cried out and started to crawl. Focusing on her, his eyes scanned the forest. "He left you here to die?" he said skeptically, looking around.

"My ankle," she whined.

He took another step and raised the pistol. There would be no quarter from Reyes. But Derrick was there, as he pushed Reyes's arm into the air and the gun discharged harmlessly. Derrick hit Reyes in the throat. Reyes choked and stumbled backward, and Derrick advanced with a menacing look on his face. Emma went for the gun, snatching it up. She aimed, but there was no clear target to hit; Derrick was too close. Reyes swung wildly, but Derrick was calm, almost serene as he ducked the punch. Reyes was off balance. Derrick stepped in, got him into a chokehold and didn't let go.

Reyes struggled, but it was too late, the life going

out of his eyes. As he slumped, Derrick let him go, his body dropping to the forest floor. Then he was moving, grabbing her hand, and they were running back the way they had come.

Back at the car, they retrieved their weapons. A soft groan made Emma's head whip around. She ran to Velasco. "Derrick, he's still alive."

Derrick opened the back door to the sedan and went over to Velasco and slipped his hands under the man's body, maneuvering him onto his shoulders, then lifting him with a strong push of his thighs.

He placed him carefully in the backseat. Emma got in behind him, belted him in and ripped off a piece of his shirt, pressing it to the wound. Velasco roused. "Ah, Emma, you are an angel," he murmured.

"You're going to be all right," she whispered, having no idea if that was true or not. Derrick texted lightning fast on his phone.

He turned to her and said, "Hang on!"

Dirt and gravel spit out from under the wheels of the car as they raced along the road, Emma doing her best to brace herself against the bumpy ride.

In minutes they were back at the Ortegas' hacienda, ready for a fight. But to her horror, the ground was littered with bodies. She grabbed Velasco's hand and placed it against his wound. "Keep up the pressure," she said and he nodded.

They exited the car and walked cautiously toward the house. The door was wide open and more bodies lay prone and bleeding in the foyer from numerous gunshot wounds. Derrick said, "Clear," when after searching the living room, he found no one alive. Upstairs, they found the nanny and several more dead guards. When they went down the hall to Gilberto's room and pushed open the door, the drug lord was absent. But there was a body facedown on the bed soaked in blood.

Derrick went to turn him over and they stepped back and gazed down at Arturo Ortega, his throat cut.

"That's another cartel's calling card," Velasco said, leaning heavily against the door frame, his hand over the gunshot wound in his shoulder. "They formed from the remnants of the *Medianoche* Cartel, swearing retribution."

"Gilberto just wants us to think he was attacked by the rival cartel," Derrick said, backing away. They headed back downstairs and into the kitchen. As Emma went around the counter, she called out, "Derrick!" Gabriela Montoya lay on her back, gasping for each breath.

Emma knelt down and supported her. "Gilberto's gone, taken your boy." Her eyes were anguished. "I tried to stop him, but he knew that I told you everything. Hurry. He's gone to the Caliche Airport. I think he's taking your nephew to Colombia. You must hurry."

She choked several times, clutching at Emma. She stiffened, then went completely lax as she died. With a heavy heart for the woman's bravery, Emma released her and rose.

Velasco had his phone in his hand as he leaned his hip against the countertop for support. "Go. I will take care of this. Good luck!" he called as they raced out of the house and got back into the sedan.

With an angry set to his jaw, Derrick said, "It's about fifteen minutes from here, Emma, a small, private airport—"

"If he gets on that plane with Matty—"

He glanced at her, the sick, naked expression in his

eyes making her throat contract. "I know. Get on the phone and call the police," he said as he gunned the car, and the speedometer rose past sixty.

She called the chief inspector of the Caliche police and he promised he would contact the forces near the small airport. She relayed the information to Derrick, his jaw clenched, his expression grim and determined.

They approached the small airport's gate at top speed, not even slowing as the sedan busted through the metal barrier and guards started running and shouting. In the distance, Emma saw a small private jet, the stairs down, and Gilberto Ortega holding her nephew stepping up into the plane.

Then that dark, silent man turned and surveyed the speeding car. He rushed into the plane and pulled in the stairs as the engine fired up for takeoff, the sound loud in the car's interior. As soon as the vehicle came to a screeching halt, Emma was out the door and rushing toward the jet, Derrick on her heels. Dread like lead in her stomach, she raced down the runway, her throat burning, tears running down her face, the dread turning to panic. Gravel from the tarmac flew from her running feet, and she stumbled, twisting her ankle, but that pain was insignificant compared to the fear racing through her system.

Even as she gained, the small plane accelerated and her heart dropped as it lifted off into the air. She was suspended by horror, rooted to the runway, the only sound penetrating her senses the powerful sound of the plane's engines taking her beloved nephew into a terrible and blood-soaked future. Suddenly cold, she clenched her fists at her sides, her gaze riveted on the silver and white plane rising even higher into the sky.

A soft breeze stirred, ruffling her hair against her

cheek, like the flutter of butterfly wings, the scent of new mown grass buried in the wind. The sweet fragrance made her insides clench even more.

Derrick stood next to her, his chest heaving as he, too, watched her sister's son get farther and farther away. She dragged her hair back, frustration and a sense of helplessness raging through her. Letting her hands fall, her mind racing, her stomach knotting, she whirled, but there was nowhere to go, nothing she could do.

She looked at Derrick, uncertainty racing through her, and she folded her arms tightly in front of her; she needed to hold everything in right now, bleakness chilling her.

Gripping her forearms, Emma tried to will away the thickness that was growing in her chest, a thickness that was rooted in monumental pain.

The banked rage in Derrick's eyes exploded, and he twisted and swore viciously. He looked at her, his eyes blazing, the veins in his neck distended with fury. "Goddammit!"

His tone filled with disgust, the air sizzling with tension as he walked away. Stopping a few feet from her, he jammed his hands on his hips and tipped his head back, trying to level out his rapid breathing. Finally, he exhaled sharply and turned to face her, his voice subdued. "I'm sorry, Emma. I'm so sorry." He bent his head and rubbed his eyes, his expression set. "We'll track him again. We'll find him!"

Her breath suddenly wouldn't come. She dropped her arms as if all feeling had left her body. Trying to fight the increasing tightness in her throat, she nodded.

Emma pressed her thumb and middle finger against her eyes to try to stall the ache that kept spreading. She knew it was going to be extremely difficult to track him now. Ortega had unlimited resources. Time was on his side, and before too long, Matty wouldn't even remember them.

That thought sliced through her like the sharpest knife. Her strength was fragmenting on her, but she hung on to it, using it to block out the pain. Her sweet baby boy wasn't going to be raised by a notorious drug lord.

She thrust her hands into her hair, trying to process the awful realization. Raking her hair back from her face again, she tried to make her mind focus, shock draining the warmth from her.

Sirens blared and people were running toward them, but Emma couldn't move.

"I'm sorry, babe." She heard the agony, felt his pain, and she clutched her stomach. Her throat so cramped her jaws ached, she sank down to the concrete; a broken sob escaped her, tears blinding her.

His face ashen, Derrick knelt beside her, his eyes shadowed by some emotion she couldn't understand. "It's going to be all right, Emma."

"Matty," she whispered brokenly.

He looked away, the muscles in his throat convulsing, and desolation stripped her bare.

"Ah, Emma," he murmured, his face contorting with raw emotion as he reached for her. "It'll be okay."

Catching him by the back of the head, Emma closed her eyes and hung on to him. Deep sobs were wrenched from her, and Derrick crushed her even closer, his fingers tangling in her hair as he tucked her face against his. "It's okay, babe," he choked out. "It's okay."

Having Derrick here to support her meant everything. It felt so damn good to lean on him. Let him comfort her. She needed that desperately. Needed him.

Overwhelmed by her feelings that one revelation set off in her, she went blindly into his arms, holding on to him with all the care and strength she possessed. With a gruff sound, he enfolded her in a fierce embrace, holding her as if she was the foundation of his world. Fighting against more tears, she closed her eyes and cradled his head against her, needing him so much she felt almost suffocated by it.

He kissed the side of her neck as he smoothed down her hair, trying to comfort her by touch alone. Then inhaling deeply, he caught her face between his hands, her chest so full she could barely breathe. She leaned her head against his jaw, the muscles there contracting. She looked up at him, the rawness in his eyes going straight to her heart.

The richness, the wholeness of her feelings nearly overwhelmed her as she slipped her arms around his neck. "I'm glad you're here with me, Derrick," she whispered vehemently.

He caught one of her hands, then laced his fingers through hers with a crushing grip. His expression scored with a range of emotions, he closed his eyes and pressed her hand against his mouth, his voice hoarse. "Emma— babe—"

Fighting against the swell of tears, Emma tore her hand free and clutched his shirt, a soft sob wrenching loose when he looked at her with his eyes so full of concern. Despite all the things that had gone wrong, this was right. So damned right.

Derrick raked her hair back, cradling her head against the curve of his neck, his breath warm against her skin. "We're alive. We can fight again. I'm not going to give up, Emma," he murmured hoarsely.

"Thank you," she whispered.

He held her tighter, his fingers spread wide as he cupped the back of her head. "I'm going to move heaven and earth to find him. I vow on my life that I will place him in your arms."

Emma's breath caught in her throat, suddenly scared, but this time it was for Derrick. Softly cupping his face, she gave him a reassuring look. "Together. Don't leave me hanging," she whispered, a hint of censure in her tone. "You promised."

Derrick stared at her, then closed his eyes and hugged her hard. "Emma…" His voice broke on the word.

"Promise."

He drew in a deep, uneven breath, his voice raw with emotion. "I promise." Moved by the depth of feeling in that hoarsely spoken declaration, Emma shifted her head, her mouth connecting with his in a kiss that was filled with so much emotion, with such open, unfettered sentiment, that it drove every conscious thought out of her mind. Rising on tiptoe, she molded herself to him as he shifted his hold, bringing her fully against him from shoulder to thigh. He held nothing back in that kiss— nothing. And she felt the fire in him—the wonderful, hot, all-consuming fire that seemed to come from his very soul. It was so overpowering.

A shout from down the runway blasted them back into reality.

Unable to check her tears, Emma tightened her hold and made an anguished sound as she opened her eyes and over his shoulder saw the plane, now a speck in the bright blue sky, disappear along with her hopes.

She couldn't believe this was happening.

She'd failed Lily. She'd lost Matty.

She couldn't shake the feeling that she was going to lose Derrick, too.

Chapter 15

Over the Pacific Ocean

Through the window of his private jet, Gilberto Ortega watched the moonlit clouds course across the sky over the dark ocean below. Beside him, Francisco was furious, delivering his outspoken tirade in a constant stream of Spanish, punctuated by butchered English when he wanted to make a particularly damning point.

"This is dangerous. Entrusting yourself and your young son to Lopez's cartel and their leader, Diego. Far worse than finding a place to lay low in a different country." His second-in-command had been vocally unhappy from the moment Gilberto had decided to make a risky decision to eliminate everyone in his organization, including his eldest son, and to start over from a new location.

"All will be well, Francisco. We have an established network in every city in the United States." He corrected Francisco's last statement. "We have something very valuable and lucrative to offer. We'll build something bigger, bolder, and my name will be whispered with fear on the lips of every man who decides to cross me.

"You should have let me stay back and kill them," he grumbled. "Reyes was a bumbling fool and now that NCIS agent and that woman are free and alive. That agent is trouble, Gilberto. I guarantee it. I know a threat when I see one and he's very, very dangerous. The St. John women can cause a lot of problems for you, including the old woman pressing the State Department about the boy. Let me handle this."

"No, Reyes will be the one with the blood on his hands. There tends to be a lot of interest in the death of a federal agent. Let Reyes earn his pay and take the heat. As for the surviving mother and grandmother, they will get lax and there will be a time to take care of them once the danger seems to have passed. We will bide our time. We have plenty of it."

He rubbed his hand over the tattoo of Santa Muerte, saying a prayer to her for his fallen employees and Arturo.

His future lay in a carrier, strapped in the seat across from him. The beginning was always so exciting, and Lily St. John's son would become Gilberto's shining legacy, as dangerous and feared as his father.

He'd make sure of it.

Caliche, Mexico

Derrick stood in the dark square of the small, peacefully sleeping city of Caliche the night after they had lost Matty. His hands in his jeans pockets, fingering his folding knife, were contracting into fists. The gun in its holster was pressing against his ribs. He wanted to kill someone, but the two main targets were hundreds of miles away now.

A man approached and said softly, "I was shocked as hell to hear from you. I thought you got out of this game a long time ago, son." His thick Southern accent was the one he was born with, but it was often hidden behind so many identities and accents, Derrick had rarely heard it.

S. Robin Browne was a veritable chameleon and almost as good at espionage as Derrick. He wasn't even sure that was his real name. Derrick straightened, glancing around the square. The guy didn't look a day over nineteen with his blond ponytail, scruffy beard and a perpetual confident smirk, a hippie company man toting more weapons on his body than anyone Derrick had ever met, who from observation knew Browne didn't need a damn one of them to take an opponent down. He was also one of the lost boys, an orphan like Derrick. "You never get out of this game," Derrick said bitterly, knowing that while lies and deception were all part of his past, they were now also part of his present.

The guy laughed softly.

"I need some information."

"Even though you pulled me away from another part of Mexico and my current mission, you saved my life, man, more times than I can count. Name it."

"I need the name of Gilberto Ortega's second-in-command."

"That's an easy one. Man, I'm not even breaking a sweat here." He bit into an apple he had been tossing in his hand as he crossed the square. He leaned against the wall. "Sadistic son of a bitch that goes by the name of Francisco Flores. You crossed paths with him?" He took another bite. "Best to kill him swiftly and cleanly. Make sure the job is done." He worked at his tooth, then took another bite of the fruit.

"Not yet," Derrick said. "He's not in the country right now, but my gut says Gilberto Ortega isn't quite done with the area he's carved out here in Mexico."

"Your gut trumps even tarot cards, psychics and any form of intel for me, man."

"Still got that warped way of looking at the world, Browne?"

"What can I say? I'm the company's joker." Then he grinned.

Derrick sighed. "I'd stake my life on Ortega coming back. He's going to keep what's his. It's going to be a bloodbath. But he's going to have a forerunner. So when Flores returns, let me know."

"You've got it." Browne finished off the apple and threw the core into a trash can a few feet away.

Derrick grabbed the man's shirtfront and said in a low and menacing voice, "If you breathe a word of this to anyone or betray me, I will come back here and kill you. We clear?"

"Crystal. I got you. This one means a lot to you. I won't take you threatening to kill me personally. But I do have a question."

"What is it?" Derrick asked and let him go.

"Does this have anything to do with that gorgeous redhead with the amazing legs and eyes and skin—" Derrick growled "—you've been paling around with?"

"So, our presence here didn't go unnoticed?"

"What kind of spook would I be if I wasn't aware of all the potential chaos going down in my little neck of the woods?" He straightened. "I'll give you a piece of advice for free. Don't get involved, man. You'll do things, dangerous things, that will get you dead because you lost your head. Screw her, but cut her loose. I'll be in touch," he said and right before Derrick's eyes, the guy walked off and simply vanished.

The fallout from Gilberto's "fake" coup, supposedly orchestrated by a rival cartel, had everyone in the area in an uproar. The rival group was trash-talking and taking all the credit; other cartels were circling around the Ortegas' vacated piece of prime drug lord real estate and the area was quickly turning into a powder keg.

Velasco had survived his gunshot wound, reported back to the attorney general who then reported back to the NCIS director, offering his condolences on the way the case had been botched by one of his own.

When Derrick had contacted Kai, she had been sympathetic and saddened by the news. She'd ordered them both back to the US. Now that Matty wasn't in Mexico, their only recourse was to go home, regroup and figure out their next steps.

They had a room at the hotel and he'd left Emma sleeping there to meet with Browne. He wasn't going to tell her anything and it tore him up inside that he had to be secretive to keep her from getting any more involved. He wasn't sure what was going to happen, but he knew he'd lied to her. Exposing Emma to any more danger just wasn't on his agenda.

He'd lied to her and he knew this jeopardized everything they had between them. He also knew what they had between them was…significant. But he knew going into this that he wasn't sure he could change.

He closed his eyes and swore softly under his breath, hitting the side of the building with the flat of his hand.

She trusted him.

And he was going to find a way to get Matty that was completely illegal and dangerous. He was going into a world she wasn't prepared for, didn't have the skills to disappear and blend into like he did. She was tough, beautiful and he was in too deep, but he'd rather lose her than have her death on his conscience or have to look into those heartbroken blue eyes every day, knowing Matty's loss was eating at her. It was in his nature and he was doomed to be a loner. It had been an illusion to think he could fight it. Putting other people ahead of himself had been what joining the CIA was all about.

He walked back to the hotel and slipped back into their room. He wasn't trying to hide anything anymore. Emma needed him now, and he needed to be there for her.

He slipped out of his suit coat, gun holster and shirt, pulling out the weapon and setting it on the bedside table. He shucked off his jeans. In his underwear, he stood beside the bed. She was curled up on her side, still asleep, and she looked so soft and vulnerable lying there.

He slipped into the bed and she shifted automatically against him, nestling her head into the hollow of his shoulder, resting her upper body against his chest, her arm going around his waist. He clenched his teeth at the exquisite sensation of having her curl around him. He dipped his head and brushed a soft, lingering kiss against her forehead, smiling a little when she made a soft sound and turned her face toward his warmth. If only things could be this simple.

Brushing back the wisps of hair clinging to her face, he kissed her again. He stared into the darkness, thinking about what had happened on that runway two days ago. He had received something from her that he had never expected to have in his life. An emotional gift. And he couldn't be sorry about it.

But what left his gut in a knot was that she had lost it the way she had. From his experience, Emma never lost it. She was pensive, heartbroken, and it hurt his heart to see her like that.

Releasing a heavy sigh, he gazed at her, his expression solemn. Even in the faint light, he could see the shadows under her eyes. Matty's loss had hit her so hard. And, he admitted, him, as well.

She stirred and he brushed a light kiss against her temple.

"Where did you go?" she whispered.

"To get some air," he whispered back.

"Any news?" she asked, her voice hopeful, and he hated that he had to be the one to dash it."

"No, sweetheart. Go back to sleep."

She caressed his waist and then his hip. Lifting herself up, she kissed his jaw. "Don't tell me what to do," she said softly, a teasing inflection in her voice.

"I'm not the bossy one," he said.

She snorted, and he rested his head against hers. He immersed himself in the scent of her, the feel of her.

"I won't let you down, Emma," he said gruffly. He looked at her, something painful happening around his heart when he saw the glimmer of tears in her eyes. Sliding his hand along her jaw until his fingers were buried in her hair, he drew her head down, the fullness in his chest making his throat tight. He took her mouth in a soft, comforting kiss. Wrapping his fingers around the back of her head, he held her still as he softly, slowly, brushed his mouth back and forth across hers, tormenting her, tormenting himself. "That is a promise," he whispered unevenly against her mouth. "Nothing is going to stop me from getting your nephew back, protecting your sister and you."

Releasing a pent-up breath in a rush, Emma slid her arms around his neck and moved on top of him. Closing his eyes against the onslaught of sensation, Derrick turned his face against her and wrapped his arms around her, wondering how in hell he would ever manage without her. Grasping a handful of hair, he clenched his jaw and turned his head against hers, something raw and wild breaking loose inside him. Inhaling raggedly, he clutched her against him. A tremor coursed through her, and she drew her knees up and pulled out of his hold.

Kissing her way down his chest, her hair cascading down his body in a sensual caress, she tugged at his shorts and pulled them off him.

His hips lifted off the bed when her mouth found him hard and pulsing. There was no way he could hide how she affected him. Her tongue swirled and he almost lost his mind. Needing her, he dragged her up his body and she forced his hands down by his head. Another tremor shuddered through her, and her body rose up, then lowered onto his throbbing erection, taking him deep inside her, where he needed to be.

Derrick clenched his jaw against the sharp, electrifying surge of feeling, his shoulders coming off the mattress as she moved once, twice against him. His heartbeat frenzied in his chest, his pulse thick and heavy, he tightened his fingers through hers in a white-knuckle grip, turning his head against the pillow.

Ah, damn. He was in love with her. It was over, and he was a goner.

Bending over him, she stroked her hands over his biceps, his shoulders, his chest, deep satisfaction purring in her throat, her breasts grazing his chest. "Derrick…" she whispered brokenly. "Oh, Derrick." Another shudder coursed through her, and her breath caught as she flexed her hips, her hot, wet tightness gripping him, stroking him, drawing him closer and closer.

An agony of sensation shot through him, and he rolled his head again, the cords of his neck taut, and he sucked in a breath through gritted teeth. He wanted her, he wanted her so badly, to just let go and come out of the shadows, to ride the hard, swelling need. Give in to her.

Then she moved again, taking him ever deeper inside her, and he went under, the fever claiming him. He groaned and flexed beneath her, driving inside her. He couldn't stop.

In the morning they were driven to the airport for a six-hour flight back to San Diego. When they landed, they grabbed their luggage and headed out of the airport. Standing in the busy meeting area, where people were hailing cabs and crowding the curb and circling around, looking for their friends and family, Emma put her hand on his arm. "Would you come with me to the hospital?"

He should really get into the office, but couldn't say no to her. They hailed a cab to her house and picked up her car, then drove to the NAB hospital.

When the elevator stopped on Lily's floor, guards were visible in the hall and outside her room. So far there hadn't been any more attempts on Lily's life, but Derrick wasn't naive in thinking that Ortega had given up. He was biding his time. That was all. It was going to be a race against the clock to get to him before all this died down and Emma and Lily were deemed out of danger.

He suspected Ortega wasn't going to let any of Matty's relatives live.

Lily looked the same, beautiful, vulnerable and young, except her bruises were healing. The doctor came into the room and said, "Hello, Ms. St. John. Your sister is doing very well. There is quite a lot of brain activity. We're optimistic."

Emma clutched his hand, squeezing hard. "Thank you, Doctor. That is such good news, something I really needed right now."

The doctor left and Derrick, too intuitive for his own good, knew she needed a hug. He pulled her against him, pressing her ashen face against his shoulder. She meant so much to him. He felt her chest heave, and she pressed her face tighter against him; then, on another uneven breath, she slid her arms around his waist and held on for dear life.

Trying to ease the sudden knot in his throat, he tightened his arms around her and rested his head on top of hers, the hard knot of tension in his belly finally letting go. He gave her a few moments to regain her equilibrium; then he began rubbing her back. It took about thirty seconds, but she finally went slack against him, and he felt her take another deep breath. Running his other hand up her neck under her hair, he shifted his head and rested his cheek against her temple.

His voice was low when he murmured, "I'm going to get us some coffee."

She settled in a chair by the bed and said, "I'm so glad you're here. Thank you." Emma nodded, turning to talk to her unconscious sister.

As he exited the room, Derrick experienced a shot

of guilt, and he felt like a first-class bastard. Inhaling heavily, he stared straight ahead and headed for the coffee machine.

An hour later they got off the elevator in the parking garage and at the car, he stopped her and said, "We have two options here, Emma. We can find a good restaurant and go for a late lunch or early dinner or we can go to my place, and I'll fix you something amazing when we get there."

He was rewarded with a shaky laugh. "I think maybe you'd better tell me if you can cook or not."

He made a face. "Details."

She smiled and flattened her hands against his back. Experiencing a flurry of emotions, he tucked his head tighter against hers and caressed the base of her skull with his thumb, her hair like silk against his hand. Waiting for the thickness in his chest to settle, he continued to stroke her neck, wishing like hell they were somewhere out of public view. He gave them both a minute, then he eased his hold a little and shifted her head so he could see her face. She looked pensive and worried.

Keeping it light, Derrick managed a smile. "So, pretty woman. What say you?"

"What are you having?" she said with a glimmer of dry humor in her eyes. "Hopefully something that doesn't begin with 'cup o'…'"

He chuckled and rested his arms on her hips, determined to keep this light. "No, I can promise you something better than just a carton and steaming water."

As though she was afraid of what he would see in her eyes, she dropped her gaze. "No restaurant, okay?" she whispered.

He gazed down at her bent head, her hair shining like metal in the sun, and his chest got tight all over again. "Pop-Tarts it is," he answered, his voice husky.

She backhanded his arm and laughed as he reached for the door and opened it for her. "Would you mind driving?"

"Not at all." Once she was tucked into the passenger's side, he got behind the wheel, took a moment to acclimate himself to the controls, then drove out of the garage.

She looked at him, the strain gone from her face, a sparkle of anticipation in her eyes, and Derrick's heart did a barrel roll in his chest. "You're good at that."

"What?"

"Managing vehicles—planes, trains, motorcycles, boats, ships, aircraft carriers. I bet you can fly anything, drive anything and absorb it in minutes. Make split-second decisions."

"If you're asking me if I was a spy, just come out and ask me."

"I got the feeling you don't want to talk about that."

Something sweet and warm unfolded in his chest, closely followed by a more sobering emotion. Feeling a little too exposed, he shifted his gaze and tugged on a loose strand of hair. "In the past, I've avoided it. But with you, it's different."

"Were you a spy, Derrick?"

"Yes, Emma. I was a CIA field officer. A spy, spook, ghost, shadow. Man in Black." He swallowed. He'd never told anyone, but it seemed right to tell Emma.

"I thought so, but having you confirm it feels...very good." He took her hand and pressed it against his thigh, covering it with his own. Her only response was to turn her hand palm up, lacing her fingers through his. When he glanced at her, she was sitting with her head tipped back against the headrest, her eyes closed, as if absorbing the quiet. She looked serene and relaxed, but he could see the rigid tension along her jawline, as though she had her teeth clenched. Derrick tightened his hold on her hand, refocusing his attention on the road, his own jaw tensing. He felt as if he was standing at the edge of a deep, dark precipice, with very little room, and if he made one wrong move… He shifted in his seat. He didn't even dare think about it.

The sun had dipped in the sky by the time they reached his house by the ocean, and he pulled into his garage, his stomach grumbling. He opened the door for her and she reached up and caressed his jaw. His lungs suddenly tight, he gave her a quick kiss on the temple.

He dragged open the patio door and led her inside, dropping her keys on the kitchen table. He grabbed a bottle of wine out of the fridge and held it up. She nodded and he poured her a glass. She settled at the bar and he placed the goblet in front of her.

Pouring himself some, he then raised it and she did, too. "To survival," he murmured. She clinked his glass and drank. He filled a pan and set it on the stove.

She laughed. "That looks like you're boiling water to me."

He gave her a sidelong glance that had her softly sighing. "You know you're god-awful handsome, right?"

"Yeah, movie star potential," he scoffed. After pulling out fixings for a salad, he started cutting tomatoes.

"You are, Derrick. Achingly handsome."

He smiled. "You're beautiful."

"Tell me how you can sympathize with me so deeply on how it would be to never get Matty back."

He picked up his wineglass and took a sip. "I have a son, Emma. One that I can't claim and can never see, interact with or support."

She gasped and choked on her wine. "Oh, Derrick." She stared at him, her eyes wide.

"It was a terrible mistake on my part. I got involved with an asset. Someone who could help with taking down a terrorist organization. It was my mission. I…fell in love with her and got her pregnant. An unmarried, pregnant woman would have been in danger." He closed his eyes. "But more important, if my handler had ever found out, I would have been pulled and the mission in jeopardy."

"What did you do?"

At the sound of the bubbling pot, he turned, reaching for the angel hair pasta, dropping the noodles into the water. "She married someone she was close to and gave birth to my son under a different man's name."

"How old is he?"

"Nine."

She got up and walked around the island and wrapped her arms around his waist. His expression serious, he ran his thumb over her bottom lip. "What is his name?"

"Israr."

"That's beautiful, sounds very masculine." She held his gaze for a moment, then looked away, running her hand along his shoulder. "I'm so sorry, Derrick. That must be so hard on you. Never to know him," she whispered, her voice uneven. "You've been through so much in your life."

He lifted her chin, forcing her to look at him, his voice gruff when he said, "It hurts every day, but I'm secure in knowing that they are both safe."

Her expression softened, and she kissed his mouth.

She held him for a moment. Then she looked at the boiling water and said, "Hmm, I think I've been hood-winked. Sure looks like boiling water and…noodles to me."

He chuckled, drawing her into a tight embrace. He closed his eyes, his heart turning over. Just like Afsana and her family, he would keep Emma safe and she would never know the agony of not having her nephew in her life.

Chapter 16

Emma sat back in her desk chair and stared out the window, frustrated beyond belief. She'd tried everything, exhausted all her contacts, but after two weeks digging and following up on even the smallest lead, she had nothing.

Her cell phone rang and when she looked at the display, she let out a soft groan. It was a call from her grandmother.

She answered. "Yes, Bess."

"I'm in the lobby of your office building. I'm coming up."

"I'm busy."

"Emma, make time. I will be there in five minutes."

She ended the call and gritted her teeth.

Emma wasn't in the mood for an argument with her battle-ax of a grandmother, but there was no way to get out of it.

Her grandmother had a perfectly cut page-boy haircut, sensible shoes and an impeccable beige suit; Emma swore she had nothing else in her closet to wear on her ruthlessly maintained body. She charged through the door exactly five minutes later. Her mouth was pinched in a line, the sanctimonious tilt of her chin and her righteous confidence she wore like armor meaning she was spoiling for a fight.

There was never any greeting with Bess. No quick hugs and smiles or hellos. She just got right to the point. "Emma, what progress have you made? The State Department tells me that until they find Matthew, they can't really start any legal proceedings. The Colombians have been cooperative, but unless they can discover where that slime drug lord has our boy, their hands are tied."

"I'm still working on it."

"It's been weeks! You call yourself a private investigator? We have to get him back before Lily wakes up."

Emma clenched and unclenched her jaw, then spoke, her voice deadly quiet. "Don't you think I know that? I'm doing the best I can," she said.

A muscle in her jaw twitched, and she drew a deep breath. "It's not good enough."

She gave her a cold smile. "It never is, Bess. I was never good enough and neither was Lily. Why do you even care? You never even acknowledged him before now. What has changed?"

She narrowed her eyes, a warning glint appearing. "Don't talk to me like that."

"Why not, *Grandmother*?"

"I am your elder and the woman that raised you. You will have respect."

"Respect is earned." Emma sighed. "I've got an appointment," Emma said, and grabbed her purse. She didn't have anywhere to go, but she couldn't stand being in her grandmother's presence anymore. Bess caught her arm and hauled her up short, and Emma jerked her arm free and turned to face her. "There's no need to talk about this anymore. I'm doing my best. I'll let you know if I find out anything."

"I want to talk to you."

"Well, I'm done talking to you."

She grabbed her arm and steered her over to a chair, her jaw set in determination. "Too bad, missy. We're going to talk anyway. Sit."

Jerking her arm free again, Emma turned to face her grandmother. "I'm not a dog."

"Sit, Emma."

With an exasperated huff, Emma sat down. Folding her arms in a defensive stance, she stared across the room. She gave herself a minute, then she spoke, her voice taut. "What is it you want to talk about?"

She released her breath in a frustrated sigh; then she said, "I have money, plenty of it. There are mercenaries out there for hire, are there not?"

Emma made a soft sound and dropped her head into her hands. "Oh, for the love of God."

When Emma raised her head, Bess met her gaze, and Emma was aware she was an inch away from losing her temper. Totally at a loss. "We can't hire mercenaries because we don't know where Matty is, Bess. We have to find him first."

An anguished look crossed her face and all the steam seemed to go out of her like a deflating balloon. Her voice caught and she reached for a chair, sinking down on the cushion. "You're right. I'm grasping at straws."

Emma had never heard that defeated, soft tone in her grandmother's voice before. She was always so…strong, distant, unapproachable. But her eyes grew moist. "All these years, I thought I was raising you both so well, to be tough, to weather anything. Lily was fragile and you both were so little when you came to me. But it was my fear and my failing that I couldn't let you in. I was so raw after your father and mother were killed. I thought I could keep from loving you, not getting hurt if something happened to you, but all I've done is drive you both away. And now Matthew… I can't bear it that he's with that man and we're all so fragmented. What you said to me was very hurtful, and I had to do a lot of soul searching the last few weeks. I'm sorry, Emma. I'm so sorry."

Emma gaped at her grandmother, unable to believe the words coming out of her mouth. She couldn't deal with this right now. She closed her eyes and said, "Bess, it's best to leave this up to me and NCIS. Please, just go home. I'll let you know when I know something. I promise."

The look in her eyes was the old Bess, strong enough to strip steel. "You promise me, Emma."

"Yes."

"And if you need money for mercenaries or anything to get him back…you'll come to me?" she demanded, her voice shaking.

She closed her eyes. Her voice hoarse. "Yes. I'll come to you."

"All right, then." Bess rose and put her hand on Emma's arm and squeezed. "Find him, Emma, and bring him home."

Immobilized with gut-wrenching pain and fear, she sat there staring at the far wall. Finally, she rose and headed for the elevators, so much pressure boiling up in her that she could barely see. She had to find him. She had to. She walked out of the building, the frenzy in her chest making her tremble, the anger and the fear mixing into explosive proportions.

She drove to Camp Pendleton and got admittance as a visitor to NCIS. She rode up in the elevator and when she stepped out, she just stood there as if she couldn't find her way. Derrick spied her and rose, the smile at seeing her fading from his face.

He came to her and she clutched at him. Without saying anything, he took her down the hall and into the conference room. "Have you heard something? What's wrong?"

"I can't find him. I've tried everything, Derrick." As if everything was crowding in on her, she wrapped her arms around herself. She worked at keeping her cool, then said, her voice barely audible, "Are you people even still looking for him?"

"Of course we're still looking," he said, just as frustrated as she was. "I'm working on it every chance I get."

Her face ashen and her voice wobbling, she said, "But it's not a priority anymore?"

He'd forced himself to remain disengaged—not allowing any kind of feeling to surface. But now, as she stood there, her animation gone, the vibrancy beat right out of her, he experienced a rush of rage. She was beside herself with worry, her sister was still in a coma and her nephew was taken by a ruthless drug lord. He wanted to kill somebody.

She tipped her head back and closed her eyes, and Derrick could see tears gathering in her lashes. "He cannot be raised by that man. I won't have it." Her despair cut him to the quick. And something gave way inside him. He covered the space separating them. He'd already crossed the line anyway, grasping her hands between his.

"Emma, you've got to trust me. He's my priority." He hadn't wanted to say anything until it was certain, but he needed to give her some hope. "I'm waiting for some intel. But until that happens, we wait."

"Intel?"

His heart stuttering, he tightened his hold, rubbing her hands between his. "I'm using contacts from when I was in service."

An unquenchable flicker of hope broke free, and she grasped his arms. "This would be solid?"

"Yes, but I'm not saying any more right now until something comes through. I don't want you involved in this anymore."

Her eyes narrowed and she pulled her hands free, her expression turning mutinous. "What? You said we were going to do this together."

"I've changed my mind and I've got to do…things to get him back. Things you can't be involved with."

Her chin lifted and her eyes flashed. "Why?"

He ran his hand through his hair. When she'd walked into the office, she'd looked like she was on the verge of panic. He didn't give that panic a chance to gather momentum. She opened her mouth again and he held up his hand. "Emma, stop."

"But Derrick. You're not being reasonable. You let me go before. You said I was helpful and valuable. What has changed? Tell me why I—"

"Because it's too damned awful, Emma," he said, his voice low and fierce.

She never took her eyes off him, and his gut clenched when she closed her eyes and swallowed. The anguished look on his face said it all. He didn't want her to see him be as ruthless and brutal as the men who took Matty.

There was law and order and polite society. Everyone lived here because men like him and Robin were doing the jobs that no one wanted to do to keep the country safe. Someone had to get their hands dirty and his were stained in blood already.

He watched her fighting her little fight, and he respected her for that. And he knew it just wasn't in her nature to go down without a struggle. She took a breath and wrapped her arms around his neck and held on tight. "Derrick," she whispered. "I would never judge you."

"I know you're not naive with the ways of the world. You were a cop, so I know that. It's just I have to…ah, dammit…do the kind of things that I left in my past. I told you I would do what it takes and it's going to take someone like me who knows how to extract information the hard way."

"What does that mean? Are you going back?"

"Yes."

"I'm going with you."

"No, Emma."

She wasn't so down and out that she couldn't even scrape up a decent dirty look. "Yes. Do you think I care what we have to do? Do you think I won't do anything in my power to have him back safe with us?"

He looked away, knowing that she might say that now, but when faced with the kind of things he was going to have to do to get the information he needed… Faced with that brutality, she would change her mind. It did matter. But that had never stopped him. "It'll be different. You think you'll be okay with it until it happens. This won't be easy and it's not legal. You've always stayed within the letter of the law as a cop, and as a PI you're also governed by laws."

"You're not?"

A cold sensation spread through his middle, and his insides bunched into a hard knot. "Not in this case. I'm leaving my badge here, and I'm not sure I'll have a job when I get back."

Clearly struggling with a whole bunch of emotions, she tipped her head back, wrestling with his plan of action. "Derrick—"

"It's just a job, Emma. I can get another one." It hurt, really hurt, to think he wouldn't be part of NCIS anymore, but he couldn't work within their parameters on this one. Just like his black op mission to shadow Rock Kaczewski in the Darién Gap, he couldn't breathe a word of this to anyone. He was as alone as he'd been in the field, the whole of his life. But without his willingness to do what needed to be done, she would surely lose that kid, just as completely as he'd lost his own, and that was something he couldn't bear. "Compared to the future that awaits Matty if we don't get him back, it's inconsequential."

"I know you're saying that for my benefit, and I know you believe that, but I also know those people mean something to you. They're special."

He closed his eyes and said in a low voice, "They are. But Emma, I'm still doing this."

"And so am I."

He huffed out a breath and they separated. He understood her need to go with him. He did, but the thought of her in danger and anywhere near Francisco Flores made his blood run cold. "All right, but you'll have to do exactly what I say every step of the way."

"Sounds familiar," she said with a ghost of a smile.

He looked down at her, humor tugging at his mouth. "Dissension in the ranks already?"

Pulling his head down, she brought his mouth into full contact with hers.

The kiss was slow, soft and so unbelievably gentle that it left him absolutely breathless, and his whole body turned to jelly. "I've got to get back to work and let you get back to yours," she whispered against his mouth. "Tonight?"

"Yes, I should be off at five."

She caressed his jaw, tipping her head to one side, her expression changing as she considered him. Finally, she spoke, her voice very soft and very husky. "Did anyone ever tell you that you make one hell of a white knight, Very Special Agent Derrick Gunn?"

Caught off guard by her comment, he stared at her. He didn't want her thinking that. He wasn't a white knight by a long shot. His intentions toward her were not pure.

Derrick woke up, the vestiges of a nightmare crowding against his now waking mind. The warmth against him made him recalibrate his thinking. He wasn't accustomed to having someone in his bed. He opened his eyes, so aware of Emma's body against his. The fading sky that preceded dawn was illuminating the room, and Derrick turned his head and looked at her; the kind of feeling that rushed through him, he wanted it every day of his life.

She was sleeping on her side, facing him, a lone leg drawn up, her breathing deep and even. The windows had been left open all night, and the room was filled with the sound of ocean waves. Bracing his weight on his elbow, he ran his hand down her bare arm; then he reached over, tugged the sheet loose and drew it over her. He watched her sleep for a long time, until parts of his body started sending him messages that had nothing to do with sleep and everything to do with getting closer to her. For an instant he indulged in the sensual memories from last night, the lovemaking off the charts as usual.

Emma sighed and shifted beside him, her hand brushing against his arm, and he glanced back down at her, suddenly feeling things he didn't want to feel, wanting things he wasn't sure he could keep, knowing he would never be able to lie in this bed again without seeing her there. The thickness in his chest climbed higher, and he rolled onto his back, resting one arm across his forehead as he stared into the gloom. This part of their relationship was damned easy—so easy.

It was the rest of it that he wasn't sure about; the uncertainty of the future never used to bother him before, but losing Matty and not getting him back could tear her apart. Losing his own son would have if he hadn't compartmentalized the whole damn thing and tucked it away. He had to because doing so would save many, many soldiers' lives.

Unsettled about his feelings for Emma, he got up and pulled on his jeans, then went over to the windows and looked at the ocean. Usually it soothed him. Today, there wasn't enough water on the planet to do that.

Casting one last look at the sleeping form in his bed, he left the room, shutting the door soundlessly behind him.

The breeze through the open patio door rattled the blinds, and Derrick closed the door, then went into the kitchen. He filled the reservoir on the coffeemaker and put fresh grounds in the basket, his movements automatic and detached. Flipping the switch to start it brewing, he went and stood in front of the patio door, a hollow feeling unfolding in him. Bracing one arm on the window frame, he stared out, wishing the hole in his gut would go away.

His life had been defined by being alone, but he'd rarely felt lonely, until now. It had been a helluvah ride, being part of the CIA. One that took him places he'd never expected to go. There had been times when his aloneness got so big, he felt cloaked by it. And he had figured he would go to the grave with that awful hole in his chest. Then *boom*. Emma. *Boom*. Love. Again. A love that held a lot of promise. He had no idea what was going to happen between them, but she was the one he wanted.

The need he had to do what was right, like when he'd sacrificed Afsana and his boy, felt the same damn way this whole mess with Matty felt. Like he was going to have to lose the woman he loved to that part of him that needed justice, needed follow-through, needed someone to get his hands dirty.

He would move heaven and earth for her.

He knew they could never just be friends. And there was no damned way he wanted them to be just lovers.

Looking away, he swallowed hard, his eyes suddenly burning. It was a hell of a thought; he had never found anyone who came close to replacing Afsana in his heart. Now Emma was there as if she had always been.

All he knew for sure was that having her, being with her, had been real for him. As real as it got. He'd never wanted to get blindsided by another woman, and lo and behold. *Bam*.

Exhaling heavily, Derrick dragged his hand down his face, then tipped his head back, trying to release the tension across his shoulders. Hell, he was going to drive himself crazy if he didn't stop thinking about it. Especially when there weren't any answers. He turned from the window, rolling his shoulders. What he needed was a long run. Instead, he headed for the shower.

When he came out, the bed was empty. He dressed in a clean pair of jeans and went out to the kitchen. She was standing at the now-open door, sipping coffee, dressed in his navy blue NCIS T-shirt. It came to about midthigh on her. He'd never seen anything look so good in that shirt.

"You had better have saved me some," he murmured, coming up to her and wrapping his arms around her waist.

She leaned into him. "Slowpokes don't usually get the rewards," she said with a laugh.

"Emma..." He tickled her and she almost sloshed her coffee.

"I left you some."

He walked over and poured himself a cup, then sipped the strong brew.

"Why didn't I buy a house on the ocean?" Her voice was filled with regret and envy.

"Yeah," he chuckled. "Why didn't you?"

He went onto the deck and tugged her after him. Folding down onto a lounge chair, he urged her onto his lap.

She snuggled up to him and shrugged. "I think I might have retired instead, getting much too engrossed in living at the beach. I had a business to run, so I thought it was best to leave the vacation living to people who could handle it. I love the ocean and it's heavenly to fall asleep with you here. It's kept me sane."

Her hair flew around in the wind like thin copper strips. Her delicate features were contemplative.

"I own an island," he said, all kinds of smugness in his tone.

Her head whipped around and she scowled. She smacked him on the bare shoulder. "Now you're just being cruel."

"No," he laughed when she made a face at him. "I... inherited it from that old tycoon who thought I was nothing but clay for him to mold. I sold everything else, but that place is paradise. It spoke to me. It's off the coast of the Bahamas, Tucked Away Cay."

She turned totally around, straddling him and set her cup on the small table next to his. She shook him. "Are you kidding me?"

He leaned his head back just so he could stare at her. "Derrick...when you look at me like that, I can't think."

"Yeah, I know."

"You're terrible."

"Yeah, I know."

She smacked him again.

He gave her an innocent look. "I'm not kidding. I'm thinking you'd look good there on the sandy beach, not a stitch on."

She shot him a startled look.

Unable to resist the draw of that daydream, he reached out and ran his finger down the swell of her breast. "Yeah, you sunbathing in the nude, playing in the surf, plenty of bounce...to your step."

"Ah, you're not talking about my step and I know it."

"You ever make soft, slow love in the surf, Emma?" he asked, his voice low and provocative.

She stared at him, transfixed, looking totally winded. As if she'd finally gotten the rush he'd been living with all morning. She closed her eyes as her chest rose, as if she couldn't catch her breath. He really expected her to tell him to stuff his soft, slow sex where the sun don't shine, but this was better. Infinitely better.

Finally getting some air into her lungs, she turned and looked at him, a dangerous glint in her eyes. "You think you're so smart," she breathed, well aware of the hard-on she was currently cradling between her bare thighs.

Then she grabbed his hair and planted a kiss on him that had him groaning and itching to get her just as naked as she would be on that beach so far away.

Laughing against her mouth, his whole body going on even more full alert, he slid his arms around her hips. "You drive me completely crazy," he murmured, tasting her mouth.

She gave his hair another yank and deepened the kiss. Derrick got really serious, really quickly, and he dragged her down against him. She made a low sound and slid her arms around his neck, and suddenly Derrick couldn't breathe, either. Grabbing the back of her head, he fought for air, his heart hammering. He changed the angle of her face, then sealed his mouth hungrily against hers. He would never get them to the bedroom in time. Never.

She moved against him, and he nearly groaned, a pulsing heat coursing through him. In desperation, he reached down, working her panties off and loosening his jeans. She tightened her knees against his hips and moved to take him deep. And he nearly lost his mind.

She clung to him when it was over, and he couldn't hold her close enough, clutching her to him, her fingers still in his hair, her face buried in the crook of his neck.

Their breaths came in heavy pants, and she slowly raised her head. At the first hint of movement, his arms tightened around hers, his fingertips digging more deeply into her hair. "Don't leave me," he whispered. He closed his eyes when she pressed a damp, heated kiss against his jaw, then dragged her lips to his, her mouth so sweet and gentle.

She raised her head, her face pensive, the magnitude of what had passed between them clearly not lost on her. "What's going to happen after we find Matty?"

"Everything will go back to normal. I'm going to make sure you're safe."

"No, Derrick, this, between us. Do you want to continue this?"

He wrapped his hand around her throat, caressing her beating pulse with his thumb. "Yes, I do."

She went to open her mouth, but he covered her lips. "No, don't say it yet. Tell me after all this is over about what you want to do with…this."

He kissed her palm just as his phone beeped. He pulled it out of his back pocket.

It was a text from Robin:

Flores is back. Showtime.

Yeah, he would wait to see how everything played out and if Emma would be interested in him after all this was over.

Chapter 17

Former Ortega Hacienda
Caliche, Mexico

"**D**on't tell me he's dead."

They had come to the abandoned house where Ortega's son, Arturo, and Mrs. Montoya had been killed. There was still a blood stain on the kitchen floor where she'd died. Flores probably had been the one to knife her and brutally kill Arturo; the bastard had liked the personal touch. The world was a little safer now that he was gone. Except they both knew there would be another one to take his place. It was the way of the world.

"Yeah, he wasn't going to give us anything anyway. Dude was a straight-up, stone-cold killer and he enjoyed every minute of it," Robin said, facing Derrick, his face bleak. No one, not even hardened operatives, got used to this.

"So that's exactly what he is. Dead. Good riddance, I say."

"I didn't expect you to do this on your own. This was my situation and I would have dealt with it."

"Look, Derrick. You're NCIS now, and I jumped the gun to leave you out of this." He held up his hand. "I know you would have done what was necessary. But I got some cartel guys to get information out of Flores. They were very cooperative and had some questions of their own anyway. This way, no harm, no foul. We're both out of it."

"My hands aren't clean, Robin."

Robin huffed a breath, setting his hands on his hips, giving Derrick a shuttered look. "None of us are. But you're clean of this and that satisfies me. I left it up to them. Believe me, they were thorough."

"I would have done what needed to be done, but thanks for what you did."

Robin nodded.

"What did he say?"

"He let slip that Ortega was rebuilding and forging a new business with Diego Lopez."

This wasn't exactly what he had planned, but he was glad Flores was dead. He was just as big a threat to Emma, Lily and Matty as Ortega. He was the kind of man who would exact revenge. So he was dead and he hadn't given up Ortega's hidey hole. Or had he?

"We didn't get enough, at least not where Ortega is hiding."

Derrick leaned against the counter. "Oh, but he did give us a clue. He told us Ortega is in bed with *Lopez's cartel*. I'm sure part of his deal with Diego Lopez is new and improved routes for their drugs to enter the US. We also know he went to Colombia. That gives me a starting point."

Robin made a face and ran his hand through his loose blond hair. "You're going to send me home with the babe, aren't you?" he whined.

"Don't call her that and yes, I need you to do this for me. I need her home safely. Watch over her."

Robin shifted and snorted. "I'm no judge of women—well except for when it comes to getting what I want—but she's not going to go into that good night quietly, my friend. She looks like a ball-buster. Kicking and screaming comes to mind and I, for one, don't want my balls within kicking distance."

He was completely right. That was exactly what Emma would do—kick and scream. She might not want to see Derrick after this. He'd promised her and he was going to break that promise for the second time. If she hadn't broken him down with those blue eyes and that determined attitude, she would be back in San Diego right now. Instead, she was out front watching their backs. "You find a way, Robin."

"Man, this blows, but I owe you big time." Derrick turned to go. Robin grabbed his arm. "But I'm not doing it because you saved my life."

"Why are you doing it?"

Robin met his eyes head-on. The guy maybe didn't look a day over nineteen, but he had the eyes of a wiser man, an old soul. "Because we're the lost boys, there's an innocent kid at stake and—I'm not going soft here—you love her. The first time you fell in love, you got the raw end of that deal made at the highest level. So because I can say 'screw you' to Uncle Sam, I'm going with this plan. For now."

"Thank you, Robin. I'll owe you." Derrick's voice came out gruff.

Those amber eyes warmed. "Nah, it's gratis. Just don't get dead. That'll really piss me off."

Derrick laughed. "You watch your back and at the end of all this, there'll be an anonymous star on the wall for you."

"Yeah, you bedazzle the hell out of it for me, huh?"

Derrick chuckled. "Copy that."

This time the warm amber lights of Robin's eyes turned steely. "Oh, and you kill that son of a bitch, too. They'll never be safe if you don't."

Derrick's jaw and voice hardened. "You can count on that." Derrick turned away. "I'm going to slip out and make my own way." He was going back into the shadows, but he was used to it, like an old friend. "Take her out of here and get to the airport."

"Have you told her?"

"Told her what?"

"That you love her."

"There's a commercial flight out in two hours. Make sure you're on it. I'm depending on you to keep her safe."

"Hey, I'm named after a famous hero and the sidekick of one of the baddest, badass superheroes of all time. I won't let you down. You know you're not alone."

Derrick didn't answer as he slipped out the back and disappeared into the forest. He picked up the rusty pickup he'd stashed in the trees along with passports with old covers from his past. He ran the risk of flagging himself with the company, but he didn't expect to be using these aliases for very long. A plan was forming, a plan that would end Ortega and his organization for good, and if he was lucky destroy a good part of Diego Lopez's business in the process. Ortega was never going to threaten the St. Johns again. He got inside just as his cell phone rang. When he looked at the display, he swore under his breath. His gut was tied up in knots and his chest was on fire.

Emma.

And even the ring of the cell sounded pissed.

As soon as he engaged the call, she shouted, "How dare you do this to me!" Her voice was shaking with fury. "You promised me."

"Your involvement ends here, Emma." He hardened his heart; he'd done it so many times in the past it was like second nature. "I need to finish this alone. He'll never see me coming this way. You stand out like a sore thumb with your gorgeous copper hair and that body. He'll remember you."

"Derrick, don't you dare be charming right now. I want you to come back here and we'll figure this out."

"No, Emma," he said, his voice clipped, then it softened when he heard her sniff. "I'm finishing it now. I don't know how long it will take me, but if I don't come back…" He wanted to say so many things. He wanted to tell her he loved her, that he wanted to be in her life permanently, that he wanted her with every bone in his body, every cell in his head, and every emotion in his heart. Instead, he whispered, "Take care."

"Derrick." Her voice broke on a sob. "Don't do this."

"Goodbye, Emma."

"Derrick!" she shouted. "If you do this, I'll never forgive—"

He closed his eyes and disconnected the call. He broke down the cell, removing the sim card and snapping it in two, then chucking it out the window. The pieces he threw out as he drove away, his eyes burning and his heart torn to shreds. She would never forgive him.

That was his answer. He'd broken her trust, betrayed her, thrown her care and commitment in her face. He wouldn't know the word *team* if it bit him on the ass.

"—you if you die." Emma closed her eyes, squeezing them tight against the tears. She was in love with him and he had the nerve to try to protect her. She could take care of herself and he knew it. This was his white knight complex getting all mixed up in this. Emma stood there, Robin in her peripheral vision, looking as calm and collected as if they were on a stroll in the park. Maybe that came with the spook territory. She tried Derrick back, but the phone just gave her a recorded error message.

She turned to Robin and grabbed his shirtfront. She pressed him back against the hacienda and shouted, "Where did he go? Tell me."

He held up his hands, his amber eyes sympathetic. "I don't know. But it wouldn't matter if I did. I wouldn't tell you. Derrick is going to need everything he has focused on this mission. If he's worrying about you, he's not at one hundred percent. And believe me, he's playing with some serious big boys. Let me do what he asked me to do for you, Emma. Keep you safe. I know him. I know him well. He's not going to give up on this, so let him go."

She couldn't let him go, but at this point she couldn't do anything to help him. But back home, there were possibilities.

When they touched down in San Diego, Emma hailed a cab. Just as she was about to tell him her destination, her cell chimed. She looked down to see it was the hospital calling. She answered while the cabbie waited and Robin settled inside and closed the door.

"Emma St. John."

"Ms. St. John, this is Lieutenant Keenan over at Coronado. I wanted to let you know that your sister woke up. She's asking for you."

"That is great news. I'm on my way."

She gave the cabbie the address and let Robin know. He grinned broadly as the cab pulled away from the curb. First Lily, then Emma was going to help Derrick, whether he wanted her to or not.

When she arrived at the hospital, she rushed up to Lily's room, Robin following her closely. When she turned down the hall, she couldn't stop herself from running. The cops at the door recognized her, smiles on their faces, but her eyes were only for her sister, sitting up in bed, looking lucid and beautiful.

With a cry of joy, she went into the room, threw her arms around her and hugged her hard. "It's so good to see you awake. I'm crushing you."

Lily's voice was full of tears. "No, you're fine. You must have been out of your mind with worry."

They parted and Lily's cornflower-blue eyes were swimming with tears. She glanced at Robin, then did a double take.

He came forward, reached out his hand. Lily put her good one in his and it engulfed her sister's tiny one. "Robin," he said. "Nice to meet you, Tinkerbell."

"Same." Her quizzical expression turned to her sister.

"It's a long story, but just know he's one of the good guys and here to help."

When she pulled her focus back to Emma, Lily's face was flushed. "Tell me everything. Where's our Matty?"

Emma closed her eyes and her sister's voice caught on a soft sob. "He's got him, doesn't he? I should have told you everything. I should have asked for your help.

But I was so scared, I didn't want anyone to know. I just wanted that nightmare to go away. I thought he would take no for an answer and would leave us alone." She covered her mouth. "What have I done, Emma? What have I done?"

After many explanations and many tears between the both of them, Lily finally went to sleep. Emma rose and backed away. Robin was standing at the door, his eyes riveted to Lily in the bed, slightly unfocused and...dazed?

She nudged him and he snapped his gaze to hers as if he'd been doing...or thinking something he shouldn't.

"What now?" he asked.

"Now we get Derrick some backup. You included."

"Emma," he said, straightening. "I'm not leaving you alone."

She grabbed his arm and pulled him out of the room. "I won't be. Come on."

NCIS Headquarters
Camp Pendleton, California

When Austin read the news coming out of Mexico, he closed his eyes. Derrick. Dammit. He knew it had been Derrick, although the report didn't explicitly mention him. He knew something was up when he'd asked Austin to cover for him. When he opened his eyes, his boss was standing in front of his desk. She would have gotten the same report.

She slammed her hands down on the metal, everything reverberating. Out of the corner of his eye, he saw Amber jump. She gave him a look that told him she'd read the report, as well. "Tell me I'm wrong."

Austin thought he would go for an I-don't-know-a-thing ploy. He looked her up and down. "Did I tell you how great you look today?" he grinned.

He looked over at Amber for support. She shook her head in a that's-not-going-to-work way, then rolled her eyes heavenward.

"So, I think that color looks great on you. You're rocking that…uh…red like a pro."

She narrowed her eyes. Her voice laced with steel. "Beck…"

"So, Francisco Flores is dead," he said in a dismissive tone. "One more scumbag out of commission. That's a good thing."

"Austin…"

"Okay, so Derrick may have been involved." She growled and he held up his hands. "I don't know."

She let out a heavy breath. "Find him, Austin. I want to talk to him."

Austin leaned back in his chair. This time his tone was worried and resigned. "I've already tried. He's gone off the grid. He's a ghost."

"Son of a bitch." Kai left and went up the stairs to TacOps. "I'll be with the director." The door slammed behind her.

His cell phone rang and he answered. It was Emma St. John and she had a plan. Austin's tight chest began to ease. He motioned Amber toward the conference room. Once inside he put it on speaker. Emma started talking.

"You got that?"

"Yeah," they said in unison and Austin smiled. "We hear you. We're in."

Jungle Near Bogotá, Colombia

If Derrick didn't hurt so damn much, he would laugh right now. Lopez's shipment team was in chaos after Derrick had continued his plan to make it look like Ortega was undermining Lopez's operation. This was the third drug shipment Derrick had disrupted in a week. Word was going to filter back to Diego and it would have Ortega's name all over it.

He hid behind a clump of palms and brush, the humidity making sweat run off him in rivulets. Sweating in the jungle was normal, but this kind of cold sweat wasn't. He tilted his hand away from his side and looked down.

Okay, he was chewed up, but it wasn't bad—except the blood running through his fingers. The bullet was still in there, just under his skin, and it might have skittered off one of his ribs, which would explain why he hurt so freaking bad. The jungle thrashed with Lopez's men looking for him. He'd never been shot, and now that he had, he couldn't recommend it. A friggin' ricochet. Well, at least that tree had slowed the velocity of the slug.

That was good, but the blood...yeah, the blood was a problem. He'd lost too much. He'd slapped a quick patch on himself while fleeing, but that was an hour back, and he hadn't dared stop long enough to really bind himself up.

On the plus side, his plot was going exactly as planned. He'd called in a crap-load of favors and his shady network had come through. He'd found Ortega within a week of hitting Bogotá, thanks to Flores dropping the intel that Ortega was in bed with Diego Lopez. Now all he had to do was evade eight armed men and get to

Ortega's estate before Lopez decided to take him out of the equation. The irrefutable evidence that Derrick had already planted and was now being whispered into Lopez's ear would seal Ortega's fate. Lopez would kill Ortega and neutralize the threat to Matty and his family.

All that was left was to get Matty out.

With the thought of the infant, Derrick unerringly went to the last time he'd kissed and held Emma. In their hotel room in Caliche before they'd ambushed Flores. What a hell of a way to spend a vacation with the woman he loved.

He closed his eyes, his throat tight. He could only hope he'd see her again long enough to place Matty in her arms.

He'd made a calculated error. He should have asked for help. Whether he wanted to acknowledge it or not, he was part of a team. NCIS was his family! The company, for all its faults, had given him the skills he needed to put this scheme in motion and he was doubly grateful for the training and the experience. Without this network, without these contacts, he would have been screwed. Matty would have been lost forever and Emma and Lily devastated.

"Hold it right there," someone said in Spanish and he turned to find one of the men who had been pursuing him pointing his weapon, his black eyes shadowed beneath the brim of his baseball cap.

Derrick closed his eyes in anguish. He was a dead man.

The guy reached for him to jerk him to his feet, but one moment he was standing there and the next he was on the ground, his cap displaced and a suppressed shot to the back of the head—a professional shot.

Then he heard footsteps and he brought up his gun, but his hand was shaking badly right now. Robin grinned at him as he stepped over the dead man.

"What are you doing here?" Derrick said, his eyes narrowing, happy to see Robin, but pissed he'd left Emma and Lily unguarded.

"Hey, me, my sniper rifle, my 9mm and big ass army knife were in the neighborhood, and that's a downright unfriendly tone, man.

"Who's watching Emma?" Derrick snapped. "And, Lily?"

At the sound of Lily's name, Robin got a look in his eye. "Even more beautiful than your babe. Even in a hospital gown, she looks like a fairy princess."

"I will kick your ass, bullet wound or no bullet wound."

Robin was too busy pushing Derrick's hand away from his side and looking at said damage. "Ooh, that looks bad. Let's get you some medical attention, *compadre.*"

"What?" Maybe Derrick had lost too much blood and he was disoriented, but there were still seven men out there hunting him. "Robin. Answer the question!"

He slipped his arm under Derrick's shoulder and hauled him to his feet. Derrick gritted his teeth and almost passed out. "Some big dude named…Tristan."

"Michaels? Amber's husband?"

"Yeah, that's the guy. Former marine sniper, could bend steel with his bare hands. I think they're covered." He helped Derrick to sit with his back pressed to a tree.

"Well, there's still seven guys out there trying to do me harm. I don't want any more holes in me."

"Roger that. Put a sock in the hole that's flapping right

now. I've got you covered," he said breezily. "I brought us some friends. More big dudes and one badass smaller dude. They insisted."

Three figures materialized out of the jungle and Derrick gaped. Austin Beck, Dexter Kaczewski and his brother Rock, in full tactical battle gear, surrounded him. Bristling with weapons and fifty-pound packs, they were a freaking active navy SEAL and two former marines.

Austin dropped his pack and set his rifle across it. He nodded to Derrick. "I'm going to whittle down the odds," he said.

"Without any weapons?"

"No, I'll be out in the dark with a knife." Derrick watched Austin the surfer dude/egghead/hacker extraordinaire melt like a seasoned commando into the jungle.

"Derrick, you look like hell," Dex said, setting his rifle next to the tree Robin had propped him against.

"Robin the Boy Wonder said you needed help, but was too bashful to ask." Rock, a mountain of six five inches of muscle, crouched down. "Don't you know, man, you're part of the fam? We inducted you after you saved my brother and his wife, then saved me and my wife. We've got your back." He raised his fist and Derrick bumped it.

Robin was working on Derrick's side and when he saw the bottle, he wanted to protest, but it was too late. Robin poured on the disinfectant.

Oh, dammit, dammit, dammit. He took a sharp breath as fire burned in the wound and agony ignited in every raw pain receptor. If he hadn't been sitting, his knees would have buckled.

"Come on, we're in the presence of superheroes," Robin said.

Rock patted Robin on the head. "He's a good sidekick."

"I'm nobody's goddamned sidekick," he ground out and cut off Derrick's chuckle when he splashed more of the antiseptic into the wound. The son of a bitch.

"I'm not a superhero," Derrick said.

"That's right. You're a secret agent man and a white knight, so buck up."

This time Dexter crouched down. "Don't worry, Derrick. We can kick his ass and you can rub salt in his wounds."

Robin grinned and said, "I'm a lover, not a fighter," right after he pressed a self-adhesive dressing to Derrick's wound. This time he passed out.

When he came to, he was across Rock's shoulders and they were heading toward a nondescript building. Austin, Robin, and Dex flanking them. There were no visible weapons, but he was sure all three of them were armed to the teeth.

Rock went through the door and as soon as the doctor saw them, he motioned them to the back. "This way, gentlemen."

Derrick was sure there wasn't one in this bunch, including him.

This was a discreet place to get a bullet wound competently seen to, the doctor a friend to every shadow and spook in this area. He asked no questions, took his pay and kept his damn mouth shut. He probed Derrick's wound with forceps after numbing the area. Then he heard the sound of metal plinking into a metal dish. The doctor got to sewing him up. It was disconcerting to be sitting here in front of four men, almost buck-ass naked, well, except for the tiny square of cloth covering his groin.

He insisted on walking on his own when they left with

painkillers and sutures holding everything together. In a small hotel, they holed up as Derrick laid out his plan.

After he told them how he was going to get off the estate with Matty, they looked at each other.

When they rose, Rock leaned over and said, "If I were you, I wouldn't tell the mother or aunt how you got that kid out."

Derrick grimaced, thinking there wouldn't be much to say to Emma when he was done with this.

He dressed in a gardener's outfit and pulled the cap low over his eyes. Grabbing the bag with his specialized gear in it, he gritted his teeth as he slung it over his shoulder.

"Are you sure you're up for this?" Austin murmured from the open door of the van as they prepared to go over to Ortega's rented estate.

"I have to be. Lopez is going to move on Ortega today. My intel is solid and I'm the only one who can get in. Wait for me at the rendezvous point."

"Yeah, maybe you should pop one of those happy pills," Robin suggested.

"I can't. I've got to be mentally and physically sound to do what I have to do. I can endure the pain. It's still mostly numb."

Fifteen minutes later he drove up to the estate, showed them his ID and they let him through. He'd been working here for little over three days, casing the area and scoping out the best route to Matty. The nanny brought the baby outside just after lunch and put him in a playpen on the balcony that overlooked the valley below. The estate was set on a bluff, an excellent deterrent to getting attacked from the rear. It was fortified in the front with armed guards and dogs.

His phone vibrated. The voice on the line was terse and brief.

"He's on his way. Fifteen minutes. Good luck."

He silently thanked the CIA operative Robin knew in Colombia who was watching Lopez for him. It was now eleven forty-five, and all hell was about to break loose. He made his way with his bag to just down the stairs from the balcony. Matty was there, sitting up and playing with a toy. He set down the bag and pulled out the harness, quickly getting himself into it. He looked at his watch and then dashed up the stairs. He clipped the nanny on the chin with his fist and she dropped to the warm tiles.

Scooping Matty up, he set him into the specially made harness to hold the baby. He cooed and smiled up at Derrick as he made sure he was secure.

"Hold it right there," Gilberto Ortega said, pointing a gun at Derrick. But he was sure the man wouldn't fire.

"Set the baby down," he said angrily, cocking a round into the chamber. "You won't get off this estate alive."

That's where he was wrong. He didn't see what was on Derrick's back. As soon as he heard the automatic weapons at the gate, he watched Ortega's face blanch and look behind him.

"You hear that, Ortega? That's your destiny coming at you like a freight train. Your legacy ends here and Matty will never be a part of it. I'm going to make sure he grows up in the loving arms of his family." At Ortega's lack of focus, Derrick had been steadily moving to the edge of the balcony. As the sound of doors bursting open and more gunfire, Derrick launched himself off the rail backward and into open air. With one hand he supported the baby's head and neck and with the other, he pulled the ripcord, gritting his teeth as the parachute opened. Over his shoulder, he saw Ortega jerk spasmodically as he was riddled with bullets. Below him the shots echoed across the jungle, sending birds flying and the chatter of monkeys to cease.

Derrick spied his team and his chest tightened. His team, his friends. Ignoring the pain scoring his side, he brought both him and Matty down for a smooth landing.

They were going home.

Chapter 18

They went back to the doctor, who checked the baby out as if it was a common occurrence in the jungles of South America for five hulking men to be toting an infant. The doctor pronounced him in fine condition and they headed back to the hotel room to pull up stakes and head home.

Once inside, Robin sniffed just as Rock said, "Derrick, you're bleeding. If you pulled out those stitches…" he said, forcing him down on the bed. "Let me take a look."

He grabbed one of the pill bottles and pulled out a bottle of water. "Take one."

"I don't—"

"The mission is over. We won. Take the freaking pill before I shove it down your throat."

Derrick took the freaking pill. Rock had at least fifty hard-packed pounds and five inches on him. *And* he was wounded. They were out of the woods. It was a trip to the airport and a commercial flight out of Bogotá.

"What is that smell?"

Dex sniffed and wrinkled his nose. "That's the little guy. Looks like he's done his *duty*."

Everyone laughed, except Robin. Then it dawned on him. "Oh, he crapped his diaper."

"Give this one a medal," Rock said from the bed where he peeled away the old bandage and Derrick breathed around the agony.

"Looks good, just a little bit of bleeding. I'll clean it and put on a fresh bandage, then it's *hasta la vista*, baby."

"Someone needs to change him," Robin said.

"You do it," Derrick growled. "Geez, you can topple governments, kill a man before he even knows he's dead, blend into the shadows, assume new identities and con a person into believing you're whomever you chose to be. I'd say you can change a diaper."

"Yeah," Dex said. "It's not rocket science."

"Dex, can't you do it? You have a kid."

"Ah, it's good practice. You never know when you'll need it in the field. Go on."

"There are some in my backpack," Derrick said. He'd been prepared for every contingency, right down to the diapers and wipes.

Rock shook his head, pressing a new dressing to his wound, but Derrick wasn't feeling any pain now. Derrick chuckled, watching the panic on Robin's face.

Dex piped up. "Just a heads-up. Watch out for—"

"Ah," Robin groused as Matty set off a stream to splash against his shirt.

"Too late," Austin chuckled, slapping Robin on the back.

The diaper change turned into a tactical operation as Rock left the bed to supervise and Dex barked orders. Austin sat down next to him.

"Kai's pissed. She's got that 'he's fired' look. Man, I tried to cover up."

"It's all right. She has every right to fire me. I went off the grid. Twice. I'm a rogue agent. But now I see I should have trusted you all to have my back. I like being on this team. I hope I have a job when I get home."

"Me, too." Austin nudged his shoulder. "You *are* part of the team. Always have been."

Derrick nodded.

"No, that's backward," Dex said, trying to shoulder his way in, but Robin muscled the bigger man over.

"Hey, don't bogart the baby. I got this," Robin said.

Austin chuckled, his eyes glinting. "So you were CIA. I always knew it."

"Yeah, I was. I'll tell you all about it when we get home." He'd given Austin a hard time so that he wouldn't get too close, but now Derrick realized that he was close to this man. They were friends, partners and teammates. "You can come over and we'll have a beer and a cookout."

"Are you sure that's not a martini, shaken not stirred?"

"You got me," Derrick said, smirking.

"Will you show me those rockets in your tailpipes?"

Derrick laughed. "You bet. I'll even let you blow up some bad guys."

"Neato torpedo!" Austin said with a huge grin on his face.

After they were in the van, Matty tucked safely in the car seat, Robin looked over at him. "You going to be okay?"

"I hope so."

"Well, with these big lugs, you've got your back pretty much covered." He shifted in his seat. "Don't even try to drink them under the table."

Dex mumbled, "Lightweight."

Rock said, "He drinks like a girl."

Robin's eyes glinted and he gave them both the finger. He rubbed the top of Matty's head. "He's lucky to have Lily as a mom. I wonder what that feels like?"

"Yeah, he does, and I bet it's freaking fantastic," Derrick said.

Robin looked out the window. "Yeah, I bet it is."

He thought about Emma with a heavy thickness clogging his throat. Her last words to him came at him like a load of bricks right to his heart: *I'll never forgive you.* Just when he realized how tight and intimate his relationship with her was, he'd screwed it up, to do something he had to do. He couldn't regret cutting her out of the action, making the decision to keep her safe. He totally couldn't regret saving Matty. Emma filled a hole inside him he'd been carrying around for way too long. She would never know what it was like to never see Matty again. He looked away as the pain from his wound made his eyes water. Yeah, that's what he was going to tell himself.

Hours later he and Robin were standing outside Emma's house, Tristan assuring them everything was secure.

"You want to come in?" Derrick asked.

Robin smiled. "Nah, it's enough to know I had a hand in this. Besides, I should stay away from that beautiful babe. She looks way too innocent for the likes of me."

"Does it help to know that she's taken? She's marrying some former commander in the navy."

Robin got a pained look on his face. "Ah, hell, that blows. Just as well. Tell Emma she's welcome and you take care. We even now?"

"Hah, we're never going to be even."

Robin laughed and shoved him slightly. "Right."

Derrick watched him walk away, then turned toward the house. Heading up the stairs, he took a deep breath. Matty cooed in his arms.

"Time to see your mom, kiddo. I bet she's missed you."

At her home, Emma moved her backgammon piece and her grandmother scowled. "You are good at this game, even when your focus is elsewhere." They had drawn closer, gone to counseling and were talking and working through their past. Bess had been a different woman, finally turning into their grandmother, not the doily-making, cookie-baking kind, but close enough.

Emma gave her a wan smile and Bess patted her arm. "Everything is going to be fine," she whispered, glancing over at Lily. With her broken arm and leg, she needed twenty-four-hour care, so Emma and Bess were trading off looking after Lily. She was listlessly staring out the window, looking wan and tired. She wasn't sleeping well and Matty's abduction was weighing heavily on her. She blamed herself for being so stupid and getting involved with Gilberto. But she'd just come off a breakup with her navy petty officer and needed solace. She'd found it with Gilberto and had ended up pregnant. Aware she was carrying his baby, she'd contacted him to let him know about his son. But when she dug into his life, she'd discovered he was a drug lord and had flatly refused to speak with him after that.

With her broken ribs, arm and leg, mending nicely, and no permanent damage from the coma, she was recovering. At least physically.

Emma was no different. There wasn't a night that didn't go by that she would wake up, aching to feel Derrick next to her, missing him and sick with worry for him and her nephew. But Robin assured her that he would take care of Derrick. She'd finally learned to trust in someone and stop having a chip on her shoulder that was begging to be knocked off. She let Derrick take the lead and save her nephew because she trusted him with his life, her life and the lives of her sister and grandmother.

Robin had jumped at the chance to find Derrick for her. And Austin and Amber were so ready to help. Amber's husband, Tristan Michaels, was checking around the house to make sure the perimeter was secure. Lord, that man was large and in charge. The Kaczewski brothers, both of them, had agreed, immediately crediting Derrick with saving them and their wives.

Tristan slipped into the room from the back patio and gave her a curt nod just as there was a knock on the door.

Emma looked at him and he moved toward it, looking through the peephole. He smiled and pulled the door open. Standing there was Derrick. Her heart and knees and every part of her felt rubbery as if she was going to collapse in a heap.

But the best part was Matty in his arms. The baby took one look at her and giggled. His laughter filled her with glee.

"Matty!" Lily yelled. "Please, bring him to me, Emma!" Derrick held him out and she took him. Her heart filled when Bess grabbed Derrick and pulled him into a hard hug. If she wasn't so overcome with emotion, she would have laughed at Derrick's stunned expression. She went to her sister and they kissed him and hugged him. When the brief reunion was over, she looked for Derrick, but he was gone.

She rose and walked over to Tristan. "Where did he go?"

"He said he was sorry, then left. I'm not sure where he went."

She bolted out the door and into the street, but it was empty.

Derrick walked into NCIS and the moment he came into view, Amber was up and running. She slammed into him, wrapping her arms around his neck. "Tristan just texted me. I'm so happy to see you."

He winced in pain and doubled over. "I'm sorry. Are you injured?"

"Gunshot. I'm fine."

"Gunn! Upstairs," Kai said with a thunderous look.

"You've got some explaining to do," Amber said with a sidelong look toward the stairs and the closed door of TacOps.

He squeezed her arm. "I'd laugh, but it hurts too much."

Kai turned and climbed the stairs and Amber murmured, "Good luck."

He entered TacOps and saw that the director was on the big screen.

"Agent Derrick Gunn, Director," Kai said.

"Back from a successful mission, but I heard you were wounded. How are you doing, and shouldn't you be in a hospital?"

"I've seen a doctor. I'm fine, sir."

"You make us proud every day, young man. Now you're on leave for the next six weeks. Job well-done."

Derrick gaped at the screen even as it went dark. Then he turned to look at Kai. "I'm not fired?"

She shook her head, an exasperated look crossing her face. "No—on the contrary, you will probably get a medal for this. If you had bothered to check with me, you would have found out that this mission to recover Matthew St. John was already sanctioned by the director and SECNAV. There was no way in hell SECNAV was going to let an infant from one of our navy personnel be raised by a drug lord. We had no intention of letting Gilberto Ortega keep him. We had a whole team on the ready and it was just missing one component."

"Me?" he said, shaking his head and laughing.

"Derrick, I can't say enough how lucky we are to have you. But from now on, rogue missions aren't kosher. *Capisce*?"

"Yes, ma'am."

"Don't 'ma'am' me with that smug look on your handsome face. Now do as the director told you and get healed. I don't want to see you back here for six weeks." Then she hugged him hard, making him wince again, but he swallowed the pain. When she separated, she gave him a chiding look. "Try to stay out of trouble until then."

He headed for the door. "Yes, ma'am." Everything had turned out perfectly, except for him and Emma. He'd ruined their chance of being together by breaking her trust.

Once again he'd had to sacrifice for the greater good. It was good she was alive and well. That she, Lily and their grandmother would have the pleasure of raising Matty.

I'll never forgive you.

Yeah, those were her final words. Bereft and completely shutting down, he didn't even bother to go home, just hailed a cab and said, "Airport."

Once there, he bought a first class ticket on the first available flight to the Bahamas. As soon as he was seated, he popped two pain killers and slept all the way

there. Groggy and feeling sick at heart, he had someone fly him over to Tucked Away Cay. He went up to
the house and went inside. His very competent British
housekeeper was there and he startled the hell out of her.

"Mrs. Carbuncle, this is an impromptu visit. Sorry I
scared the bejesus out of you."

"Would you like something to eat? I can make something in a jiff."

Derrick exhaled unevenly and shook his head. "No.
Thanks. I'm just going to lie down for a bit. He turned
and headed for his bedroom, not sure how much longer he could hang on to the rising pressure in his chest.

Derrick had his foot on the stair when Mrs. Carbuncle
said, "I will be here for another hour, Mr. Gunn. Please
let me know if you'd like me to make something for you
before I go."

Without turning around, Derrick struggled with the
tightness in his throat, the burning in his eyes. "Thank
you. Carry on." He went up the stairs and his body finally shut down on him. He didn't feel a whole hell of
a lot better when he woke up, but his head was clearer,
and he could think halfway rationally.

Sitting up in bed, he felt as if something heavy was
pressing on his chest. With a soft, pained sound, he
moved, his wound protesting...loudly. The medication
must be wearing off. After checking the clock to see
when he'd last taken it, he saw that he was due for another dose. He'd been asleep for eighteen hours straight.

Padding into the bathroom, he peeled away the dressing; reaching into the cabinet and pressing on a water-
proof bandage, he turned on the water, letting it warm
while he took his pills.

Staring at himself in the mirror, he noted his haggard appearance, the dark circles under his eyes. He'd been pushing himself with so little sleep for the last few weeks. Now he could rest.

His throat tightened. He would rest much more easily in Emma's arms. Damn, he wanted her. Even with the pain, his body reacted to the thought of her closeness. As he walked into the open shower, he got an erection, the hard throbbing between his legs making him press his hands against the wall and let the hot water rush over him.

Want her. Want her. Want her.

Then he straightened. Was he an idiot? He hadn't even spoken to her. Hadn't said anything or given her a chance to tell him to take a hike. Maybe. He abruptly shut off the water and walked out, drying himself off.

He had automatically receded to the shadows, gone into hiding to lick his wounds when he realized he was no longer that man. Emma was his and they had something special together. He'd be a complete fool not to give them a chance to work this out. She had told him she wanted him in her life permanently.

He hadn't given her his answer. Well, he was damn well going back to San Diego and telling her. Telling her he loved her. Telling her that he was sorry, ask her to forgive him. She'd probably said those words in the heat of the moment. If he'd been thinking straight, he could have been in her arms right now.

Swearing softly, soaking wet, he headed for his closet, then realized he was dripping all over the floor. Swearing even louder, he headed back to the bathroom and grabbed a towel.

He heard something, and came out of his bedroom. "Mrs. Carbuncle?" he yelled. But there was no answer.

He must be hearing things. He dried off as he walked back into his bedroom. Pulling open the closet, he grabbed a pair of baseball-inspired gray sweatpants with black and yellow banding at the waist and the knee. He shrugged into a yellow Polo and grunted when he pulled it over his head.

Grabbing his wallet and keys, he headed for the door. Downstairs, he went to step onto the wide porch, but stopped dead when he saw a women's tank top covering the WEL of his welcome mat. He looked up and froze. On the newel post at the bottom of the stairs was a...bra. He closed the door and walked down the stairs, picking up the lacy nothing by its strap. He brought the concoction to his nose and breathed deep. His heart lurched and his eyes popped open.

Emma.

Then he spied the shorts on a bush leading down his path to the beach. When he followed it, he saw a pair of matching panties hanging from a palm frond. He gripped his side as he sped up.

When he hit the sand, he saw the top of her coppery head, lying prone in one of his beach chairs. For a moment he couldn't breathe; he couldn't move.

"This was your fantasy, Derrick, and you're just going to stand there like a dummy? It was no easy feat to use my skills to discover you owned this island, then to fly to the mainland and hire a small plane to fly me here."

He expelled a breath, rubbing at his eyes, his shoulders tight. Then he felt her hands curl around his wrists. He opened his eyes and she smiled, snapping his world right back into place.

His voice thick, he said huskily, "Emma, I love you. I was coming to tell you that."

She tilted her head, leaning heavily into him. "Nice opening, but then, you are a charming bastard."

He wrapped his arms around her, so thankful. "I thought you said you would never forgive me."

"If you had waited until I finished my sentence, you would have heard it right. I said I would never forgive you if you died. I love you, Derrick, so much. I was more afraid of losing my independence than I was in letting go and trusting you. I understand why you wanted me out of it. You were more highly qualified and pulled it off without a hitch."

"There was one hitch."

"What?"

"I got shot."

Her mouth dropped open. "And you're standing here letting me prattle on. Holy cow, sit down." She led him to the lounge chair and he sank down on it. She sat down next to him. "Shouldn't you be in the hospital?"

"No. I think I'm healing as we speak. You've healed me, Emma. You gave me what I needed to let the past go and move forward in the future out of the shadows and into the light. I never want to let you go."

"You don't have to. Ask me now what I want to do with…" she kissed him softly "…this."

"Tell me what you want, babe. I'm all ears."

She leaned over and kissed him again. "You. Me. Permanently. Working together to make a future for us. That's what I want."

"Look at that," he said softly. "We're both on the same page."

"I'd say you were a tad overdressed."

"I've been, uh, shot."

She pulled his shirt over his head. "I'll be gentle."

"It hurts, Emma."

"I'll kiss it and make it better." He shut up after that and let her pull down his pants and underwear. He kicked off his flip-flops and stepped out of the material.

"You said something about slow, sweet love in the surf. Let's go try that out. I'll take good care of you."

When they stepped into the warm ocean, she pushed him down. "Hmmm," she said with a catch in her voice as she straddled him. "Just the way I like you. Flat on your back and under my mercy."

"You promised to be gentle."

"I did, but I didn't say anything about not torturing you."

"Oh, damn," he whispered. "What a way to go."

Epilogue

One month later

"**I**'m not so keen on goats."

Derrick glanced at his son. Just after he and Emma had reconciled, he got word that Afsana, her husband, Raffi, and their two children, Israr and Emad, were in terrible danger. The terrorists they had worked so hard to put away had fragmented into a splinter group and were now aware of her part in bringing down their leaders. They were now after them. Derrick, the Kaczewski brothers, Tristan Michaels and Robin took care of that threat, and the family was given asylum in the US.

After a harrowing few days, Afsana, Raffi and the kids were now in the States and Afsana and her family were safe. Derrick found them a farm near San Diego, which they filled with goats. Derrick had shown up in their small town while tracking navy SEAL Dexter Kaczewski and Senator Piper Jones; she had gone missing while visiting her wounded brother. That had seemed like a lifetime ago, before he'd met Emma and had fallen deeply in love with her.

Israr had asked so many questions because of their resemblance to each other. Afsana had confirmed that Derrick was his father, deciding that lying to her son wasn't healthy for anyone involved. Once they were in the States, Afsana had told Derrick Israr wanted to get to know him and now here they were, on their second outing.

"These are the kind that you can comb and make sweaters out of their hair," Derrick said. He switched the tackle box to his other hand and opened the gate to allow them to take a short cut across the meadow, where cashmere goats cropped grass. With the threat to their lives, Afsana had to leave all her own animals behind in their small village.

Israr rolled his eyes. "Sounds like it's more than just feeding and milking now."

Derrick laughed. They had just recently been down to the pond to fish, something Israr loved. After being in an arid country, Israr was thrilled to be this close to not only the pond, but the ocean. His brother Emad loved to watch the surfers. Austin had promised him lessons and that kid was over the moon.

He and Israr were feeling their way through this new relationship, as it had only been two weeks since they had to flee Afghanistan. They went through the gate that led to the main property and stopped at the barn to put away their fishing poles and tackle. The string of catfish needed cleaning, as well.

Afsana and Raffi had been grateful and generous in allowing Derrick to visit often, not only to see how they were doing, but to start getting to know his son. Both

Israr's parents had been open to the idea, understanding that it was both Israr's and Derrick's right to take this step.

Of course, the boy was only nine and his understanding about grown-up situations was limited; the strife of war and unrest had already touched him. But here Derrick was certain he and his family could live out their lives in safety and peace.

He set the fish on the board to fillet them. Rolling up his sleeves, he thoroughly cleaned the area and reached for a knife while Israr stood next to him.

"So, other than goats, how do you feel about going to school here?" He started cutting the catfish, one after the other.

He shrugged. "I went to school in Afghanistan. Not so hard."

Israr and Emad both spoke very good English. Afsana had taught them herself, making sure her sons were fluent. Maybe it had always been in the back of her mind that she would have to leave someday. He wasn't sure.

"I don't want this to be uncomfortable between us, Israr. You can ask me questions and I'll try my best to answer them."

"Mother said this is painful for you and I shouldn't be too intrusive."

He finished the last of the fish and went to the small sink and washed his hands. Drying them, he turned to Israr. "It is painful for me. How much has your mother told you about the situation?"

"Only that you and she were close but that she loved me and wanted me."

Derrick leaned back, his heart contracting. "I worked

for the government. That's all I can tell you about that. What I did was secret."

Israr nodded. "I know." His dark eyes met Derrick's. "Did you want me?" The tentativeness in Israr's voice made Derrick's heart contract even more.

Derrick took a breath, all the remembered pain from his childhood echoed in Israr's voice. "Yeah." Impulsively, he dragged the kid against him and wrapped his arms around him. It felt so good to hold him. "I wanted you. But the circumstances were dangerous." His arms tightened as he cupped the boy's head. "Your mom and I, we were in love. I was reckless and should have been more careful. I couldn't be there when you were born or acknowledge you because of that danger. Do you understand?" He released Israr, but gently held him by his upper arms, crouching slightly so he could look him in the face. His voice uneven, he clenched his jaw. "It's important that you know I wanted to be part of your life, but I couldn't."

For a moment Israr searched Derrick's eyes, his young face pinched, moisture glistening in his blue depths. Then his face cleared and he said, his voice stronger. "I understand. We can be together now. Know each other."

"Yes, that is a promise. We'll be friends since you already have a mom and a dad. I'll be here as much as you want. It's up to you."

"I want that, Derrick. Would it be okay if I call you *Mal*?"

"That's friend in Pashto."

Israr nodded. "Yes, but to me, it means more. 'Derrick' seems too formal."

"Mal it is, then."

Derrick straightened. "Let's get these fish into the house."

With a smile, Israr grabbed the cooler and Derrick slipped his arm across the boy's shoulders.

Later, after the celebration dinner, Derrick found Emma standing on the edge of the property looking up at the night sky. "Hey, what are you doing out here?"

"Taking in the scenery and enjoying the night."

There was a burst of laughter from the house and Emma gave him a soft smile. "They are settling in very well."

He nodded as he came up behind her and wrapped his arms around her, pressing her back to his chest. Burying his face into her hair, he breathed in her unique scent.

"How do you feel about all this? Afsana and I were in love and now I'm helping to support her family with the son we made together, both boys now a part of my life."

She turned in his arms and cupped his face. "I think that it's wonderful that you've gotten the opportunity to know him. It's tragic what happened, and it's going to be a transition for them to get acclimated to the States, but I'm fully with you on this. I want you to be happy, and I know that our love is strong and true. What we have isn't diminished by what you and she had."

He kissed her softly, her warm lips responsive. "You are amazing," he said, pressing his forehead to hers. "Thank you for understanding how much this means to me." Derrick looked at Emma and tightened his arms around her. "I'm totally all right with it. He's close and they're safe. That's all that matters."

She nodded. "I love you, Derrick."

Now seemed like the right time. He was going to take her to a fancy restaurant to do this but after the crisis with Afsana, he just didn't see the need to be anything but honest.

He cupped her face and said, "I love you, too. Will you marry me?"

She gasped when she saw the ring box he pulled out of his pocket.

"Derrick…" She threw her arms around his neck, her shoulders shaking.

He cupped her head, his heart rolling over. "Don't cry, babe. This was supposed to make you happy."

She released him, tears streaming down her cheeks. "I am happy. These are happy tears, you beautiful man." She kissed him on the mouth, the salt of her joy mingling in with the sweetness of her kiss.

Contentment flowed over him as he slipped the ring on her finger. His life had changed so much in such a short time. He now had everything he'd ever wanted: his son, a job that challenged and fulfilled him with an awesome team, and the woman of his dreams agreeing to be his for the rest of his life.

No more shadows; no more hiding and no more pain. It was pushed out by the bliss filling his chest as much as Emma filled his arms.

A month later, they were married on Tucked Away Cay with their family and friends all around them.

Afsana sought him out as he was watching Lily and Emma play in the surf with Matty during the reception.

"Thank you for saving us."

"Of course. I meant it when I said you could depend on me."

She nodded, looking pensive. "I loved you so much, Derrick. I would have been willing to do anything. But saving so many lives—there was really no choice."

"I know. You have been such an amazing asset. And I loved you so very much."

She linked her arm with his. "But now we're content. Are we not?"

"We are."

"I can see that you love her as much as I love my Raffi." She looked at him, her face serious. "Now that there are no constraints, you can get to know your son."

"I can." Derrick smiled, feeling as if the last thing he'd been missing in his life had clicked into place. He looked out to where the two boys were laughing, helping their father grill hamburgers and hot dogs.

"He wants to get to know you," she said softly.

"That means everything. He wants to call me Mal." Derrick's heart tightened. To get this chance to nurture this relationship with his son, to get to know him—he was overcome for a moment.

Later on that night, after everyone had left the island for the mainland, Emma snuggled up to him. "Are you sure you don't have a white horse stashed away somewhere?"

"Yeah, I confess, I've got it in the same place with all the shiny armor. Now, stop talking, Mrs. Gunn, and kiss me, or this knight will perish from the loneliness."

"Oh, you'll never be lonely again," she whispered and kissed him.

She was right; he'd found the life he'd always wanted, with the warmth of friends and family and the love of his life. He wasn't alone anymore, no longer a lost boy. He'd discovered himself in Emma's arms and they would keep each other safe for the rest of their lives.

* * * * *

If you loved this story, don't miss the other thrilling romances in Karen Anders's
TO PROTECT AND SERVE *series:*

HER ALPHA MARINE
A SEAL TO SAVE HER
HER MASTER DEFENDER
JOINT ENGAGEMENT
DESIGNATED TARGET
AT HIS COMMAND

All available now from
Mills & Boon!

MILLS & BOON®

INTRIGUE
Romantic Suspense

A SEDUCTIVE COMBINATION OF DANGER AND DESIRE

A sneak peek at next month's titles...

In stores from 19th October 2017:

- **Shadows in the Night** – Heather Graham *and*
  Colton K-9 Cop – Addison Fox
- **Daddy Defender** – Janie Crouch *and*
  Reluctant Hero – Debra Webb & Regan Black
- **Mr. Taken** – Danica Winters *and*
  Small-Town Face-Off – Tyler Anne Snell

Romantic Suspense

- **The Billionaire's Colton Threat** – Geri Krotow
- **Stranded with the Navy SEAL** – Susan Cliff

Just can't wait?
Buy our books online before they hit the shops!
www.millsandboon.co.uk

Also available as eBooks.